THE SNOW RATTLERS

Books by Shepard Rifkin:

The Murderer Vine
What Ship? Where Bound?
McQuaid

THE SNOW RATTLERS

by Shepard Rifkin

G. P. Putnam's Sons
New York

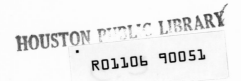
Copyright © 1977 by Shepard Rifkin

Library of Congress Cataloging in Publication Data
Rifkin, Shepard.
   The snow rattlers.
   I. Title. P4.R565Sn [PS3568.I365] 813'.5'4 76-23311

SBN: 399-11880-2

PRINTED IN THE UNITED STATES OF AMERICA

I want to thank all who have helped me with their time and advice. Most prominent are: the homicide detectives of New York City's Homicide Zone 1, particularly Detective Mel Waxman; Yeffe Kimball, of New York City; and Curtis Cook, of Zuni.

Snow Rattler (*Crotalus atrox niveus*). U.S. Southwest. A rattlesnake with a snow habitat. A completely imaginary subspecies which sometimes exists.

Scalise had left the light spinning on his patrol car. It was raining, one of those hard autumn night rains, and it was after dark, so there were red blotches skittering around and around on the shining wet asphalt of East Seventieth Street near Madison. The block was too well-bred to have someone lying dead upstairs with a real honest-to-God Apache lance stuck through him.

Dorsey, my partner, double-parked the seven-year-old squad car beside a green owner-driven Rolls-Royce, and we ran through the hard downpour to the front door. I rang the bell and huddled for cover underneath the carved limestone lintel.

"Hung over?" Dorsey asked. He had good peripheral vision. If they would start rating hangovers on the Beaufort Wind Scale, which rates a flat calm at zero and a hurricane at twelve, I would rate Force Eleven. I gave him a sour look and rang again. "Whadda we got?" Dorsey asked.

I had picked up the phone in the Squad Room while he was watching TV. "Some guy killed with a lance."

"Junkie?" he asked indifferently. I shrugged. It wasn't likely, seeing that this was Oliver Sorensen's house. Not only was he the richest man in the block—and that in itself was an achievement around that block—but he was also one of the richest men in the country. I didn't like that at all. All sorts of extraneous matters get introduced when you deal with rich people. I sighed. That would have to be dealt with eventually. Just to think about it gave my headache another boost to its flywheel.

I could see right through the massive wrought-iron gate into the lobby through the heavy plate-glass door. The lobby was paved with big rectangular slabs of a pale green marble specially imported from a small quarry in Yugoslavia. I knew all this, not because I adored rich people and doted on the society columns, but because there had been a long article in the Sunday *Times* about Mrs. Sorensen and her collection of modern paintings and her American Indian art collection. I read it with some annoyance. She was giving an open invitation to any good thief who wanted to case the neighborhood.

On the far wall of the lobby I could see the big painting by Stuart Davis that the Modern Museum was lusting after. It had numbers all over it. Its charm escaped me, but on the other hand I liked to get up at three in the morning on my days off and go fishing, an occupation many sensitive people consider idiotic.

In the middle of the lobby was a long oak table. Pilgrim period, mid-1660s. On it was a four-hundred-year-old bowl from Acoma pueblo, filled with imported fresh violets. Just the bowl was worth about seven hundred bucks. I looked at it sourly. If I could read the *Times* and get that information, and if I could afford twenty cents for the *Times*, so could every burglar in town.

Dorsey cursed and shoved his big red hand over my shoulder and pressed the bell. I didn't wear a hat and the cold rain was dripping inside my coat collar. I hunched up to get more of the McQuaid body under the lintel. I still stuck out somewhat. I could lose five pounds. I looked at the Rolls; the license plate said OS. Oliver Sorensen. Eighteen coats of paint, hand-rubbed. Loudest sound at ninety, the clock ticking on the dashboard.

More rain down my collar. I had a feeling I was not going to like anything tonight.

*   *   *

"They're all excited up there!" Scalise said as he opened the door. Not as excited as you, kid, I thought. Scalise was only a cop for three months. I grunted. He looked at us wide-eyed. We were real live detectives.

We walked across the lobby. The marble was a cool, translucent green; I had the impression I was walking on top of a swimming pool. Di Benedetto was walking down a spiral staircase across the lobby. I felt better. He was a detective from the Precinct Investigative Unit. I did not have to make drawings for Di Benedetto. He was one of those blond Italians from Trieste.

"Ah, the golden guinea," I said.

"You insult me, you sunnabeetch, I keel you," he said equably. He turned to Dorsey. "Hi, Dorsey."

"Hi."

Dorsey didn't care much for Di Benedetto. Di Benedetto didn't like people who called him guinea behind his back.

"Scalise," Di Benedetto said.

"Yes, sir."

"Go on up and stay with them."

"Yes, sir!" Scalise said, and went up the spiral staircase two steps at a time.

I reached out a finger to touch the violets in the bowl.

"They're real," Di Benedetto said. "This joint's got class. I got a lecture from Mrs. S. This marble's from a quarry near Spoleto. The iron grille—"

"Who gives a shit?" said Dorsey.

11

Di Benedetto stared at him. I would have liked to kick Dorsey in the ass, but you have to live with your partner.

"You think the murderer left a label behind with his name and current address? You guys are gonna have to sweat on this one. So relax."

"Yeah," I said. "Take it easy, Dorsey."

"The grille used to be a gate in front of a Dominican monastery near Toledo, and I don't mean Ohio. The basket is Pomo, and the table is fifteenth-century Scottish. Gimme your coats."

We handed him our coats. "Fifteenth century?" I asked.

"I got a tour from the madam. That's some broad. You gotta see *this*." At one end of the cloakroom was a washbasin. "This is carved outta a solid chunk of Ferrara rose marble," he said. "The handles are from a design by Cellini. I don't want you guys to see the toilet. You'll lose control. Follow me, please."

He led the way across the marble floor. He walked straight toward a mirror till I thought he was going to walk into it, suddenly grabbed what I had thought was an ornamental brass knob, and pulled. It was the door to an elevator.

"Lissen, this Sorensen is something, but his wife is something else. She's half Apache, half Mexican. Oh boy, what a setup!"

We stepped into the elevator. There was a Chinese rug on the floor, oiled walnut paneling, and three crystal vases, each with a yellow rose sticking out of it.

He gave us a fast rundown on the Sorensens as the elevator rose slowly five floors.

Sorensen had found a uranium mine in southeast Utah in the late forties and cleaned up. Then he took charge of the stock issues and cleaned up on *that*; then he sold out just in time and sank that into offshore oil-drilling just before that became fashionable. When he was in Utah he loved Mickey Mouse cartoons. He bought himself a DC-6, rented a pilot, put in a TV, and every afternoon had the pilot take her up to ten thousand and go around in circles while he drank a six-pack and watched Mickey coming in loud and clear from L.A.

Later he found better ways of spending money. He met a beautiful half Apache, half Mexican girl who was a waitress in a greasy spoon down in Moab. She handled him the way Quanah Parker used to handle horses. She broke him to the saddle in jig time, pried him from the busted porch of his shack at Escalante, took away the Winchester which he used to keep on a rack back of the driver's seat of his pickup to shoot rattlesnakes, took away the pickup, took away the shack, and kicked his ass across country to Manhattan. She made him buy a townhouse in the East Seventies, had it redone completely for a million and a half, not counting the antiques, and broke into society the way an Apache would infiltrate a soldier's bivouac. Park Avenue looked around in the morning to find her triumphantly waving scalps.

Di Benedetto finished his wrapup.

"You're in a good mood," I said.

"Damian," he said, grinning, "old buddy, if you knew what you're getting into you would run down the PC himself heading for the George Washington Bridge. This guy has had himself a number-one heist plus a dead body. And it ain't easy stuff like diamonds or negotiable bonds or currency."

I knew what he meant. I had some good informants who had contacts with crooked jewelers, fences, crooked brokers, or mob characters at Las Vegas, the best place to launder money.

"What is it, Mike? Break it to me gently."

"Very valuable American Indian carvings. Old Eskimo ivory. And a first printing of the Declaration of Independence."

Oh, Jesus. I didn't know anyone in those fields. The Department's idiot computer had selected Johnny Green to run the Stolen Art Unit because he had spent one year in the Art Student's League on the GI Bill. And he did that because he didn't feel like working for a living. I knew Green. I dumped

13

him one night in a bar five years ago because he started feeling up my date. He would not be friendly. I would have to work with him on this. I did not look forward to it.

The elevator hissed to a stop. You could have placed a carpenter's level across the gap and the air bubble would have centered perfectly. There are enormous advantages in being rich.

"No, you ain't, old buddy," Di Benedetto said, reading my mind about Green. "He left yesterday for a three-week vacation."

Worse and worse. That's how my mind was working those days. I have a homicide, I haven't even gone up to look over the scene, and here I am worrying about how to track down some of the stolen pieces. Because I had a feeling that the search for those would turn out to be the hard part. I was to find out out that I was all wet.

"Who was first on the scene?"

"Scalise."

Dorsey was standing behind us with his hands clasped behind his back. He never moved unless I told him what to do. I was two months senior to him in the department, and he was entirely willing to let me have all the responsibility. He had made detective and all he wanted to do was to coast gently to his pension.

"Who's gonna take notes?" he asked.

"Me," I said shortly. I could read my writing; he had trouble reading his own. "All right," I said. "Let's go."

Di Benedetto led us down the hall, past a signed Matisse, past a mahogany sideboard that must have set Sorensen back at least fifteen thousand, and into a big room which had been turned into a museum. There was no other way to describe it.

Big Navajo rugs lay scattered on the oak floor. There were little recesses scooped out of the white walls. In them were set little ivory carvings, little fetish dolls, wampum belts, necklaces. All were beautifully lit by indirect spotlights set even further back in the wall recesses. Older rugs hung from the walls. Paintings of Indian chiefs lined the walls.

14

"You wanna see the people?" Di Benedetto asked.

"Nah," Dorsey said. "Let's see the corpus delicti." He liked to use the two words.

Di Benedetto pointed back of us.

"There," he said.

* * *

The body lay on the floor. It faced upward, the mouth open, the eyes staring at the ceiling. It wore the uniform of a private guard. Just over the heart a long lance was sticking out. Another lance was jammed into the floor next to him.

Scalise was staring at it from the doorway.

"Touch anything?"

My voice was sharp. Even experienced detectives do stupid things. Dorsey once ground out his cigar in an ashtray in a homicide scene, and I spent four hours looking for a suspect who smoked cigars before I found out that dumb dodo was responsible.

Scalise said as soon as he saw the body and realized it was dead he stepped back out of the room and wouldn't let anyone inside. Very good.

"I'm gonna call forensic," Dorsey said. He was very good at that.

"And the ME?"

"Yeah, sure, the ME," Dorsey said, suspecting irony. But I can control my face. He went out to make the call. Di Benedetto stood in the middle of the room, not touching anything. It was Dorsey's and my responsibility, and he shoved his hands in his pockets, like many detectives do, in order to resist the temptation to pick up things. He was very interested in everything I was doing.

The window was closed. Metalized strips ran around the edges of both panes of glass. If the glass had been broken, and if this resulted in the strips being severed, an automatic alarm would ring. The glass wasn't broken, but a circle of glass two feet in diameter had been neatly cut out of the heart of the lower windowpane. Big enough for a man to

15

slide through. I walked across the room. The windowsill was six inches wide. There was no dust on it. And so there were no traces of anyone having stepped on it or rested his hands on it. Fingerprints? Later.

I poked my head out the hole and looked upward. The roof was twelve feet above. A man could have come down on a rope ladder, done what he did, and returned up the ladder. There should be signs of dust or dirt on the floor if he had come from a dusty roof. I looked very carefully at the floor, getting down on my hands and knees to do so. The floor was immaculate. But then it had been raining hard for hours. There would have been no dust on the roof, and therefore no dust to track around inside the museum.

There had been a control panel inside the entrance hallway downstairs. I noticed that when I entered a green light flashed red; when the door closed it became green. I asked Dorsey to go downstairs and look at the panel and tell me what happened when I opened the window of the museum. I waited five minutes and opened the window. Dorsey came back and said that a little red light had appeared on the panel and that a bell had rung at the same time. They really had the joint wired, then. Why not? The article had said that the modern paintings and the American Indian stuff were worth over thirteen million bucks. If it were my house I'd have a thirty-foot-deep moat all around the house, jammed full of irritated cobras.

But it wasn't my house. All I had was a two-room apartment with a convertible sofa and a worn rug. I liked my bed and I wanted to be in it. All alone this time.

"The ME's here," said Di Benedetto. He looked as if he were impressed.

"Big deal," I said.

* * *

It was not the ME. It was an assistant ME. His name was Bernard. He came in, nodded at me and, still keeping his dripping raincoat on, shoved his hands in his pockets, bent down, and looked at the open eyes of the dead guard with his usual expression of competent boredom. He unglued a hand, pulled the eyelid of the left eye down even further, and then let it go. He stood up again and yawned. It was no act. He was tired and bored. He wanted to get back to the morgue and work some more on his book about unusual murders. This had the look of a completely ordinary murder. He held out his hands, palms upward, looked at me, and nodded.

In Bernard's kind of visual shorthand this meant that we had here a completely obvious homicide, done by the weapon that was lodged in his chest, and that there was no reason to suspect any other cause of death. Then he buttoned up his raincoat, nodded again, and left.

"He always like that?" Di Benedetto asked.

"Sure."

Di Benedetto looked into the hallway. "Oh, goody," he said. "Forensic's here."

Connolly and Mauriello walked in. Connolly was the photographer; Mauriello took the prints. They set down their attaché cases. They looked like successful young businessmen out to get a nice contract. Connolly was slender and handsome; Mauriello always managed to look bored, as anyone would do if he had to crawl around windows and tables with a camel's-hair brush and blow gently. Mauriello looked sourly at Di Benedetto. "You guys always bitch when we don't come in eleven seconds. Well, for crissakes, we was over in Brooklyn, and then we hadda go up to the Bronx. Some teams gotta wait six hours. You guys are way ahead, so stop whining. Hi, Damian, Dorsey."

Dorsey grunted.

"Tom. Why don't you check out the roof?"

Dorsey grunted again and left.

"What's the matter with Dorsey?" Connolly asked, opening his bag of tricks.

"He is aggrieved at me somewhat," I said, watching Connolly rig his Leica with the strobe.

"Yeah? Why?"

"He was watching Cagney on TV in the Squad Room when I caught this one. He wanted to wait till Cagney shoots the old engineer, but I said no."

"Yeah. *White Heat!* Great movie!" All cops love old Cagney movies. They all root for him and when he finally gets shot by a cop, there is a moment of sadness felt for an erring brother.

"Sure," I said, "but Dorsey, to my personal knowledge, has seen the goddamn thing eight times. I made him come."

"All set," Connolly said. "Whaddya want?"

"Outside shot. Room from door. Room from each end. Full shot of body. Close-up of chest. Close-up of each lance. Shot of window from door."

I itemized all I wanted.

"And then I want a lovely three-quarter of me."

He began shooting. I watched him. He was fast and accurate. When he finished I had him dust the window, the window frame, the glass on the floor, and the lance handles. When he finished he looked up.

"Nothing. Smudges."

"Lance handles?"

"Clean."

"You figure gloves?"

"Yeah."

I wasn't surprised. It all looked very professional. Very smooth. There were no prints and I was sure there wouldn't be any anywhere. I was sure of that. But there was one consolation. If it was a professional job it had to be done by someone who specialized in that line of work. And if he had done it before, the chances were very good that he had slipped up somewhere and done time.

I felt better. I knelt down beside the corpse. I took out my wallet. I had a long one. Inside I kept a pair of thin rubber gloves and a few glassine envelopes. I took out the gloves and put them on. I grabbed the lance in the guard's body close to the blade and pulled gently. No good. I pulled harder and it came out with a slight smacking sound, almost the sound of a kiss. It didn't bother me. Nothing bothered me.

Hardly anything, that is. If he had been dead two weeks in August before being found, that would have bothered me somewhat. But this was a nice clean killing. Some dark blood welled up for a second, then stopped. If the heart wasn't pumping, that was par for the course.

The blade had slid sideways into the heart, between the ribs. If the murderer had held the shaft just a quarter turn to the left or right, the guard would only have had himself a flesh wound, since the broad blade wouldn't have passed through the two adjoining ribs.

That was interesting. If the murderer had known that little item in advance, then it was clearly murder. If he hadn't, an eventual defense of manslaughter was possible. The way the assistant DA's nag you, we homicide detectives get used to planning trial strategy that far ahead.

The shaft was about an inch and a half in diameter. It had been split open to take the narrow tang of the blade, then it had been tightly wrapped around and around to hold the split end firmly over the tang.

I keep a Bausch and Lomb folding magnifying glass in my righthand coat pocket. It was bordered with tortoise shell. It had been a joke present from my sister when I had graduated from the Academy. I had unfortunately let slip one day that my big aim in life was to make detective. I had developed other aims, but I still remembered her contemptuous remarks with some annoyance, even after all these years.

I stood up and walked to a good light. I flipped the glass open and brought the blade up. There were old brown stains darkening the sinew windings. Overlaying the old stains were new stains, still damp, with the musky odor of fresh blood. That blade must have seen a lot of action in its time.

I set the blade down carefully against the wall. I walked over to the window. I poked my head and shoulders out through the hole that had been cut out of the bottom half. It had just just stopped raining and the heavy downpour had washed the car-fume stink out of the air. I took a few deep breaths while I still had the time to see what fresh air

19

smelled like. I had wide shoulders. If I could go through the hole easily so could just about anybody. I inserted myself back into the room and thought as I stripped off the thin rubber gloves and put them back in the wallet.

If the guy who had done it had been around, he had a rap sheet. If he had a rap sheet he had been fingerprinted. So then all I had to do was find him, print him, and compare prints. Easy. If there were any prints. And if I could find him. First, I'd have to check out the modus operandi files. Then I'd find out whose idea of a hot time it would be to steal American Indian art. Then I'd nose around till I located the bastard. Then I'd locate some of the pieces. Then I'd tie him to the art. That way I'd be able to prove he had once possessed the stolen articles. Big deal. Did that mean he had killed the guard? If it did I'd eat the rear bumper off the Rolls downstairs. The more I thought about it the worse my headache became.

Dorsey came back. He had borrowed Scalise's flashlight.

"Howja make out, Tom?"

"Aw, nothin' there," he said, indifferently.

"Yeah?"

"Yeah."

He yawned and kept twisting the flashlight in his hands.

I didn't think he'd look things over as carefully as I would. He was just coasting on to the pension. He didn't care much about anything anymore.

"Rain washed everything away, anyway."

He sat in a chair, turned on the flashlight, and swept the beam back and forth over the dead guard.

"When they takin' him away?"

"Your guess is as good as mine. And not that I'm sensitive, but do you mind cuttin' that out?"

"Sure, sure." He clicked it off. He yawned. He fished out a battered toothpick and began dredging away. Suppose I went to Lieutenant Slavitch and said that Dorsey wasn't pulling his weight. First, I'd get marked lousy. Second, it wouldn't do any good, because Slavitch would love it if I put in for transfer. He did not love me and I did not love him.

Dorsey picked out a luscious piece of old hamburger and rechewed it somewhat.

"Walked around up there, nothing there, right?"

"Yah."

Stupid jerk. The soles of his feet were completely dry. He was coasting.

"OK. Tommy, why don't you write everything up to now while I go talk to the people?"

"Sure," he said, pleased. That would let him sit down and bullshit, his favorite occupation. I could fill in anything he missed, which would be plenty.

"That Scalise's flashlight?"

"Yeah."

"I'll bring it to him."

I held out my hand and he gave it to me with some reluctance. But instead of going into the drawing room with the Sorensens, I made for the roof. A board platform had been laid down, a large red circus tent had been set up in the middle, and big potted trees and shrubs in large redwood tubs surrounded the tent. Smaller tubs crammed with chrysanthemums surrounded the edge of the flooring. The sides of the tent could be rolled up if the weather was nice. The tent was very solidly anchored with steel cables. The cables were bolted to steel rods which were bolted to the supporting roof beams. It looked very strong. Very nice on a hot day. It was nice to be rich.

Fire escapes broke up outlines in an ugly way, so both the architect and whoever had redone the Sorensen house had decided the Sorensens deserved to die inside rather than survive out in the open air on that ugly safety device. If the Sorensens spent a million and a half in redoing their pad and didn't insist on a fire escape, who was I to care? Besides, a fire escape made access easier for a thief. Great logic there.

I walked over to the coping at the edge of the roof. Twelve

21

feet straight down was the window with the round hole in it. The coping was made of stone. It was three inches thick. It surmounted a brick wall which was three feet high. There was a very slight scratch on the inner edge of the coping, and ten inches straight down from that scratch on the coping, and in line with the scratch, was another slight scratch on the brick wall.

If someone were to anchor a rope with a heavy iron loop on the coping, and then slide down on it to the window, that would be two reasonable marks to leave behind.

I walked across the roof and looked down the other three sides. Nothing. No way to climb up. The front was covered with heavy, arched carvings above each window. It looked as if someone had tried to compress a French chateau into a forty-foot frontage. A lot of carving all jammed together so that there'd be something to look at every four inches. When I leaned over I could see the bronze plaque beside the front door. It said *Sorensen* in what medieval script would look like if it took orders from Sorensen, who obviously was used to giving orders. Even in the darkness it shone like the noonday sun. That got polished every day, or else.

But no way to climb up. Not in full view of the street, early in the evening. No way. I swung around and walked to the west side of the building. I faced a tall apartment house. I threw my head back and counted. Thirty-two stories. It fronted on Fifth Avenue. And the side that faced the Sorensen house had a fire escape. But the outer edge of the railing was ten feet from the Sorensen coping.

A problem? I didn't think so. Not for the person who had done everything else earlier in the evening. He could have thrown a grapnel hook across, anchoring it to one of the wire cables which supported the tent. He could then have made his end fast to the fire escape railing, and then made his way across upside down on the rope. Like the way we used to do it when I was in training at Camp Lejeune, down in the boondocks.

Then he could have shifted the grapnel to the coping, made another line fast to it, and slid down and cut open the window glass. Bundle up the stuff, kill the guard, tie a line around the loot, climb up, haul up the stuff, shift the grapnel to the coping, crawl back to the fire escape on the other building, pull back the loot, flip off the grapnel, haul it back, and so to home, having done a neat evening's work.

It needed some looking into, but I bet that was the way it had been done.

I went downstairs. Dorsey was still writing. I walked downstairs via the spiral staircase. On the floor below the museum I saw Scalise. He was leaning against the door-jamb, and on a low couch crammed with brown leather cushions I saw a woman of sullen beauty.

She had a skin which looked like apricots flushing through a delicate brown haze. Her hair was jet black with a few strands of gray which looked like silver wire woven against black marble. I approved of her breasts. She wore a red wool dress. Our eyes locked. She began to swing one long leg slowly back and forth.

"Christ," she said wearily, "another one."

Her hard blue eyes went up and down my body insolently. I wondered if I was dressed decently enough to be allowed in her zillion-dollar house. I thought I looked respectable enough. My fly was zipped shut. She kept staring at me with a faint smile. I knew I was supposed to say something, but I was in no mood for chatter, and that's what she was after. She gave me the feeling that anything I said would be handled like a serve at tennis, and she looked like she was poised to smash any of my feeble serves right past me. I never got on well with rich people, and if she provoked me I might say something I would regret. I decided it would be best for me to postpone my chat with the Sorensens until I had looked around some more and could do a little smashing over the net myself. I nodded and withdrew.

* * *

Dorsey had had himself a bright idea. He had acted upon it in a most praiseworthy manner. He had gone next door and canvassed the whole house—at least, those apartments on the Sorensen side. No one had seen or heard anything unusual that evening.

I was somewhat suspicious.

"How'd you do it so fast?" I asked.

"Called 'em up from the switchboard down in the lobby."

Well, that's one way. It's hard to tell if anyone is lying when all you've got to go on is their voice. It works better if you can look at them and at their apartment, and if anything seems off-key, then you might have a little bone there to gnaw at. But it's easier sitting down and calling them one by one. Another reason why it was rough working with Dorsey.

"Yeah," I said calmly. "Listen, Tom, why don't you see what you can dig up on the servants while I check out the buildings in the back and other side?"

"Sure, Damian." Sure, Damian. He liked that. More sitting on his ass. More work for me. No point bitching to Slavitch when Dorsey would be putting in his papers so soon. I sighed and walked into the apartment house next door. A rubber mat had been laid down from the door into the middle of the lobby. A door on my right opened into the staircase well. It would open if there had been a knob on it, but there wasn't any. It could only be opened from the inside. It was designed to prevent anyone from opening it from the lobby side if the doorman weren't around. But there was no doorman. There was only the elevator man.

He was sitting on a walnut bench next to the elevator with his arms folded. He looked like a footman in one of those nineteenth-century paintings: the kind who sat on the back of royal carriages. He had a sour expression and looked at me in an unfriendly way. He wore a white bow tie and white gloves, and he obviously had to be forced into them by threats of death.

I stood on the rubber mat. I had opened my raincoat because I was beginning to steam inside. Even the forty-foot dash between the two houses had gotten my hair drenched.

24

I took out a comb and combed my dripping hair. I put the comb back. He did not know me and disapproved of me.

"Sir?" he said coldly.

Good. I like suspicious elevator men. If I lived in that house that's the kind of screening I would like for my guests—most of whom would be refused admittance.

I dug out my gold shield. It helps.

"Anyone come in or out of this building in the last two hours who doesn't live here?"

"Nope."

"Any way of getting in that side door from the lobby?"

"Nope. It's gotta be opened from the inside."

"How do you do that?"

"You gotta go to the second floor in the elevator, then walk down one flight, and then open it."

The buzzer rang.

"Be right down," he said, and closed the elevator door.

I took out my laminated ID card and, inserting it between the door and the jamb, pushed it down. The lock clicked open. I got my fingernails inside and pulled the big door open.

I let it close again.

The elevator came down again. A sour, well-dressed man stepped out, gave me a suspicious look. OK. Very good. This habit has a high survival value and will be passed on in the genes to the next generation. The elevator man walked out with him and blew his whistle for a taxi. He must have waked at least a hundred people. OK. No objections. Rank has its privileges. A cab stopped. The elevator man came back in.

"Where's the doorman?"

"You kiddin'?"

"What's the rent?"

"Starts at eight hundred."

"And no doorman?"

"Oil went up, out went the doorman. They raised the rent because of the oil, but fired him anyway, the sonsabitches."

25

"Yeah, rough. Not so safe."

"Safe, hell. I don't give a shit for anyone who can afford to pay eight hundred. I just ain't got no one to talk to. You try workin' all by yourself eight hours a night! And I ain't allowed to read. An' I got to wear this horse's ass of a bow tie an' I got to sit with my hands on my knees!"

"You got me to talk to now. How about a ride?"

He let me off at the sixth floor. I walked to the end of the corridor. On the floor, just inside the fire escape, were a few little pools of water, the kind that might be made by someone stepping inside the corridor after a jaunt on the fire escape.

I knocked on the door closest to the fire escape. A suspicious eye peered at me from the peephole. I held up my shield.

"Oh! One second!"

I heard a window being opened. A few seconds later two locks unclicked and a chain was removed. A skinny nervous girl stood there. Three more stood behind her. They all looked nervous. They were all in their early twenties. I caught the typical pungent aroma of marijuana. Opening the windows wasn't enough.

"Good evening, ladies," I said, politely. "I'm just going to open the window and get on the fire escape here. I just don't want you getting nervous. OK?"

The girl behind the door swallowed nervously. "Sure, sure," she said, flushing with relief.

"That's all, ladies," I said. The door closed. I put on my rubber gloves, pulled the catch back, released the latch, and slid the window open by inserting a thumb into each corner of the frame, a place where it wasn't likely that anyone had placed his hand. The window opened with a squealing noise. I stepped out onto the fire escape.

There was the Sorensen roof, a few feet below. There were no signs of scraping or wear on the fire escape railing. I climbed back in again. I closed the window with my rubber gloves, took them off.

I examined the fire escapes on the next two floors. Higher than that would not be necessary, the angle of climb would be too steep. On the outside railing of the fire escape on the eighth floor I saw a few minute scratches. Maybe. And maybe not.

I walked down to the sixth floor and knocked on the door of Marijuana Mansion.

Once more, the clicking and sliding of bolts and latches and the rattle of the chain. I couldn't blame them. There was a lot of young, delectable female flesh there. It didn't appeal to me. I liked mature female flesh, in my age group. Someone like Mrs. Sorensen. I liked that kind of cool, heavy-lidded challenging stare. I liked forty-year-old women with long legs.

"Anyone hear any noises from the fire escape?"

They shook their heads.

"Anyone hear the window being opened out there?"

No.

"Anyone been outside during the last three hours?" The rain had started three hours ago.

Hesitation. They all shook their heads. Liars.

"Sure now?"

Vigorous nodding of heads.

"Thank you, ladies."

Smiles of relief.

I walked down the six flights. I used my handkerchief to twist the doorknob open. The elevator operator was sitting on his bench, looking like he'd like to strangle the landlord.

"You didn't hafta to walk down," he said. "You coulda rung."

I nodded.

"Anyone from 6-A been out tonight?"

"Yeah. One of 'em went out and come back. About nine. I took 'er up. She yelled at me to speed up."

"Speed up?"

"Make the elevator go faster. I just looked at 'er. I don't talk back to the tenants. You do that just once an' you're out

27

on your ass. Them four girls share the rent. Dirty little cheap bitches."

So what else is new? I told him I'd have someone dusting for prints. I buttoned up and stepped outside. It was still raining. I stopped by the iron gate of the service entrance of his building. There was a five-foot-wide areaway between the apartment house and the Sorensen house. On the right side, against the base of the Sorensen house, lay a small brown paper bag, just about where it would end up if thrown hurriedly from a sixth-floor window. I picked it up and opened it and smelled it. It was no surprise to me to find that it was half full of marijuana.

Lying bitch. She'd gone out to make a buy. She must have had some going back; it distorts perception of time. That would account for the little darling yelling at the elevator man to speed it up. I remembered the story about a pot smoker standing on a street corner with a friend when a motorcycle suddenly went by at a hundred and twenty. He turned and said, "Man, I thought he'd *never* leave."

I tore open the bag and dumped the pot into the gutter. I watched it flow along to the sewer grating and slide inside. Something else for the poor fish in the river to deal with.

* * *

The morgue wagon had come and gone. Forensic had gone next door to check out the doorknob on the lobby door and the windowsill on the sixth floor. I'd have their report early next morning. If I cared to work overtime without pay, that is. I didn't feel like it. Five P.M. would be good enough. But Forensic said he'd be willing to give me the result before he went home.

I walked to the corner drugstore and sipped a cup of coffee while I did some thinking. There were no sleep-in servants. The housekeeper, the porter, and the two maids had left at six. Since the Sorensens had gone out for an early dinner, the cook had gone out.

28

Dorsey had gotten their addresses and left to talk to them. He had left with ink, a pad, and fingerprint cards. He'd take the necessary elimination prints faster than Forensic and save us some time tomorrow. I didn't think any of them were involved with the murder or theft, but you never know, maybe they had fingered the job. Dorsey was good at smelling out that kind of operation.

Lots of details, lots of running around and barking. Lots of problems. I didn't like the smell this case was beginning to give off. I paid the check and left.

I went back to the Sorensen house. Scalise was standing outside the drawing room where I had left Mrs. Sorensen half an hour before. He nodded respectfully as I entered. Her husband had now joined her.

They stared at me in silence. Sorensen was a short, broad-shouldered man with gray hair and big brown hands. He was leaning back in a white leather armchair that was all squared off, with flat arms. Those foot-wide flat arms were a decorator's delight. I hated them. You couldn't slump back in them for a snooze, you couldn't throw a leg over the arm. My armchair is made of brown leather and looks as if it had been dragged behind a truck all around Manhattan. I fit inside it like a hand in a glove. Sorensen had an annoyed look. No wonder. He must have hated that chair in a simmering rage. He exuded an irritated power which had been locked into a badly designed environment, just like a wild bull forced to spend the night in a closet. His eyes locked onto me with an almost perceptible snap. His legs were thrust out as far as they could go and his arms were folded. I would hate to be a small uranium deposit he was after. He looked as though he could lower his head and go right through a brick wall. Right now he looked as if he was considering it seriously. But through me first.

"Who are you?" he snapped.

I looked at him silently for a few seconds. I didn't like his arrogant tone, but it was his house, there had been a murder in it, and lots of his valuable things had been stolen. Be-

29

sides, he helped pay my salary. I would like to pay him back his pro rata contribution, which would be something like a quarter, and then express myself frankly and obscenely. I refrained.

"Detective Sergeant McQuaid. Third Division Homicide."

He considered this for a while. I looked around some more. *The Readers' Digest Year Book* was in his lap. There was a full set of it, all bound in red leather, in the big walnut bookcase on the west wall. They were playing chess. Between the two of them was a chess table four feet square, made of alternating black and white marble slabs. They were in the middle of a game, and she was winning. She had balanced her elbows on her knees, her chin resting on her joined palms. Her index fingers pushed up at the corners of her eyes till they were almond-shaped slits. It made her look like a blue-eyed Chinese.

"Your move, sucker," she said. "Don't keep Sherlock waiting." Her slow, sultry voice drifted over the sentence like a drugged butterfly. There was a faint contemptuous air about her which I didn't like. It was mixed with the calm, sure arrogance which almost always accompanies great wealth. Her blue eyes challenged me. It was clear that she had to win at anything she did. Sorensen frowned at the board and reached out for a knight. Each of the pieces was six inches tall and carved out of marble. It sure was nice to own all the uranium in the United States.

Mauriello came in. I asked him to take the Sorensens' prints.

"You think *we* killed 'im?" he snorted.

"No sir," I said patiently. I had already been reprimanded for insulting an influential citizen whose attitude I disapproved of. I was determined to be polite all the way tonight. "These are what we call elimination prints. When we find them around the room or on your art we eliminate them from consideration." They grudgingly permitted Mauriello to roll their fingers back and forth across the paper. I asked

30

for palm prints. Maybe the thief had used his palms to push up the window and *then* put on his gloves.

"Fat chance," muttered Mauriello, but he did it. "That all you want?" he asked, when he had finished.

"Yeah. Here, that is." I took him outside and described the kind of prints I wanted him to look for on the outside and inside of the windows on the building next door.

"Be ready about eleven tomorrow. You comin' down to look at 'em?"

"Yeah, sure." It would be easier on him and I needed friends.

Mauriello went in again, pretending to take another print off the window, but what he really wanted was to look at Mrs. Sorensen.

"Sergeant," Sorensen said.

"Sir?"

"Will you please tell me what the hell's goin' on, all these detectives comin' in and askin' questions, then you comin' an' askin' the same questions? Looks like you guys don't know nothin' 'bout organization." He was angry. I soothed him with a brief description of the Precinct Investigative Unit system and how I tied into it. She kept restlessly tapping her toes while I was talking. I noticed them out of the corner of my eye when I was talking. I explained that I had objections to the PIU myself, but that it was an attempt to create a more efficient department, and not due to sheer stupidity. He was interested, as I thought he would be. A man who had created a vast fortune by buying up and reorganizing badly run companies would be.

"Oh, Oliver, for Christ's sake!"

I turned to her. "Mrs. Sorensen, can I have a detailed list of everything that was stolen?"

She jerked a thumb at her husband with a bored look.

"I'll do better than that," he said, getting up heavily. He left the room.

"Yep," she said, throwing her head back and letting the smoke escape from her nostrils. "He'll get a detailed list, all

31

right. He's got color photographs of each piece. He's got them measured in millimeters. He's got them weighed in milligrams, too. He's very methodical, is ol' Oliver. He screws me every third Wednesday at fourteen minutes after eleven. For exactly seven and a half minutes. But who am I to complain? That's how he made his money. He's got affidavits from every dealer 'bout provenance. You know what provenance is, Sherlock?"

This kind of talk, although interesting, always made me restless. I never liked to hear a wife tear down her husband even when it was necessary during an investigation. I wanted to tell her she must have liked that money an awful lot. And that's why she put up with it. She had no sympathy from me.

"Well?" she demanded.

"Sure I know what provenance is," I said politely. "It's the capital of Rhode Island. "She flashed a sudden grin and patted the couch beside her. I remained standing.

"I don't like you much," she said. "We're not gonna get along, I can see that, sure as God made little red apples. Where are all those cops?"

"All gone."

"They was crowdin' in here like cattle round a salt lick. One ol' deppity sheriff 'd straighten it all out real quick."

"Yes, ma'am." I wasn't going to get involved in that kind of a squabble.

"Siddown for crissakes!"

I thought she must be a little drunk, but I didn't see any bottles around. But that was just the way she was. Angry, loose, loud, intense. As if she'd been drinking alone for a couple hours, thinking and brooding. This was her standard operating procedure. She was a very hard woman to handle. I felt sorry for Sorensen, but this is what happened very frequently with rich, successful businessmen. It was like sleeping in bed with a hundred-and-twenty-pound scorpion.

I sat down. At the other end of the couch. It was a very

32

comfortable couch, and I sank down in it till I reached bottom. Goose down locked inside fine, supple brown leather. Ten feet long. At least a thousand bucks. She noticed my surprised, pleased face. She was very perceptive.

"Like it, McQuaid?"

"Yes." I couldn't prevaricate or play games with her. She liked things blunt and to the point.

"How 'bout me, McQuaid? I was born in a lousy shanty on the outskirts of Phoenix. It was made out of empty five-gallon cans my pop had scrounged from the town dump. An' some scraps of lumber. I didn't get a store-boughten dress till I was eight. Wore ol' flour sacks. Didn't get to buy a pair of shoes till I was ten. Wore shoes an' wore-out sneakers I found in the dump. Slept on burlap bags. Bet you did better."

"Yes."

"Your ol' man die from a shotgun blast?"

"No." I didn't care for the way the conversation was going. I was there to detect my way around a homicide and burglary, and she had picked up the ball and was going through me the way Texas A & M would go through a Vassar scrimmage line. And I knew that if I tried to stop her, however politely, I'd regret it. I kept my mouth shut. What the hell, I *might* pick up something interesting.

"Mine did. When I was seven some son of a bitch deppity come over to him in a juke joint when he come in and tried to get a drink. They wouldn't sell him liquor 'cause he was an Indian, an' he got mad an' knocked over the juke box. That Anglo deppity come over to tell 'im to git, an' my ol' man never got for no one. He knocked the deppity on his fat ass, an' he went out to his car an' come back with his sawed-off. My pop started to take it away from him an' that was the end of my ol' man."

Strangely enough, her voice did not get louder. It softened and slowed down, as if it were some kind of an animal—a mountain lion, for instance, that was stalking me, waiting to spring at my throat at the correct second.

33

It made me feel wary and apprehensive. I did not see the point of this story.

"They had no call to kill 'im. They had no call to kill a drunk Apache who wasn't hurtin' no one. Just a stinkin' juke box he was killed over. An' so he was killed by a lousy cop."

So that was the climax she was aiming at. She had slowed down even more, and I thought that now is the time when she will raise her voice and drench it with hatred. But she fooled me. She simply slowed down and pronounced each word as if she were carving it out of a hard, recalcitrant wood. She was completely in control. Like an Indian chief in council.

So she hated cops. So did a lot of people. I felt sorry for her father. But that incident was the kind of thing that escalates without anyone really wanting it to. It could have happened to me. I was sorry that her father was killed when she was just a little kid running around in a dress made from flour sacks, but that didn't give her a license to lay it on heavy.

"What did the couch set you back?"

"Eighteen big ones." The flush over her high cheekbones was subsiding. Good. Maybe we would not come to blows.

"Very nice."

She took a deep breath, knocked the ash off her cigarette, and stuck it back in a corner of her mouth, flung both arms sideways along the back of the couch, and pivoted her hips towards me with a sudden jerk of her pelvis. The movement of her arms over the back of the couch thrust her full breasts forward till they strained against her dress, and the little wiggle of her ass was like a sudden convulsive movement in coitus. This lady was advertising her availability just after she had finished announcing her hatred of cops. It spelled poison, and I would do very well to go the other way for many reasons, the least of which was that if she ever locked her ankles in the small of my back I had no doubt that she would crack two or three vertebrae as if they were paper-shell pecans.

Mr. Sorensen came into the room. I sighed with relief. He held a small filing box which was lined with asbestos. He set it down on the chess table, sat down in a low armchair next to me, put on a pair of horn-rimmed glasses, and pulled out a stack of five manila folders.

"These are the stolen pieces," he said. He sighed and leaned back.

I opened the first folder. Inside was a superb eight-by-ten color photograph of a carved ivory bird's head with mother of pearl inlays. It was three inches tall, as indicated by a ten-inch scale running along the edge of the photograph. More careful examination showed it to be a grotesque bird god, with human feet on which it was squatting. The huge beak jutted straight out over its body, which was carved with subtle and flowing curves. There was an air of quiet menace and malicious humor about it. The back of the photograph read *Hohokam. Southwest Arizona. Walrus ivory. Ca.* A.D *580.* Then followed its long history, ending up with the name of the dealer who had sold it to the Sorensens.

The next photograph showed a grotesque carved wooden figure, shaped like a man. It was eight inches tall. The head and neck were painted red, the body a faded black, and the arms were the natural color of the wood. The genitals were faintly prominent. I looked on the back. This was Kan Hotidan, the tree-dweller spirit of the Wahpeton band of the Ogallala of North Dakota.

"Ogallala?" I said.

"You say 'Sioux,'" she said.

I read on. Kan Hotidan was a powerful forest elf. He lived in tree stumps. His magic was greatly feared, since he enchanted travelers. However, he could ensure success in hunting. I could use him myself.

I looked at her for a moment. Her hair had fallen in front of her face. She ran her nails across her forehead, pulled back her hair as if she were pulling back a curtain in order to reveal a stage. Then she shook her hair back over her ears. It was the fastest hairdo I had ever seen.

She looked like a sports car which could do two-twenty

without any strain. The kind that would roll over and bite unless you had it under perfect control. I looked for a second at her husband. I had the feeling that for all his bull-like strength he didn't look as if he could handle her on a fast curve. It would be like trying to downshift on a gearbox that had been locked into high gear. What I got from her was a feeling of savage, unlimited power. Get her going and it would be like sitting on a twelve-cylinder engine with the accelerator jammed to the floorboard. Just hang on and ride her till the gas tank was empty? Nope. Too dangerous.

"Look," she said dryly. "Ol had a man from Parke-Bernet make a written evaluation on the back of each of them pictures."

It was all very intelligent and very helpful to me. He was the kind of man who translated all these carvings and necklaces into dollars. These figures danced in his head like sugarplums all night long, I'd bet. Holding hands with each little dancing dollar value was another one: their future values, based on two factors—inflation and the normal increase in value. This in turn was based on the consideration as to whether the artifacts would still be considered collectibles by those people who had enough money to bid heavily at auctions.

I knew the type well from my days on the Robbery Squad. It's a normal kind of behavior and I respect it. Oh, I respect it a lot. And God forgive me for a financial failure, I also despise it. But I was paid to look for stolen things and not to sit around despising people who paid my salary.

Next to the carved little figure of Kan Hotidan was a twelve-inch-tall square wooden box, carved out of a single piece of oak. A sheaf of feathers was lashed to the rear, so that they sprayed above the top. A buffalo skull was incised on the top half, and lower down was a snake figure.

"What's this?" I asked.

"That symbolizes the tree stump where Kan Hotidan lives," Sorensen said moodily. "There's only three of those goddamn things known. I mean, up to now. This one's

36

worth seventy, eighty thousand. Price goes up fifteen percent every year, goddamnit. Look at this thing, will yuh?"

He took a folder from me with a brusque jerk and slid out the eight by ten. The photograph showed a white belt with two black parallel lines running its entire length. "This is a covenant belt," he said with a sour, irritated tone. "It's made from black and white wampum. It—"

"Tell 'im what it's worth, Ol," she said.

"How the hell do I know?" he growled. "Paid one thousand for it to some Mohawk up at Canajoharie. But that was ten years ago. It—"

"I don't know what a covenant belt is," I said.

"It marks the peace treaty between the British and the Mohawks. About seventeen hundred fifty. Right, Lizzie?"

"If you say so."

He looked at her sharply. "Come on, Lizzie," he said with annoyance. "You're the Indian expert round here."

She took the photograph from him. "Yep. Seventeen fifty. The guy Ol bought it from said his great-great-grandfather was the chief. The old Mohawks got very good memories. They passed their history down in long talks. If he said seventeen fifty it's seventeen fifty. Those two parallel stripes mean that both the British and the Mohawks would travel on separate but parallel paths and neither would interfere with the other 'cept in cases of murder or robbery." She suddenly grinned. "Jus' what we got here, right, Sergeant?"

"Yes, ma'am."

"This ol' Mohawk jus' couldn't resist Ol's money. He didn't want to sell at first. Said it was his people's heritage."

"I get that shit all the time," Sorensen boasted. "But all I gotta do is wave a little more cash each time an' they'll break their necks snappin' at it."

"Sure, Ol," she said. "Tell the sergeant how you got it."

"We were in his cabin," Sorensen said. "Pretty cold outside. Kerosene stove. They was all wearin' their coats. Why? Not enough money for kerosene. I had offered him a thousand bucks the day before. He said no. I went to the bank in the mornin' an' got rolls of quarters. I broke 'em open and put them all in a suitcase. When he said no again I jus' upended the suitcase on his bed. He said, 'Take the belt, mister."

"Ol sure is smart," she said with a note of faint sarcasm.

"You bet I'm smart," he said. "That's how come I built this here collection, an' don't you forget it!"

"Ol," she said softly, "I ain't *ever* forgettin' it."

"After all," he said, "those Indian friends of yours used to kill each other 'fore the whites came here, they used to steal each other's grain an' all."

This kind of marital squabble could go on all day, and invigorating though it might be to the participants, it was not very interesting for bystanders. What I was hearing was obviously a long-standing quarrel wherein he played the bad white man and she played the noble Indian. It was an intriguing variation on the ordinary husband-wife conflict situation, but I had a lot of things to do, and while I might learn something about their relationship I had no one to pass on this gossip to except Dorsey and Dorsey wouldn't give, as he would say, a flying fuck.

"Well," I said. "What else?" I pulled out another photograph. It showed a peace pipe. About two and a half feet long, carved from oak; one end displayed a bunch of eagle feathers, each one was linked to the next by a necklace of black and white beads. On the lower half of the pipe there had been carved the head of a deer; a few inches below that a turtle; and below that, just above the quill end of the feathers, was the head of a mountain goat. From the other end of the pipe to the carving of the deer head ran a mass of red and yellow beads in an abstract yet formalized pattern. The end of the beaded pattern was signalized by a group of tiny, brilliant feathers which may have come from woodpeckers; these feathers were bound tightly to the pipe by a simple brown cord, wrapped several times around the shaft.

"Very old," Sorensen said. "Maybe Blackfoot. Maybe Cheyenne."

Two more. I slid out a photograph.

No explanation needed for this one. It was a tomahawk. But it had a long, slender oak shaft on which was inlaid silver decorations. The blade was narrow. The top edge went out at right angles from the shaft; the bottom edge curved gently downward, then swung in a fine curve till it met the straight top edge. The other end of the blade projected backward into a delicate hammer tip; it looked like a tack hammer. The bottom end of the shaft tapered somewhat till it was encircled by a silver band; then it tapered a little more till it was as wide around as my thumb. It was a beautifully made murder instrument, and as finely made, in its way, as the Detective Special which was nestling, ready to go, in my left armpit.

One more.

I picked up the folder. What caught my eye was its heading. Neatly lettered across it were the simple words: *First Printing of The Declaration of Independence, 1776.*

Oh no, I thought, oh *no.*

I've recovered stolen Mercedes Benzes, Patek Philippe gold pocket watches with chimes striking the quarter, as well as the half hour, a rare tropical beetle collection owned by a Mellon, and a netsuke collection which I found in someone's freezer unit. He had forgotten he had put it there for safekeeping and reported it stolen in a great tizzy, but I checked out the freezer, which people put things in and forget about. Once I recovered a diamond necklace which had been stolen from a very rich girl at a party. It was the only thing she was wearing at the time.

But the Declaration of Independence?

I let out a long, low whistle.

"Yep," Sorensen said unhappily.

"It's *his* baby," she said with contempt. There was an edge to her voice I didn't understand. I would have to see if I could ferret it out.

He looked at her over the top edge of his glasses. The skin over his cheekbones flushed red, but his voice was under perfect control.

"Yep," he said again. "There's only two others. One's at

Harvard, the other's in the Library of Congress. And I've got the third. You're damn tootin' it's my baby. I guess you could sort of say the Indian stuff is hers."

So they had divided up the museum contents. She got the Indian material and he took the other stuff. OK with me. Perfectly normal behavior. I once knew a guy who collected barbed wire while his wife was hot for brass candlesticks. There was a mutual tolerance between them, and there had to be such a thing or else they would have been at each others' throats. Yet here, at the Sorensens', there seemed to be some extra emotion invested as to who claimed what. There was something weird in the air, and I couldn't put my finger on it. She obviously loved the Indian part of the collection, and just as obviously she was not exactly grieving over its loss, and he was pissed off at her because it was clear she didn't give a goddamn about the missing Declaration.

It was too late to strain the brain. I decided to get a good night's sleep. In the morning, refreshed, I would look at the ME report, look at the fingerprint results and check them out at the Bureau of Criminal Identification, talk it over with Dorsey and see what he had dug up, and then see if I could come up with a neat little theory.

Or even a sloppy little theory.

I stood up. "I'll be moving along," I said. I tapped the eight by tens. "Mind if I take these along?"

"Nope," Sorensen said.

"Don't let anyone take 'em from you," she said mockingly. It was not meant kindly. The smoke was dribbling from her nose. When I was in high school we all believed that any woman who smoked that way was passionately fond of screwing. I never believed it, but now that Lizz was sprawled backwards on that big couch with arms outflung, the cigarette dangling from her mouth and her bare toes slowly rolling a bishop back and forth on the chess table as she stared at me, I would be happy to buy that high school conviction.

Sorensen stood up and took my elbow firmly in his big paw. He steered me through the room and into the elevator.

40

We went to the ground floor. He steered me over the green marble slabs till we were next to the long oak table with the Acoma bowl. I was mystified.

The violets in the bowl had the intense blue of turquoise. Sorensen was very observant, as are most successful people. "Got a standin' order with a florist," he said abruptly. "Fresh flowers through the whole goddamn six floors every goddamn day. One hundred goddamn bucks. Every goddamn day. When I think what it adds up to a year, I go loco. But she likes 'em. You try an' get those things back. They mean a lot to her, bein' half Indian. Me, I'm pure Mormon. I don't give a shit. All I care about is the Declaration. There just ain't no goin' and buyin' another one. Period. You find it for me an' I'll slip you a bonus. Quiet. Between you and me. OK?"

He gave me a long, hard look. A bonus was not a bribe. But it was a gratuity. And gratuities were not kosher.

"And in cash," he said, not understanding my silence.

"You don't read me," I said.

"Twenty-five thousand. In twenties."

If I took it, he would understand all the little subtleties involved. It would be cash, no record would be kept, and he'd keep his mouth shut.

"Christ," he said. "A hundred bucks a day! I used to live for a year on a hundred bucks! Well, whaddya say?" he asked, squeezing my upper arm.

Now he had whipped up a problem. I earned good money. But I blew it as fast as I earned it. Horses. Women. Vacations. Nobody would ever know I had that extra twenty-five. No one except Sorensen and his wife and me. That would always give him an edge. I mean, he would probably never even think about me once I had found the stuff and he had given me that nice little bonus. But if he'd ever think about me, I'd be the detective who had broken departmental regulations. It wouldn't mean a damn thing to him. He didn't deal the way he did, with foreign governments and governors and regulatory agencies, without spreading money around. He didn't even think about them.

It was just the cost of doing business. It was just a little grease to make the wheels go easy without squeaking. He didn't even think about it.

And I think that it was just that which griped me. He would never think about me. And I wanted him to think about me. He would think about me and say to himself in amazement, "That guy McQuaid, I offered him twenty-five big ones, not for a bribe or anything like that, and he told me to go take a flying fuck!"

Some dialogue. I needed time to think about whether I should deliver it or not. I excused myself and went into the little toilet beside the spiral staircase. I dunked my hands in a washbasin carved out of a solid hunk of yellow marble and dried them on a yellow linen towel embroidered with tiny yellow roses. Yellow, boy. Color of uranium? Outside in the street sat his Silver Cloud Rolls, eighteen coats of paint, handrubbed, each one. The loudest sound at ninety miles an hour, the clock ticking on the dashboard. How come they permitted that loathsome racket?

Money. So where did I get off, telling him to shove it? I carefully folded the towel and hung it absentmindedly on the heated towel rack, instead of throwing it into the bin set under the sink. It's your lower-middle-class background, McQuaid.

Why not take the money? I'd be doing the job as best as I could, anyway. I wouldn't be trying harder because of the promise of the bonus. If he wanted to hand me a little tip, why not take it?

Well, I knew why not.

Because he'd always think I'd be making the extra effort for the money. The sort of extra effort I'd never make if he'd been a penniless cripple confined to his room who'd had his TV set stolen. A guy who couldn't afford another one. If the cripple had his smarts and had jotted down the set number I'd bust my ass to find it—if I were still on the Burglary Squad, that is.

But Sorensen would never believe it.

And that's why I wouldn't take the money. He'd think

42

he'd pressed the right button to motivate me. He was telling me, in other words, that he thought I was a piece of easily handled shit. Oh, the hell with it, I said to myself. There goes an easy twenty-five grand. I punched the washbasin in resigned exasperation. There were times when I resented this strange puritanical streak which ran under the nominal Catholic heart of this particular McQuaid.

*   *   *

Dorsey had taken the squad car when he went uptown. I lived only seven blocks away in an old rent-controlled brownstone off Second Avenue. I plodded along in the rain till I got home.

The Sorensens had no monopoly on marble. They let some get away. I had an old oak bureau, and I had found a white marble top in the street a couple of years ago. I lugged it upstairs. It had scalloped edges and the fit wasn't too good, it had sinister yellow stains, but I liked it.

I emptied my pockets and dumped the change and keys on the marble. I liked the friendly clatter they made. I slid my police .38 under my pillow, took a shower, and fell into bed. The pillow was too soft and I felt the hard mass of the gun through it. I was used to it, it didn't bother me anymore. Sweet dreams.

I took a bus downtown. We had a new building, and it had taken me some time to get used to it. It was too new. I didn't feel comfortable. New desks, new chairs, good lighting. When I went up the stairs I noticed with approval that the pale green walls already were developing a blurred smear at shoulder height, as if reluctant people leaned against the wall as they went upstairs. But I had never noticed anyone leaning against the wall, and for the fiftieth time I wondered how the hell that smear had got there.

I pushed open the swinging gate just inside the door. Dorsey was already there, doing his four-finger imitation of a gorilla typing.

"Hi, Dorsey," I said.

He grunted. "Pissed off," he said. He jerked his head at Lieutenant Slavitch's office. "I took the car uptown to talk to those people last night, right? Last one I talked to lived up by the city line. Where do I live?"

"Yonkers." I always answer rhetorical questions.

"Right. So I take the car home. Because why bring it downtown again? No one's gonna use it anyway, right? And I had to talk to another guy livin' way east in Eastchester next day anyway. So Slavitch chews my ass for goin' home with police property. He made a big deal out of it."

Everything was a big deal with Slavitch. Under the plate glass desktop in his office was a big chart that covered the entire desk. Daylight assaults were blue. Daylight homicides were red. Night assaults, green. Night homicides, yellow. The chart also showed the sectors, the reported value of goods taken, if any, and the percentages of cases closed. Also worked into it were the weapons used. It looked very snazzy. Slavitch was very proud of it.

I picked up a DD5 and covered both sides of it with my report. This was harder to do than anyone would think. The DA didn't want you to put down everything because the defense attorneys had a right to look at it. When they looked at it, they'd know how to build an effective case against the State's case. So the DA asked you to keep out some important details. On the other hand, the bosses wanted you to put down everything, so they'd know what you'd done and found out, so then they could second-guess you as they sat on their asses back of their desks. Solution: write down essential data in your notebook. Counter-solution: the defense had a right to examine your notebook. Counter counter-solution: write your notebook in such a way that only you could understand your notes, yet, at the same time, in such a way that the court would accept it as truthful if the hieroglyphics were pointed out with your help. Oh, it was a world full of challenges.

As soon as I pulled the DD5 out of the typewriter Lieutenant Slavitch came out of his office, picked up Dorsey's and my DD5's, and went back inside, carefully closing the door.

"What does he do in there with the reports?" Dorsey muttered, "jack off?"

"Don't be vulgar," I said. "What about last night?"

"They look clean. I checked out their former employers, in case they had faked their references before they came to work for Sorensen. Clean. That's some broad, that Mrs. Sorensen. I'd like to sink my tomahawk into her ishkabbible. She appeal to you, Damian?"

Anyone would appeal to Dorsey after his wife, a tense, bitter, overweight, religious bitch whose only interest in life was going to church and breeding Siamese cats.

"That's too big a hunk of woman for me," I said. "I'd have to keep shooting into the floor beside her to make her dance. Too independent. She makes her husband trot nice and easy."

But I hadn't answered his question. The answer was, yes, she did appeal to me.

Slavitch suddenly whipped open his door and said, in his usual monotone, "McQuaid, Dorsey." He closed the door. That was typical of him. Now we would have to knock to get permission to enter. Little power games. He was big on that. Little people are usually big on that.

"Prick," Dorsey muttered. I banged shave-and-a-haircut-two-bits on his door and Slavitch invited us in; it was clear he hadn't liked the way I'd knocked, but he had decided not to make an issue of it. He held a handful of colored crayons in his right hand. His left hand drummed on our two reports.

"I read your DD5's," he said coldly. I was twisting my head to find out what purple meant. Purple was brand new. I think he was playing time of day against unsuccessful plea-bargaining, or some such exotic combination. You never know what you'll come up with. The phone rang. Slavitch picked it up. "Yes, sir," he said respectfully. Dorsey and I drifted out of earshot to give him privacy. Dorsey looked at the handful of crayons and whispered, "Jerkin' off, I tell ya, Damian."

"Why must all your images be rudely sexual?" I said.

"Aw, cut it out," he said amiably. "What the hell good is all that horsin' around gonna do? Solve crimes?"

"The Department is fond of computers," I said. "Slavitch doesn't know computers from rye bread, but he knows they love charts downtown."

"Kissin' ass?"

"Still vulgar, but essentially accurate."

"Yes, sir," Slavitch was saying. "Yes, of course. Yes, sir. Yes, sir."

I had been daydreaming. I could talk to Dorsey and listen to him and make my interjections and responses as if I were an altar boy, and I could do it all without thinking. My daydreaming concerned me and Mrs. Sorensen, and her long legs. I had her straddling me, wearing only her shirt. The shirt was open, and she was bending down and brushing her breasts across my mouth, while she was figure-eighting with her hips.

I stopped daydreaming. I didn't like the sound of all those yes, sirs. I smelled trouble. The kind of trouble a pissed-off billionaire could stir up.

Slavitch hung up. "Know who that was?" he asked heavily.

This was no time to make jokes. I shook my head.

"The PC."

Even Dorsey stopped chewing his gum.

"Sorensen called the PC just now," he said. "He got through right away."

We digested that for a while. The only way I could get through to the police commissioner was to hurl myself in front of his car on his way out of Headquarters.

"The PC told me to handle this discreetly. You guys talk to any reporters yet? You type up an unusual on this yet?"

We shook our heads. Unusuals were made out on all major cases and all homicides. They called the attention of the chief of detectives to what we considered important cases, were hung up on clipboards as well, and reporters would flip through them and decide whether or not they'd like to follow any of them up for a story.

Slavitch got up and came back with the carbon. He tore it up and threw it in the wastebasket.

"Right," he said. "From now on, hand me your DD5's personally."

"You mean we don't make a folder?"

"Make a folder, sure. But it'll be kept here in my office. If word gets around to the papers, it's your ass. Hear that?"

I didn't like his style, but the meaning was clear.

Dorsey spoke after a few seconds. "Yeah," he growled, "but when he reports it to the insurance company, how the hell we gonna keep it quiet?"

Slavitch took off the glass table top. He set it carefully against the wall. He sat down, opened a desk drawer, and pulled out a carefully typed page. He picked up his crayons and prepared to transfer the data to his goddamn chart.

"Sorensen wanted to know why you guys left at midnight instead of working straight through the night. I told him there was an overtime question involved. He said he'd be happy to pay for any overtime involved."

He hadn't answered Dorsey's question, which I considered pretty crucial. Sometimes Slavitch answered these questions, but in his own good time. You had to be patient. While I was being patient I toyed with the idea of a Sorensen overtime check floating through the vast, interlocked labyrinth of the Police Department, Finance Administration, Comptroller's Office, and the Mayor's Office; I imagined the incredible mass of documents in quadruplicate which the correspondence would generate. I thought it was a good idea. For every so often one carbon from that paper cyclone would land on Slavitch's desk. He'd have to make a record of it and answer it in quadruplicate. At least the typing would keep him away from his art work.

Dorsey repeated stubbornly, "Like I said, Lieutenant, how

47

we gonna keep it quiet when he reports it to the insurance company?"

Good for Dorsey. I waited.

"He's not going to report it to the insurance company," Slavitch said.

* * *

I sat at my desk, my fingers laced behind my head. I had convinced myself I thought better that way, but what I was probably doing was imitating my father, who had an amazing ability to ferret out my childhood crimes and put the fear of God and of him into myself at a very early age.

No insurance company notification. Interesting. Why? He'd have to bear all the loss. No filing of a claim? No restitution. Strike out "interesting." Insert "Very interesting."

Motivation? Usual response from such people: because so much criminal attention would be drawn to their house, their property, their persons. All the crooks in the world would be tumbling over one another in their eagerness to burglarize the joint again, or even kidnap either or both of them.

Possible. But all things are possible. I shifted the problem to the area of probability. And I stopped. A loss of a million or so? To reject compensation to which you're entitled? Even if you're a billionaire? Not likely. Possible? Yes. Probable? I just didn't know. Maybe if I had a billion I wouldn't get excited over a million-dollar loss. Maybe.

Gut feeling on this, McQuaid, please. Gut feeling didn't buy the Sorensen story. No logic for gut feelings unfortunately. That's why they're gut feelings. Something beyond conscious logic is where they're born and start nosing around, scratching away quietly at your carefully formed logic. Experience had taught me to listen for those little, almost imperceptible noises. Listen hard. And keep your mouth shut. I sighed and unclasped my fingers and stood up.

The dealer who had sold the Declaration of Independence to the Sorensens was Henry Blakiston. His shop was on Madison at 68th Street. A window with a few books displayed in it, all leather-bound, all very thick, all very expensive. The center of the display was occupied by a Shakespeare, First Folio. London, 1623, eighty-seven thousand. His current catalogue, with color illustrations, was also elegantly offered. The catalogue itself was priced at sixty-five. Not cents. Dollars. It was a very high-class joint. It did not resemble the corner candy store in my block where I used to pore over comic books until the owner came out and chased me away.

I pressed a button beside the door. These days you never walked into stores on Madison. They had to look you over first. A young gentleman drifted over the rug like a dandelion seed. He looked at me. How are you supposed to look when someone is deciding whether or not you're reliable? I tried to appear kind, truthful, and reverent. I noticed he was wearing a lovely little necklace made of tiny gold links which clung to his neck like a leech. My look became unkind. His face stiffened and he turned away.

I rapped my knuckles sharply against the window. When he turned around my gold shield was flat against the plate glass. He opened the door reluctantly and stared at me. The stare was meant to inform that I was persona non grata, or, in English, a shithead.

"What can I do for you?" he asked frostily. The sentence sounded like a row of icicles snapping off one after the other. The tone said that what I could do for him would be to drop dead.

"Are you Mr. Blakiston?"

His delicate shoulders shrugged. His eyebrows went up. It was a virtuoso performance in gesture, and its purpose was to tell me that I was some kind of a jerk not to know who Blakiston was.

"Let me know as soon as the house lights go down," I said.

"Huh?"

Smart he wasn't.

"Do you need help, sir?" A voice materialized back of me. The voice was very assured, very aware of each rich little vowel, each terminal consonant. The joint was beginning to look like a home for failed actors.

"Mr. Blakiston?"

He nodded. A senior member, this one, in his silvery sixties, very soigné, very suave. That type could not sell me the *Times* at the newsstand price. He did very well with a lot of other people, however. But the world is full of other people. And I stopped long ago being surprised what they found impressive, entertaining, or instructive. He was very small, and had very small hard gray eyes. He had a very expensive haircut, hair just touching his collar. He smelled good, too. Not pansy. Just the correct tinge of faint masculinity. Not a macho smell. This was a man who measured himself out in teaspoons. And level teaspoons. Nothing heaped over the horizontal.

He wore a polka-dot bow tie and a blue chambray work shirt. Not a shirt made to *look* like a blue chambray work shirt, but a real honest-to-God workingman's shirt. This had put him one up on everyone in his circle. But he then took everyone's queen with his very, very expensive Knize blue cashmere jacket, hand-tailored. Say five-fifty. White linen trousers, clinging lovingly to his round little ass. A hundred-seventy-five-dollar pair of hand-lasted English brogues. He probably had his own personal last filed away somewhere in a London shop. He had a round buttonface with an expensive Caribbean tan. This had to be a tough little son of a bitch. This was the kind of man who could sell a sheet of paper for half a million bucks and make you feel honored. He'd make a very good chief of detectives.

I exhibited my shield as if it were on display in Tiffany's window. He looked at it gravely, narrowly, and somewhat sourly, as if it were a small and rather fourth-rate Rembrandt etching, with several damp stains and a massive tear right into the plate impression.

"A Cellini it ain't," I said.

He grinned suddenly.

"Can I talk to you?"

"Of course. Forgive my bad manners." I did not dislike him so much. He led the way to the rear, past his assistant, who was now doing Catherine the Great as he wielded a feather duster around the massive gilt frame of a large engraving of a ruined prison interior, full of broken marble columns and diagonal shafts of light. I paused for a second. He waited.

"Nice," I said.

"A Piranesi. All the detectives like it. That's how I can tell they're detectives. This way, please."

He pushed open a big oak door. It swung open easily on its well-oiled hinges and closed behind us with a rich big-door sound. It was a big room, and the books here were much bigger than those in the window. He sat behind his big desk and looked at a row of dials set in a pale brown metal housing. He noticed my interested look.

"Humidity. Temperature. Acid content of outside air. It's chemically treated to remove all sulphuric compounds. You interested?"

"Sure." Always let them talk. You never know what useful morsels you can gobble up.

"All right. The sulphur in the air has an affair with the tannin used in the leather-manufacturing process. The result is sulphuric acid, which eats away at the binding and ruins it. Now tell me, what was stolen, and from whom?"

I hadn't mentioned anything being stolen, but he was smart enough to know that I was not interested in buying any rarities. "The Declaration of Independence."

"Oh, Christ. Oh, goddamnit!"

51

Was it an act? No, he was too smart to overdo anything.

"Sorensen told you he bought it from me?"

"Yeah."

"I sold it to him for seven hundred fifty. It's worth a million by now."

"Listen," I said, "I don't understand. Why should one sheet of paper bring so much? When a book like that Shakespeare in the window doesn't even bring a hundred thousand? Damn, that's a lot of money for a sheet of paper only a little bigger than the *Daily News*."

"Yes. You know they printed up thousands?"

I shook my head.

"Yes. They handed them out like leaflets. Pasted them on walls."

"Why didn't people save them?"

"Who saves leaflets? Do you? The ones on the walls eventually wore away. People save books because they look important, because they can be kept conveniently in book cases. How can you keep a big sheet of paper? Books were expensive then. People saw a point in keeping them. Not throwaways. People passed the Declaration from hand to hand to be read, and eventually they all disintegrated from the wear. That's why only four or five are left. And that sheet of paper deals with the very beginning of the United States; all first things in any field are valuable simply because they're the first. Every American would like to own the Declaration. There are plenty of rich Americans, and the competitive bidding for the extremely rare copy that might show up explains the high price. As for the Shakespeare you saw in the window, why, they're comparatively plentiful."

A good explanation. Nothing overdone. There are advantages in level teaspoons. Perhaps my first judgment had been too harsh.

"And now the goddamn thing is gone!" He slammed his fist on the table.

"You sound sorry."

"Yes and no. Yes, because I made a decent profit on the sale, and no because I had a feeling this would happen."

All this was interesting.

"Why?"

"I first offered it to Harvard. By the way, the only other copy known is in the Library of Congress. Harvard was afraid Columbia might take it, but Columbia was broke. Harvard just had her library acquisition fund cut, and asked me to hold it for a year, but the overhead here is too high. I offered it to Sorensen because I had heard his wife was in the market for very rare colonial Americana. She bought it."

"But I don't understand why you were sorry."

"Harvard has excellent security for her rare pieces. And what does Sorensen have? Two front doors. That is, a grille which is kept locked, and a front door which is double-locked. A back door, kept double-locked at all times. Barred windows on the first and second floors. All the windows hooked into an alarm system which would immpediately report any broken glass—as long as that metallic strip is broken. A twenty-four-hour guard, which isn't bad—but suppose someone were to overpower the guard and shut off the alarm system? They could walk out with anything they wanted."

He sounded like a Burglary Squad detective. Or an expert second-story man analyzing a rich prospect.

"Do you generally examine the house before you sell something valuable?"

He looked at me as if I had a small pointed head.

"I have neither the time, the inclination, nor any particular interest for that. Besides, I would be told to peddle my papers elsewhere. I took a deep interest in this sale for one reason: the Declaration is irreplaceable if stolen or destroyed."

"Do you think it will be destroyed?"

He looked troubled. "I hope not. My feeling is that anyone who stole it—even if he were uneducated—would still know enough about American history to treat it with care. How was the robbery conducted?"

"Your question is not clear."

"I mean, was it smash and grab? Or was anything else taken which might indicate that the thief was knowledgeable?"

"I should say knowledgeable."

"Good!" he said with relief. "Then the thief is probably quite shrewd, probably not insane, and therefore will not destroy it in a fit of pique or rage if his demands for the return are not met. I feel somewhat better now than when you had just told me the Declaration was stolen. Not ecstatic, you understand. Just a little relieved."

He stood up and walked around the room with his hands in his pockets. I let him circulate. I did some thinking myself. Why should anyone take just the five artifacts and the Declaration? They were the best pieces. Maybe that was the reason. On the other hand, wouldn't a professional thief take all he could? They took up very little additional room. Puzzling.

But it was still a weird aggregation: five art objects *and* the Declaration. I started looking for a pattern. The pieces were carefully picked by someone who really knew his American Indian art. That much was clear. I didn't get the linkage of Indian art *plus* the Declaration. Once more, was it because those together were the most valuable in the collection? Maybe.

And maybe not. It was a thought to tuck away for a rainy day.

"Who might buy the Declaration?" I asked. Blakiston shrugged. "Who the hell knows?" he asked with some sharpness. "If they knew it was stolen, you mean? If they knew of its rarity? No one would buy it unless he were crazy. Consider the problem: the point of owning it—for normal people—is to be able to boast of its rarity and cost. You must be able to evoke envy in the breasts of all who see

54

it. That's a serious consideration for many wealthy collectors, believe you me, Lieutenant."

"Sergeant."

He grinned. "I didn't think you'd object to a promotion."

I looked at him again. He was used to dealing with wealthy customers who must have been in some awe of his knowledge; he probably, with his superior intelligence and his asperity, was somewhat feared and kowtowed to by his staff. He was used to manipulating people. On the other hand, I did not like being manipulated. I could see our little affair running into breakers ahead. It would be a good idea for me to keep my mouth shut.

He went on. "The idea of anyone stealing it and gloating over it in private is a concept which would start and stop with Edgar Allan Poe." He paused. I looked at him impassively.

"You know," he said. "Poe."

"Poe? P.O.E?"

He said nothing. His face began to acquire a certain hardness, which was his way of showing dislike. He nodded, with difficulty.

"Yeah," I said pleasantly. "I heard of him. We got him in the Police Academy. We're pretty well educated, us cops."

His face was impassive.

"Yep," I went on, "Edgar Allan. He invented the brass casing for cartridges, right?"

"I think you're making fun of me," he said stiffly.

"I think it would be best if you went on, Mr. Blakiston."

"Yes. That's all." He sat down behind his desk and looked at a point two inches above the top of my head. It was very clear he was wishing I would drop dead.

"Sir," I said, "know anyone in the rare book collecting field who's crazy?"

"Lots. They're all a little bit crazy. You have to be a little nuts to spend your days gloating over the fact, for instance, that you have the first state of the first issue of the first edition of Conrad's *Lord Jim,* wherein, on page seventeen, line six, the word 'thought' is spelled with the g and h reversed. This makes it worth thirty dollars more than the rest of the edition, which is spelled correctly. You have to be crazy to think that that's important. But there's a lot of people who get excited about things like *that.*" He sighed. "But I make money out of such stupidities."

I preferred him when he was lecturing and caught up in his subject. His casual chitchat annoyed me.

He went on. "There was a Spanish collector once who flattered himself upon being the possessor of a rare incunabulum. A cradle book. A book published before fifteen hundred. He had the only copy known. His friends envied him. One day someone showed up with a duplicate. He killed the man and burned the victim's house and destroyed the other copy. He died happy on the gallows."

"Now *that's* crazy," I said, impressed.

"Yes. But I think you'd like to know if I'm acquainted with someone of that degree of insanity, someone who wanted the Declaration so badly that he might even want to murder someone to get it?"

I had said nothing about the guard being murdered. Nor had it been in the papers.

"Yes."

"The answer to your question is that I know no one like that."

His gaze had now lowered till he was looking directly at me.

But on the other hand, maybe he did know someone of that degree of insanity; someone who had commissioned him to get a copy of the Declaration. Even if a death would be necessary. Crazy theory? Ask any homicide detective. He'd have even weirder stories. Crazy or not, it was worth checking out. I'd ask Dorsey to work on it. The exercise would be good for him, and he had the advantage over me that he didn't flare up the way I did when dealing with some arrogant bastard like Blakiston. Dorsey had been coasting too long. A little spurt before he reached the finish line would jazz up his tired blood. And I could see where this was going to turn out to be a long, puzzling, and confusing case, involving a lot of pavement pounding and knocking on a lot of doors, and behind one of those doors might very well be a bullet with my name on it. I wanted Dorsey's name on it too. That way the risk would be cut 50 percent. The people I was meeting were all turning out to be much too smart. The odds were not good.

"How about someone taking it for the insurance?"

"That makes sense. Someone will probably approach the insurance company."

And that might be you, you conniving son of a bitch.

"Yep," I said. "How about the thief approaching other dealers?"

"Not likely. But always possible. There's no distinguishing marks on the Declaration so that it could be identified as belonging to someone. No little library stamp, for instance."

He was lecturing again. He continued. "What might be done is this: someone might buy it from the thief. For a nice low price. Say fifty thousand cash, small bills, no questions asked. Then he would launder its provenance, by running it through a series of dealers on the Continent."

"That's not clear to me."

"OK. Suppose you want to buy a Declaration, but you want to make damn sure your copy hasn't been stolen. Because if it has, your title is no good. So the dealer will point out that some respectable dealer in France, or Germany, or wherever, had located it in some castle, or some church attic, together with a file of letters written home by an officer serving with the British Army here during the Revolution. Or letters written home by a Hessian officer. Or a French officer with Rochambeau. Obviously the Declaration had been sent along as an interesting souvenir. The letters, by the way, will be authentic. Such collections *do* turn up every year or so. All one has to do is wait, buy up the collection of letters, and announce your discovery. The more reputable the dealer, the more convincing the story, and the

57

more impeccable the provenance. And this way it might very well appear on the market again, making a very handsome profit for all."

"Know any crooked dealers?"

Blakiston smiled. He wasn't answering that one.

Time for me to go. Nothing much here. On the other hand, maybe quite a lot. A little information, nothing special. What a political reporter would call a backgrounder. Nothing to put down in those damned DD5's, but at least I wasn't stumbling around in unexplored territory. I had been handed a nice little map.

* * *

Carey, the detective who set up the first Homicide Squad in New York City, sometime in the 1880s, wrote in his autobiography that he always looked for a pattern. It doesn't sound original now, but all observations made for the first time never sound original ninety-five years later. He would look at all the little bits of evidence; look at the surroundings; he would look at *everything,* he wrote, as if they all formed pieces of a jigsaw puzzle. He would move them around in all directions, without any preconceived ideas, until he saw a design. He never looked for a specific design; he never superimposed his thinking on the scattered pieces, he never wrenched pieces out of their natural places. He just let the pieces in the puzzle do the talking.

I do it too. I have respect for my superiors.

So I looked. Something surfaced briefly out of the jumble and then fell back once more. So I drove up to the Amerindian Museum. It was a new building, all plate glass and gray marble, with fountains playing between big, tall carved wooden totem poles. It was just north of the United Nations and fronted the East River. They had taken the big Northwest Coast war canoe from the lobby of the American Museum of Natural History and set it down smack in the middle of the entrance hall. I was glad to see some traditions being upheld in this ugly exercise in geometry. The canoe still held all those paddlers, really leaning into it, with the witch doctor standing on the platform in the stern, all got up like a bear. It reminded me of Lieutenant Slavitch and the Third Homicide Squad.

The woman at the reception desk to one side of the lobby listened to my problem. "You'd better see Professor Lundberg," she said. "Room 504. Take that elevator, please."

When I got off the elevator I passed row after row of shelves on which were arranged clay pots, arrowheads, and clay baskets. When you've seen one arrowhead, you've seen them all, although, of course, when I saw a note under one arrowhead I stopped with interest. It pointed out that war arrows were attached at right angles to the feathers so that they would penetrate between the ribs. Hunting arrows, on the other hand, were fired at animals walking on all fours. Their ribs were vertical. Therefore, the arrowheads were placed vertically in relation to the feathers. Now, that was interesting. I could have taken up the profession of homicide detective among the Iroquois five hundred years ago. This musing was broken when I arrived in front of a door which said PROFESSOR FRANK LUNDBERG in gilt letters three inches high. Underneath was lettered, CHIEF, DEPARTMENT OF SOUTHWESTERN ANTHROPOLOGY. This only deserved one inch. I could see who rated around here.

I knocked. A sharp, commanding voice, brusque and impatient, snapped at me to come in. I did not care much for the owner of the voice. I opened the door. I had always thought of anthropologists the same way people tended to think of professors—rather thin men with horn-rimmed glasses, tanned from being outdoors, but still quite frail.

Lundberg was a big man in his late thirties. Two little knots of muscle bunched tensely at each jawline. His eyes were set deeply in his square, hard face like chips of gray ice. He wore a very good suit of brown tweed which looked like he had wrapped old bricks in it; his expensive English brogues looked like he had kicked the bricks about five miles down the road. I would have taken him for a mining engineer who'd struck it rich and who lived alone. He wore a yellow shirt with button-down collar and a knitted brown tie. It was clear he didn't give a goddamn about what was fashionable and what wasn't, and that he didn't give a goddamn what anyone thought about him. He looked like he'd be a tough customer on any level.

He spoke abruptly, shoving aside a bunch of galley proofs he'd been working on when I interrupted him. His tone was both arrogant and annoyed.

"Well, what is it? I haven't got all day."

"I have," I said gently.

This usually works. They are either not sure that they heard right or they try to figure out exactly what I want and its implications for them. The average response is that they become somewhat wary and somewhat more polite.

"The girl downstairs said you're some sort of a detective."

"Yes. Homicide."

"Well, what do you want with me? I haven't killed anyone in the last ten minutes." He chuckled in appreciation at his lousy joke, but he chuckled alone. When he had finished I put on my heavy voice. I let it get as heavy as lead and I spoke slowly. The weight of the whole New York City Police Department was in it, and that's a heavy weight. The whole bit totaled a politely phrased admonition to straighten out or he'd find his ass jammed up tight against his solar plexus. But not in so many words. Oh, no. We had a Civilian Complaint Review Board. It was just my tone, which approached atomic weight two oh seven point one. Which is, if I remember my high school chemistry, good old lead.

When he had run out of pompous small talk about his awareness of his duties as a citizen, I mentioned that I wanted to talk to a knowledgeable person about American Indians and their art.

"I thought you said you were a homicide detective," he said suspiciously.

"It's a felony murder."

"I don't understand."

"A murder committed during a felony, and there I am, front and center."

"And you want to talk to me."

Yes, you dumb son of a bitch, or anyone who works there, preferably someone smarter. Time to butter him up.

"I'd like some information on American Indians. And I'm told you're the number one man in that field."

"You want a lecture, Sergeant. I don't give lectures. Go down the hall. Room 506. Dr. Kimri. Good-bye." He picked up a pen, worked it into position as if it were some sort of an Amerindian offensive weapon, and began to insert little caret marks on his galleys, drawing lines to the margins and writing in a tiny, meticulous script, very unlike his impulsive, brusque personality. As far as he was concerned, I was now officially dead. I seemed to keep running into citizens who didn't like me. I didn't mind that. I don't want to be loved; all I want is accurate information which would eventually lead to a true bill by the Grand Jury. If I got that they could spit all over either one of the brown Harris tweed jackets I owned. I could always send in the cleaning bill to the chief of detectives.

The phone rang on his desk. I stood up. I heard some incoherent, angry conversation on the other end of the line. Lundberg said, "Your whole department is a royal pain in the ass!" He slammed down the phone so hard I thought it would shatter, rose from his chair, and barreled through the room at the door, completely disregarding me. He was built like a bear just out of hibernation; he looked shaggy; the suit was too big for him. I sucked my gut as he lumbered by on his way out, his face filled with the joy of battle. His ancestors were probably Vikings, and I bet he relished an occasional battle. The whole thing looked like a bureaucratic squabble. I had too many of those at Squad Headquarters to want to poke my nose in this one.

Room 506 sported letters only one inch tall. Dr. Shoshana

Kimri. Israeli? A woman. Probably fat, with thick horn-rims. Closely cropped hair, the better to comb out the lice she'd be picking up in native hovels. I knocked. Behind the door a husky contralto called out, "Come een."

I opened the door. She was sitting at a desk piled high with papers and letters. The hair was not closely cropped. She was not fat. The only thing I guessed right were the horn-rims. She had hoisted up the blond hair on top of her head and had stuck it in place with a lot of hairpins. Some of the loose golden strands cascaded onto her shoulders. Her eyes were the same intense blue I had last noticed when I went fishing off Jamaica, a deep intense blue. Her cheekbones were high and set wide apart. Her chin came to a point. She looked like a golden cat.

"Dr. Kimri?"

"Yes."

"Dr. Lundberg said you'd talk to me."

"Yes. He phoned very now. No! Just now?"

"Just now."

"Thank you. English is a bandit language. Damn fool language. You are a detective?"

"Yes."

"Ah. Let us go out. I am sick at sitting here. We walk."

She walked in front of me with quick, short strides. Her shoes went *thump thump thump,* like an enthusiastic puppy's tail banging against a floor. She was a touch over five feet, and I was pleased to be in back of her. She had a spirited little ass that made you want to clutch it with both hands. It was just like a basketball cut in half and then placed together side by side. They looked like someone was dribbling them gently toward some heavenly basket. She wore tiny round gold earrings and no other jewelry. She did not look like the usual anthropological lady, who usually wore the jewelry and costumes of the country where she had served her time. She wore a steel Rolex.

We stopped at the end of the hall. A window there opened out on the East River and a back view of one of the totem poles.

"Yes, please."

"I—"

The phone was ringing in her office. She held out her hands helplessly and marched back quickly, her arms swinging like a British grenadier's. I followed slowly, wondering when the hell I'd get someone to talk to me in this glass mausoleum.

By the time I had reached her office I heard Lundberg's voice crackling on the phone. I was beginning to dislike it more and more. It was not only loud, but it had a sharp, drilling quality which would laser through a granite wall. He was spluttering something about "Keresan towns, goddamnit!" I have very good ears for eavesdropping, developed during the years when I did undercover work on narcotics. Then he added something about shoving the bills for the turquoise up someone's ass. Then I heard the receiver slam down on his end. She hung up with an embarrassed smile, as if I had witnessed some family scene which she found distasteful. She saw I was curious.

"Ah, you see, he is annoyed. But you will understan'. We were working in Zia, one of the towns where they speak Keresan, one of the pueblo languages. Professor Lundberg is one of the very few whites who speak Keresan. So, we were doing dendrochronology. You know?"

Yes, I knew that meant telling the age of wood from counting tree rings. I said that.

"We had came—come? Yes, come. We had come there to see how old the houses were. We can tell now backwards to the exact year. But the governor of the pueblo would not let us make the core sample. He said the spirit of the house would go out through the hole and never come back. So Dr. Lundberg just said not to worry. He said he knew how to make spirits happy. All he had to do was buy top-grade, robin's-egg-blue turquoise and plug up the holes with those. So the old men talked it over and said it was good. So we drilled the holes and took our cores, and put turquoises in the holes and everyone was happy. Dr. Lundberg knows how Indians think."

"So everyone was happy except someone in this building."

"Yes. That is Mr. Brownlow. The chief accountant. The fight is now he will not pay for turquoises. To pacfy spirits."

"Pacify."

"Yes, pacify. He says spirits do not exist. So he cannot allow a purchase which says they exist. He says we will all be laughed to."

"At."

"At. Very hard language. So this is what they are fighting at."

"About." I sat down on the other side of her desk.

"Yes. You find it funny?"

"Yes."

"Well. I suppose it is."

"Do you believe in spirits?"

She frowned. She put the tips of her fingers together, the way my mother used to do when she was playing church and steeple, here are the people. A strand of her blond hair suddenly escaped from one of the hairpins and eddied gently downwards in front of her face. She blew it absentmindedly out of the way. I began to hope Dr. Lundberg would go away somewhere on a long anthropological trip.

"Oh, that is a hard question. The old Indians believe in them. And some of them are very wise. They think of these things all the time. Most of their knowledge is not written to? Down? Am I smarter than they are because I have three degrees? No. You see, I have not answered you. You think bad of me, you think I do not want to answer. You see, I am not sure what I think. But ask Dr. Lundberg if he believes in spirits."

I smiled.

"Oh, yes, yes," she said earnestly. "He goes to their peyote ceremonies. The medicine woman of the Comanches has adopted him." She pointed to the wall behind me. I turned. A feather was mounted against a red velvet background; the whole was nicely framed in old oak. "She blessed it for him very hard. It brings good fortune. Its special medicine is that it keeps away ghosts."

"What's it doing here?"

"Oh. Well, I don't sleep good. He loaned it to me so I will not have bad dreams. But Dr. Lundberg, we talk about him, please. The Indians like him. They tell him things and he doesn't write them down. They like that, but the museum is not happy about it. He doesn't care what the museum thinks." Her eyes were glowing with admiration. I decided I would get nowhere with Dr. Kimri. She went on. "He goes to Washington and tells the Senators they are dumb sons of bitches when Indian fishing rights come up, he says that right out loud."

"You like him?"

This was a hard question, apparently. After a few seconds she said curtly, "Sometimes." Then she let out a short, explosive, annoyed exhalation and stood there, silent. She gave me the feel of a guitar string suddenly plucked, quivering and full of tension. I couldn't tell for sure what she was mad at. I thought briefly of the great difference between her and Mrs. Sorensen. Lizzie had a lazy, relaxed quality to her, but it was the kind of an easy, supple, fluid relaxation you can see in a mountain lion lying flat on top of a big rock watching the trail below. Let her see something worth sinking her teeth into and she'd rocket off that rock so fast she'd be nothing but a blur. On the other hand, Shoshana always seemed to be vibrating. She'd spring, yes, but it would never come as a surprise.

"Let us go somewhere quiet," she said coldly. I found the change in temperature puzzling.

"It's not noisy here," I pointed out accurately.

"It will be noisy soon," she said.

As if on cue the door opened and Dr. Lundberg poked his shaggy head inside. She looked at me and raised her eyebrows as if to say, See?

"Shoshana—er, Doctor—"

"Yes?"

65

"I hope you'll excuse me, but I have to dig something out of the filing cabinet."

"What?"

This stopped him, but only momentarily. He said easily, "That file on the Folsom points. There's a couple photos there I need for my article for the *American Archaeologist*."

Her face was developing an annoyed flush. This kind of tennis could go on forever. I put a stop to it.

"No, that's all right," I said. "Dr. Kimri and I will just step out for a cup of coffee across the street."

"But—"

"No problem at all," I said. "Just take your time."

She draped a gray cashmere cardigan over her shoulders and walked out. I followed. Her heels made an angry drumbeat. I turned around to look at Dr. Lundberg. Seeing me look at him made him move from his leaning stance against the filing cabinet to an industrious riffling through it. It was clear he wasn't really looking for anything. The back of his neck was red. It was also clear that he hated me. I followed her down the corridor. I let her get in front of me. I didn't want any confidences involving a lovers' quarrel and how rotten he was and how misunderstood she was. I don't want anyone richocheting into my arms. I prefer a deliberate kind of movement. So I let her walk off her anger.

She only reached my shoulder, but she moved so fast that her legs seemed to make a blur as she entered the elevator. She tapped her foot nervously till the elevator stopped at the ground floor. She was out like a shot, and now that she was walking across the marbled lobby floor her heels sounded like a typewriter. She walked out into the street, buttoning up her cardigan. I paused at a luncheonette but she kept on steaming by. She was in a fury. "He is stupid, childish!" she muttered, and I realized she was intent on walking till she had calmed down. It was chilly in the street, and I paused to button up my six-year-old topcoat, the one with a knife slash under the right arm. My tailor had neatly rewoven it for six bucks.

"You're slow, slow!" she said angrily, calling from fifty feet ahead. She waited impatiently till I came up alongside.

"You've got all the heat of righteous indignation keeping you warm as a bug in a rug," I said.

"Bug in a rug," she said suspiciously. "What is that?"

By the time I had explained, we had gone three blocks from the museum. We had passed four places where we could have taken coffee. She had calmed down, and she picked out luncheonette number five. We sat down.

"We went out because I know him," she said. "If we had sitten down in the cafeteria in the museum he comes in in three minutes, drinks coffee from the next table, and gives me a look like a sick cow. I cannot stand this look. He wants to own me. I hate it! Brrrr!" she shivered. "Enough of my problem! What is yours?"

I told her about the death, how it happened, and what had been stolen. I told her nothing more. I had been warned by Slavitch to keep it in the family. I took out the portfolio. As soon as she saw the first photograph she stiffened.

"I know this piece! I will tell you who has been robbed. The Sorensens."

"How do you know?"

"I *know*," she said impatiently. "What else?"

She riffled through the other photographs. "Yes," she muttered to herself. "Yes. Yes. Yes, yes!"

She put them down and drummed on them with her fingertips. Short as she was, her fingers were long and slender. "How do I know?" she demanded abruptly. "Because when they were sold at Parke-Bernet we bid for them. She has more money than the museum. She won. Dirty beetch!"

"Bitch?" I repeated, amused by her vehemence.

"Yes. Beetch! I went up to her at the auction and told her what I was. I said, it was important pieces for the museum. They will fill in our collection. She said no. So I ask her to be the donor. I know these people, *big* income tax deduction. She could come in late at night and show it to her friends. She get special treatment. Some times this trick is good. She say no. She smile a lot, like this."

Here Shoshana imitated a contemptuous arrogant sneer.

"I start to hate her. I said she would get a plaque of bronze next to the pieces with her name. I said she would get a lifetime pass. I said she would get her color picture in our yearly report to the trustees. I say she would be allowed to come in Mondays with all her friends when we are closed. I am wild to get those things, I promise her anything, *anything.* I was in her house—have you been there?"

"Yes."

"She was playing chess with her husband and eating peanuts. Break the shell, drop shell on floor, eat, break shell, drop on floor, eat. Pig! She did not give me any. She did not say a *word,* and when I was finished talking all she said was—oh, how can I forget it!—all she said was, with that smile, was, 'Haul ass.'"

"What did you say?"

"I say, 'I beg your pardon?' Because at that time I did not know what these words meaned. So she explained. So now I get mad. This was not a good idea. So I stand up and said, 'How would you like a punch in the nose?'"

This was good dialogue and I was enjoying it. "What did she say?"

"She say nothing. She stand up fast, fast! I got out quick."

That's what I'd call good thinking. "Then what?" I asked.

"So, nothing happened. Then a year later I was asked to write a book on American Indian art, which was going to be full of big, beautiful color photographs. I wrote her asking permission to take pictures of her collection. She sent back my letter all tore up in small pieces."

"She has a good memory."

"Oh, yes. You know what I think of her." The plastic spoon she was holding snapped.

"Yes. Very clear."

She tapped the table with her broken spoon. "These pictures, Sergeant. They are exact what I need for my book. Can I borrow them for a day?"

So she'd copy them, they'd appear in her book, and two or three years from now Slavitch would call me into his office and mark me all over with his crayons. No, thanks.

"Well," I said, "after I show them around town a couple days, I don't know why not."

"Ah!" she said jubilantly, giving me a big warm smile. Her face looked like the sun had just come out of a cloudbank. But when she'd ask me again for them, I'd have my information out of her. And then I'd tell her why not. A little dirty, but then that's the way she was playing it herself. I was playing it to solve a murder and a burglary, and she was playing it to make a better book.

"Oh, very good, vairry good! Now, how can I help you?"

I put my palm on the photographs. "Just tell me where to look for these." Begin at the beginning.

"I would guess whoever took them, he took the best. Yes. So he knows his field. So he takes the best pieces. Then, where will he go with them? To museums with good collections needing good pieces. Museums just beginning, very anxious for good pieces to make a nucleus for a collection. To make people come to the museum. To make a reputation for the curator. To encourage gifts, not like that beetch. For them, a high price is still a good investment."

"And private buyers?"

"Of course."

"Suppose they know the piece is stolen?"

"Now, you deal with eccentric people, yes? Some of them don't not care. They won't show it. They lock it up and look at it. Then they put it away till they feel they want to look at it again. Oh, yes, there are such people."

"You mean they won't even show it to their friends?"

"No, to no one. They look alone."

She stroked her spoon, bending over and crooning.

"Beautiful. You are so *beautiful*. I loff you. All mine!" She straightened up. "See how they do it?"

"Dealers?"

"Very dangerous. It would be too dangerous to sell it here. To sell to a European collector, to sell quietly, yes, possible. But risky."

I thanked her. "Yes, yes, all right," she said, standing up abruptly, as if this had been a pleasant vacation and now she had to face real problems. I was getting used to her sudden sharp little movements. Coupled with her small size, they made me think of an intelligent chipmunk. I liked her enough to bring her home and keep her in a small box with torn-up newspaper on the bottom. But I doubted that she could be housebroken.

"One thing," she said. "You say one lance was stuck into the floor?"

"Yep. Vandalism."

"Maybe. But there is something you might not know about Indians," she said.

"Yes?" I said politely, prepared for a lecture on anthropology.

"Putting a lance into the trail that way," she said, "was a declaration of war." The thought immediately flashed into my head that there was a connection between that and the Declaration of Independence. The thought was crazy, but in this business you learn to pay attention to crazy thoughts.

But then I dropped the idea, because her face clouded in anger. "Oh," she muttered. "There he is. Hiding in that doorway across the street. What a donkey!"

I turned to look.

Sure enough, the distinguished professor was standing inside the apartment house lobby across the street. His arms were folded. I looked at her. She had doubled up her hands into fists, and was smacking the table with them. Anger made her look very attractive. Her boyfriend may not have known how to tail, but he sure knew how to pick 'em.

70

* * *

She said she wanted to drink another cup of coffee. I left her there and walked back to the museum to pick up my car. He had his head buried deep in a newspaper and he didn't even see me. I suppose he was sure I wouldn't come out so soon. That I'd be busy trying to seduce Shoshana. I had a lot of people to talk to and things to think about: check out MO's down at Headquarters; go up and see the Sorensens and find out which of their recent guests were very interested in Indian art—enough to have their own collections—*that* was a shot in the dark and just displayed frantic behavior on my part; and, last but not least, why someone had driven a lance one inch deep into an oak plank. That isn't easy. Try it sometime. It took more than idle vandalism. It took a personal kind of rage. But why? Against whom?

I started the car and pulled out into the street. I made a right onto First Avenue and spotted her walking furiously across the avenue. I double-parked and watched her. She wasn't wearing a girdle. She didn't need one. The professor shrank back even deeper into the lobby and opened the *Times* even wider. He may have known all about Folsom points, but he didn't know shit from Shinola about shadowing. She didn't even look into the lobby as she steamed by. He dropped the paper to look at her, tried peering into the restaurant, obviously convinced I was still inside. The car stalled. I tried starting her up and this time Lundberg finally noticed me. He kept peering nervously over the paper at me. He clearly wanted to go chasing after her, but he didn't want me to see him come out of the lobby. He was too big to play games like that. Finally the engine caught.

The NYPD squad cars sometimes worked. I took pity on the professor and pulled out. I could see him in my rearview mirror. His face was swollen hard with rage. I felt sorry for Shoshana, but I was sure she could handle herself. But I smelled trouble from that angle. I didn't need her help that badly. Trouble is what I go out of my way to avoid unless I'm paid for it, and the Department was not paying me to have an affair with her, even though she was a very tasty dish. I stopped at a street phone and called the Two Seven.

"Jerry Allen, please."

"He's off today."

So I phoned him at home and got him in. Jerry was half white, half Cherokee. The guys on his squad called him Chief. When I explained why I had called he was not pleased.

"Lissen, Damian, I don't know anything about Indians, for crissakes! Whyncha go to the Amerindian Museum?"

"Great idea. Come up with another one."

"Damian, I really don't know—Edith, I'm on the phone! How about hittin' those bars on Atlantic Avenue around Hicks Street? They got a bar there where a lot of Mohawks hang out."

I knew about them. Construction workers in high steel. Yeah. Very knowledgeable about Indian artifacts. Very sensitive types.

"Any other ideas?"

"I—Edith, cut it out. Whatever it is, I don't want—hey, Damian, maybe she's got something. I just got this invitation in the mail. There's some Comanche painter havin' a show on Madison Avenue, and the openin' is today, you lucky boy. Carlisle Gallery. Four to seven, drinks on the house. His name is Tom Black Buffalo. He's gotta know moren' me, kiddo."

Well, maybe. Maybe not. It was worth a shot. Sherlock Holmes used to brood, chat with Watson, and then do his bit. There was never any waste motion. All of his leads panned out. Never a wasted trip. He should have been a New York City detective. I don't think he would have been so hot. And Dorsey was no Watson, either.

On the other hand maybe Holmes was a better bloodhound. I had to sniff every trail. Even a goddamn art opening. I cut over to Madison. The heap only stalled twice. I planned to personally congratulate the mechanics when I took it in later. With two well-chosen words.

* * *

It looked like an expensive gallery, very Madison Avenue. A big painting of a horse stood in each window, in a heavy, gilt-covered frame to give it the weight of an Old Master. This Eve Carlisle looked like shrewd operator at work. She would have to be to survive at the rentals demanded of successful galleries.

Above the horse in the left painting hung a ghost horse riding the clouds; above the horse in the right painting floated a war bonnet. They didn't look like kids' paintings, the way the real old Indian paintings on things like buffalo robes always looked to me, a somewhat less than amateur expert in the field.

These horses looked like real horses, as if Tom Black Buffalo had studied horse anatomy and gone to art school.

I went in. The place was packed. People were holding champagne glasses. This was a classy opening. The noise was enormous. Faded Levi skirts and turquoise necklaces and concho belts were everywhere. I noticed some of the brown faces and straight black hair of Indians, but they weren't wearing the Levi's or the expensive necklaces; they were dressed conservatively. I moved to the temporary bar and took champagne. I sipped it. It didn't taste like vinegar. Someone—Eve?—was putting out good money. I wished her heavy sales. I sipped it some more, this time not so carefully, staring at a heavyset, broad-shouldered man who was bursting out of a pinstripe like an overstuffed sausage. He wore a white shirt with pearl snaps and a bow tie made of small blue and white beads, and black oxfords with tassels. By the cluster of deferential people around him I knew he was Tom Black Buffalo. I looked around the walls.

There was a painting of an old man bending over a shield

73

of buffalo hide on which he was meticulously painting symbols. Another painting showed a vast encampment of tepees spreading across a mountain valley. It looked like the kind of painting deliberately made to appeal to white customers; none of them had the flavor of the Indian drawings and buffalo-robe paintings which I remembered as a kid in the American Museum of Natural History.

I wandered over to a table and picked up a catalogue of the show. Expensive color work; very nice paper. More money being spent. Tom Black Buffalo looked like a good investment. He had studied at the Art Students League in New York. The Slade in London. Someone had to pay for that expensive education. The horse paintings in the window were going for five thousand each, and I could see by the little red "sold" star slapped on each frame that he had already picked up ten thousand less the cost of the champagne. I moved close and waited till he glanced at me.

"Good afternoon, sir," I said. "I'm enjoying your paintings."

"Thank you, sir," said Tom Black Buffalo politely. He sported a rich, unctuous baritone, as if he had studied voice projection at the same time he was learning to stretch canvas, playing it careful; after all, there was a big audience out there for snake-oil salesmen. I instinctively disliked him. "May I ask which one?" he asked, curling his agile tongue around each consonant and slowly twirling the stem of his champagne glass.

The son of a bitch had caught me flatfooted. "The one in the window," I said, remembering in time that it had been sold.

"Ah, yes," he said, looking at me with contempt. "The horsey." He was clearly somewhat loaded and ready to take on any available paleface who rode into his traditional hunting territory. He was probably feeling that since the whole USA had been his once, any white was fair game. It was very good champagne.

"Oh, but I *really* like it," I said. I was not going to respond

74

with hostility to a possible informant, especially when things were rough enough already. I loaded sincerity into my voice.

"Going to buy it?"

"I would like to," I said regretfully, "but I see it's been sold."

"No, it isn't. That's *her* idea," he said crisply, jerking his head toward a slender, white-haired woman of fifty. I had noticed her before. She had been weaving in and out of the crowd with the practiced ease of the skillful hostess. So that was Eve Carlisle. She slithered in and out of the crowd like an oiled snake. Her hair was plastered flat against her skull and her mouth was a red slit. She never looked at anyone when she talked to them. Her eyes were constantly prowling.

"Typical white cleverness. People will want my other paintings even more when they see how popular I am. You want it, it's yours."

"I wonder if I could ask some more questions about it first," I said, sorry I had ever started up with this guy.

"Why? You want it, take it. You don't want it, don't bullshit."

A fine philosophy, and one which I heartily susbscribed to.

"I guess I don't want it," I said, feeling I had blown everything.

He turned his back to me in silent contempt and swept another glass from the bar. Score: Indians, 1, Custer, 0. I wasn't going to ask him anything. If I would now produce my shield he'd probably regard that little move the way Custer's bugle for the charge was regarded on June 26, 1876. I just needed more practice in talking to Indians. The lesson was to avoid bullshit. I had blown it with Tom Black Buffalo.

"How do you like the show?"

It was Eve Carlisle. She had a husky, caressing kind of voice which could make you warm all over, but not after

75

you'd learned that the "sold" sticker was a phony. Her teeth had a faint yellow tinge and the incisors projected a little too much. She was a bitch wolf in heat, but not for sex; for money.

"I don't know much about painting," I said, looking around the room the way she did when she was talking. I was looking for Indians to talk to. She didn't like the fact that I wasn't looking at her.

"Is that why you're not looking at me?"

I looked at her. This was someone whom I'd better be friendly with; it was clear she knew a lot of Indians, having sent out the invitation list. "It's the only reason," I said. "You're a very attractive woman, but I'm very interested in Indians and their art, especially the way some of them have adopted traditional European painting techniques." It was easy to bullshit bullshitters, I had long ago found that out; the problem was not to overdo it and to know when to stop.

"Yes," she said, mollified. I was looking at her busily. She had a basically fine face; the figure was much too slender for my taste, but her ears were small and well-shaped. There is always something attractive to be found in the ugliest of women, and she was by no means ugly. It wasn't hard to look at her at all, and that's what she wanted. Since I was also interested in buying paintings, she now had the best of all possible worlds.

"Just stopping by to look at Sitting Bull? So is everyone else, goddamnit." She seemed tired and bored.

"Are there many Indians here?"

"Oh, God, are they! The whole goddamn Indian population of New York City. Did you come to look at the paintings or at Indians?" She was beginning to flare up; I had given her the pretext to blow steam. She had kept it all locked under a tied-down safety valve all afternoon. "If the latter, please go to the Amerindian Museum and don't waste my time. The rent's too high here and I've got the feeling that not a single goddamn redskin is going to buy a single painting of Tom Black Bullshit." She took a long drink. There was no point in playing games anymore.

76

I leaned close. "I'm a detective," I said.

"No, you're not. I know the guy on the Art Squad."

"I know him too," I said. "He's on vacation." I palmed my shield and displayed it so that no one saw it.

It didn't register. She had had too much champagne and she wasn't listening or watching me closely.

"Just another body taking up space and sucking up my Veuve Cliquot at eighty-seven fifty the case! What do you want to know? Whatever it is, you won't find it out from me. This is my first show by a redskin and I'm getting good and sick of being told where to go and where to shove it, believe you me!"

"I see you've been scalped by Tom Black Buffalo."

"You can call it that. What did you say you were?"

"A homicide detective."

"That's all I need. Business is lousy, they're all getting in here, Black Bullshit lacks the charm to seduce lady art critics and screw good reviews out of them, and now a homicide detective shows up! You better come into my office."

We pushed through the crowd. Brown high cheekbones dominated. Several women wore cheap, shabby cotton dresses, cheap shoes, and scarves over their heads. No wonder Carlisle was sick when she looked the crowd over for prospective buyers. Sitting in a corner on the only chair was a very old Indian woman surrounded by attentive younger Indians. Her face was cobwebbed with a fine network of wrinkles. She wore a cheap red print dress and white sneakers and brown cotton stockings.

"Will you look at that!" Carlisle muttered in exasperation.

"Who's that?"

Carlisle was holding open the door to her tiny office. "How the hell do I know?" she demanded in her perpetually annoyed tone. "Some old Indian broad they treat like Queen Shit. Look at the way she's dressed, for crissakes! It sure gives the joint class. Come on in and suck the gaspipe with me. How I'm going to survive the day I sure as hell don't know. Goddamnit it all to hell."

She opened the door wider. I paused for a few more seconds in the doorway, looking at the old lady's wrinkled face.

She had to be in her nineties. There was an air of great, placid calm about her, not cowlike, but shrewd and sharp. I could have used her for my grandmother instead of the harsh, brusque, harassed, tired old woman who was always scrubbing clothes and bawling out my grandfather, who simply preferred to stay in the corner saloon until she was safely asleep. The Indians around her were pressing canapes and champagne upon her. I liked their deferential, respectful, affectionate attitudes. I had read that old Indians were honored. It was good to know that it was true. Maybe when I got to be ninety respectful baby detectives would cluster about my knee and listen to my quavering voice relate legends of the nineteen seventies.

I heard Carlisle let out an exasperated breath. I turned and went in. The door clicked shut behind us. It was a very tiny room, not much bigger than a closet. She was already sitting behind a small desk; I managed to force a chair into an angle where it faced hers, and I slid along the wall until I could wiggle my behind onto the chair.

"Tom Bullshit said this place was so small you couldn't cuss out a cat without getting fur in your mouth. I'll say one thing about these Westerners, they sure got a flair for colorful speech. They sure do, by gum," she said, with mock admiration. "Well, pardner, what's it all about?"

She was as hard as a magnesium alloy chisel and she was going to dig to the bottom of all this in jig time, and I better not forget it. I had a feeling I wasn't going to like her much. Or even slightly. Or even at all.

* * *

I was right. She listened with obvious impatience, crossing her arms. She got up and sat on a corner of her desk, nervously swinging one slender leg back and forth. The

78

room was filled with painting racks, half-empty coffee containers with cigarette butts floating in them, news releases, cartons of blank envelopes, and a pile of stamps over which she had spilled coffee. I touched the stack. The coffee was completely dry and the sheets were glued together. Sloppy broad.

When I had finished talking she said abruptly, "That's it?"

"Yes."

"Well, for crissakes!"

That seemed to be her favorite phrase. "I can't help you," she said crisply. "If anyone offers the stuff to me I'll give you a call." She fooled me. I thought she'd be prying, twisting and levering here and there. I was surprised.

"Thanks." I shoved my hands in my pockets and looked at her a little longer than I should, given the situation. She misunderstood. I was thinking that I'd hate to do the Wamsutta waltz with her. She'd lie there directing traffic like a Wehrmacht sergeant on military police duty. A shame, too. If I could throw a couple of copies of *Art News* on that sour expression and climb into bed, the rest of her might peel down to something about as half nice as Mrs. Sorensen. And that would be a lot.

"What's the matter?" she said sharply.

"Thinking," I said. I turned, but she slid between me and the door. She leaned her torso against me, making sure that her right breast pressed against my upper arm. She turned and bent down over her desk, pushing her behind against my groin. She picked up a pen and wrote for a couple of seconds on one of her business cards, with her tight little ass reminding everying I owned down there of delicious little joys.

"Privacy is what I like," she said." Here's my home phone and my apartment address. In case you'd like to continue this investigation. I might remember useful information under clever interrogation. Would you like to—er—question me?"

"I might."

"Good. Anytime." I had the feeling that there'd be nothing to be discovered up in her apartment building except whether there was a thirteenth floor, or whether it skipped from twelve to fourteen, or whether thirteen was called twelve-A. I could always amuse myself with this data and so leave her place with the feeling that I'd picked up something valuable. But the more I thought about it the more I thought I'd be a lot better off not only dropping my elevator research project but investigating the Silver Fox as well. I must have been getting older. There was just nothing there and I had gone past the stage where I'd leap into bed with anything. My standards were improving. Or I was getting older.

* * *

I stood and drank another glass of champagne. If it wasn't the best in the world, it wasn't the worst. I put the glass down and walked toward the old lady. When lost, take any road. She was sitting with her hands clasped placidly in her lap and a smile on her seamed face. She looked like the most interesting person in the room. She had once been very beautiful. Her eyes had the sheen of black onyx and her teeth were a brilliant white. They looked like they were her own. I positioned myself at the edge of the group and wormed my way closer. She was talking very softly and I couldn't hear her.

"What's she saying?" I asked.

Someone said, "She is sending her heart back over the years."

I wriggled in more. She noticed me. Her face closed up as if she had slammed a door. One of the young Indians near her had been grinning at what she had just said. Now he turned and saw me. His face closed shut like a beartrap. Now that I was close I saw that her fingers, lying so quietly in her lap, looked like five pairs of nutcrackers, so swollen

80

with arthritis they were. I was next to her by now, holding my drink and trying to appear that I wasn't the cause of the sudden icy chill. I was very persona non grata. I was the original wallflower. Oh, hell, nothing to lose. I put my drink on a table in front of the small table carrying the guest book which none of the Indians had bothered to sign and I took out my small manila envelope with the three-by-five reproductions I had made of the bigger photographs. I slid out the treaty belt photo and carefully placed it on her lap.

The conversation froze. One of the young men of the Screw McQuaid Society reached out a big brown hand and took it gently from her lap. He was stocky, with broad shoulders, the kind that being shorter than you, comes in low, boring at your belly like a tank with rocket launchers. He wore a beaded headband and shoulder-length black hair. He stared at the photo a few seconds. His face didn't seem to change, but it darkened a bit, the way a sunlit field changes color when a small cloud passes in front of the sun. I was making a lot of people annoyed today, that was for sure.

"Where'd you get it?"

"It's not mine."

"Why you shove it in her face?"

I didn't *shove* it in her face, and I wanted to attract her attention, you dumb dodo, is what I wanted to say. I was considering that response, but she ended that possible response by taking the photo back from him.

"Old belt," she said. Her voice was husky and sweet, and now that I was very close, she smelled like woodsmoke. Her voice didn't sound hostile.

"Yes," I said. "It's an Onondaga treaty belt."

"Yes. Very important. You Indian?"

I shook my head.

He said, "You like to suck around Indians and feel important?"

All this was like a cross-examination by a nasty lawyer, But I was determined to be patient.

"Not particularly."

"Like to prove to Indians you're not like the other white shits?"

"Nope."

"Want to tell us what great Indian art you've collected?"

"Not so's you'd notice."

I was an uncooperative witness. He was beginning to get madder and madder and I had had enough of Let's Kill Custer; I didn't want this quiet little query for some useful information to build up steam into a confrontation. I decided that my light, casual tone would only serve to piss him off some more. What I had best do now would be to eat some humble pie.

I suddenly stepped close to him. He did not expect this and he jerked his head backward a bit, like a barroom fighter taking his jaw out of danger. He had shaved that morning, and judging by the number of small razor cuts scattered around his broad, flat face he must have had a hell of a hangover. Some of the veins in his eyes were still inflamed. He did not look as if he would be able to stand any noise louder than kitten making her way across a deep-piled rug.

I spoke softy. "My name's Damian McQuaid." And then I waited expectantly.

This took him a little aback, and after a pause he growled, "I'm Howard Lame Deer."

I took his elbow. He allowed me, principally because he was startled and unsure what to do in this novel situation, to take him out of the group. "I've got some more pictures," I said, when we were at the edge of the gallery. I handed them over without waiting for his reaction. He leaned against the wall and riffled through them. He was very Indian about it, very impassive, like Chinese when you arrest them. He handed them back.

"What are you, a dealer?" His tone expressed his opinion of dealers, which was that they were several hundred feet lower than a rattlesnake's balls.

"I'm a detective."

"Bullshit."

82

I showed him the shield.

"Crap."

I showed him my ID with my picture on it. He grunted.

"You lookin' to finger me for Custer?"

I could easily see I would soon be up to my ass in Custer jokes. I could also see he'd been in plenty of jails.

"No. These were all stolen."

"So what? One thief stealin' 'em from another thief. So what?"

I said patiently, "I'd like to know if you'd have an idea who might buy them."

He stared at me and then gave me a big, wide grin. "You mean you're so goddamn dumb you'd pick out the first Indian you run across and ask *him*? Man, you must be *desperate*."

Desperate I was, yes. And sometimes the most unlikely people have been known to take pity on desperate detectives. Maybe it's the maternal instinct, maybe it's that people are flattered by the thought that someone needs their help and is asking politely for it. I can't figure it out very well, all I know is that it sometimes works.

"That's right," I said, watching the old lady talk and laugh, and once in a while fall silent. He caught my glance at her. "Indians talk only when they have something to say," he said. "Not like whites—they fill up empty time with yappin'. She just said she wants to let her mind go away and think about something." He looked at me. I was learning something from Indians. I kept my mouth shut.

"You ain't doin' well at all. Pathetic, man." His tone informed me I could take a flying fuck for all he cared. I decided my theory of pity being a prime source of data could also go with me on that flying fuck. I started to think over where I might try next. The Smithsonian? Senator Fred Harris of Oklahoma? After all, he was married to a Comanche. FBI? They had to have at least *one* Indian agent. I mean I hoped they did.

"What makes you think I'd know any dealers?"

"I see you're in a gallery."

"Yeah, you got somethin' there," he said grudgingly. "I mean, if you saw me beatin' wild rice with a stick in a Wisconsin swamp, and if you asked me then if I knew any dealers, you'd be an A-number-one prize asshole. I mean, you got logic on your side comin' here. I gotta admit that."

I waited. He went on, "You're the first New York detective I ever spoke to. Man, I couldn't make you at first. I figured you for some kind of fruit. You sure don't look like no Dakota cop." There was grudging admiration in his voice for a change. Time to raid the Sioux encampment.

What I wanted was privacy. Howard Lame Deer looked like he could be nursed up to informant status if delicately handled. With his knowledgeable air of cops and that criminal slang, he probably had a rap sheet as long as a subway car. And if he had a rap sheet maybe he had a charge pending somewhere, maybe he was out on bail and not supposed to leave the state; maybe was on parole and ditto. There were all sorts of entrancing possibilities jumping around Lame Deer. Maybe I could latch onto something nasty, work out a deal with some DA somewhere, and then proceed to grind Howard down till he would sing. Yes, a little privacy was indicated.

"How about a drink?"

"Yeah, you bet." He put down the champagne. "I could go for some real firewater instead of this French horsepiss."

A charming fellow, Howard.

*　*　*

There was an elegant little bar around the corner. He refused to sit at a booth on the grounds that everyone would think we were a couple of fags. There wasn't anyone at the far end of the bar, so I went along with that request. I excused myself and phoned the squad. Dorsey answered.

We had divided up the chase. He would take care of the homicide angle, I would track down the art work. If he thought he was close to the murderer he'd call me and we'd check it together, partners to the end. I knew he'd like it that way; he liked the old, familiar paths, the drift from bar to bar, checking out the guard's friends and associates to see if it was an inside heist with a sudden falling out at the end, settled by a weapon of opportunity, as the DA would call it. The division of labor was OK with me.

But the robbery was beginning to look too carefully planned. People didn't work out such careful details and then kill the inside man. It was all too carefully planned, expertly carried out, and to blow it all at the end with an act of impulsive violence—and line up the guard first—it just didn't hang together. It was much too complicated for an easy answer, and one thing I was sure of: Dorsey wouldn't come up with the answer.

That was OK with Dorsey. A quiet day driving around in a squad car, asking a few questions in a few uptown bars, a few beers, a good roast beef sandwich, driving back to HQ, typing up his DD5 slowly and carefully, with all sorts of details which Slavitch liked, a few laughs with the boys, then home. It was a safe and sane way to spend his declining years.

"Any luck?" I asked.

"Nah. Usual shit. The guy's wife didn't spend time crying. They wasn't getting along well anyways, the neighbors said. No kids. She works as a typist, nobody's gonna miss him, no parents. How you makin' out with that Sorensen broad?"

"Nothing yet."

"Some dish. She's the kind of dame who'd shake your hand and absentmindedly scratch her pussy at the same time."

That wasn't my analysis of the lady, but then Dorsey was so afraid to stray that he fantasized with wild exuberance.

I hung up and went back. The barstools were upholstered in a pale pink fabric. There was a backrest on each stool, which showed constructive thinking on the owner's part. A pink carpet would take care of anyone not saved by the back rest. It was a place for serious drinkers. Back of the bar was a big round mirror with a thick gold-leaf frame embossed with fat little cupids tumbling over each other. No woman over thirty would sit in front of the mirror, although two women far past that age were sitting at the the other end of the bar where they could watch the plump little gods and goddesses cuddling as they drank themselves slowly into their afternoon fog.

Howard had grabbed himself a stool right in front of the mirror. He was too big for the chairback, and when he leaned back it cracked. Then he bent forward and placed both palms flat on the bar, as if he were considering whether to vault over it to get at the liquor more quickly.

The bartender looked at him warily.

"Two bourbons with water," I said. Everyone west of the Appalachians drinks bourbon. Howard Lame Deer grunted approval. "Jeeze, my ma'd like that mirror," he said. I had the feeling that if he thought for a few seconds on that subject he'd wind up carrying it out. I put a twenty-dollar bill on the bar and let the change rest. It was a sign to Howard that there'd be more drinks. He took his mind off the mirror and drank his shot in one gulp without any water. Then he set down the empty glass and gave me an inquiring look.

"Set 'em up again," I said. The bartender filled his glass and set another one next to my first one. I had only taken a sip. Howard Lame Deer stared at the bartender, who started to wash several already clean glasses. "I make you nervous?" Howard asked. The bartender might be able to handle a woman with three martinis, but I didn't think he'd do too well with Howard.

I once knew a sergeant in the Mounted Squadron who used to tell the recruits, "You got a balky, mean horse, just put a handful of salt in his mouth and give him something else to think about."

"If I was the bartender here any guy with a beaded headband would make *me* nervous," I said. "Let me ask you a question or two, Mr. Lame Deer."

"What's *your* name?"

"McQuaid." I sighed. "Damian McQuaid." The two drinks must have shaken his mind back into his last night's drunk.

"So you're an anthropologist," he sneered. "Big fuckin' deal. I don't hand out no information on Sioux sex life. Got that?"

Oh, boy. It took a couple minutes before I straightened him out and proved all over again that I was a detective. People were drifting in from the offices for a cocktail, and the low-pitched hum of well-bred voices was beginning to surround us. But the third bourbon made him talk louder. He had a big chest and there was no way to make him pipe down, outside of hitting him over the head with a bar-stool—and the thought became tempting after a few seconds.

"So you wanna know where those things are?" he demanded, like a bull bellowing over a pasture fence.

"Yes," I said quietly, hoping that my example would influence him.

"Dicks are pricks," he said, piercingly and succinctly.

The bartender winced. I didn't care for the remark myself, but I listened politely.

"Why should I tell you anything? I mean, even if I know, why should I tell you?"

"Because we're friends," I said calmly. It's called the Big Lie technique, and you never know what illogical statement will move a drunk.

"You gonna appeal to me as a citizen, forget it. I ain't a citizen, I'm a ward. I can fight your fuckin' wars for you, but I can't get a bank loan."

No one fought my wars for me, I fought in Korea for my-self. Everyone was listening. The bartender was glancing at the phone. But if he called now, he'd only get his ass chewed out by the cop, and each time a bar is reported for a fight, it goes down on your Alcohol Control Board record. Too many and you're a no-no. Howard wound up with, "So whoever's got that stuff, I hope they keep it, and shove it up your ass, McQuaid."

That was a hell of payment for my three bourbons at a buck fifty a throw. I looked at him, wanting to bang that mirror over his head, and I said, "Mr. Lame Deer, suppose someone comes into your house. He steals your TV and radio and clothes. And suppose you came to me and asked me to help you." I was sorry I had started this analogy, it sounded phony even to me, but everyone was listening. So I plunged grimly ahead to get it over with. "So how'd you like it if I told you I hoped he would keep it because he was white and you were Indian?"

"Ahhh, bullshit!"

I silently agreed.

"McQuaid, whoever grabbed this stuff, it was either stolen by white soldiers or bought when the owner was drunk on your cheap whiskey. I don't owe you nothin'. And I hope some Indian took it and is gonna keep it. Howjah like that?"

I liked it very much. That was a very good thought on Howard Lame Deer's part. That was worth three bourbons and a few insults hurled in my direction. I was ashamed of myself for not having thought of it myself. A smile spread over my face. Mr. Lame Deer had been set for a glorious bar brawl and here I was, just smiling at him. He stared at me, very disappointed. My grin grew even wider. He obviously thought he had to do something more, so he did it. He threw his glass at my face.

*　*　*

The glass missed me, but two ice cubes hit me on the right cheek. They stung. He kept his left hand flat on the bar and pulled back his right for a punch. Out of the corner of my eye I saw the bartender begin to dial 911. None of this

88

would look good on my record. Howard Lame Deer swung. It was wide as a merry-go-round. I stepped inside it and as his arm swung around my right shoulder I put my right palm on his big chest and shoved. The swing had put him off balance, and my easy push sent him backward together with the barstool. I was off my stool and kneeling beside him as he struggled upward to a sitting position. He was very mad, but I put him in an armlock, and after a few seconds he subsided, since it was very painful.

"Friends?"

"Yeah."

I let him go and we both stood up. We set our stools upright and climbed on them.

"The same," I said to the bartender. He had wiped up the scattered ice cubes and picked up the glass, which wasn't broken.

"I—I can't serve him," the bartender said. He swallowed. A siren was coming up Madison. The bartender looked relieved. I could have sworn that his ears swiveled toward the street. I heard two car doors bang shut as the howl of the siren wound down to a low, vicious purr. Scalise came in first, his hand near his gun butt. His face wore a tense, nervous expression.

"All right," he said, looking tough. "What's goin' on here?"

"Hello, Scalise."

"Who—" he began, but then he recognized me. "It's the brains," he said for the benefit of his partner, who nodded. Scalise sighed. His hand left the neighborhood of his gun. He would live another day. "Everything under control?" he asked.

"Sure," I said. "My friend here wanted to see if I could put an armlock on him if he threw a punch. I just showed him I could." Scalise and his partner left. I stared at the bartender, who obviously was finding it hard to believe that a detective would be telling such horrible lies to two cops.

"Two more, please," I repeated. He took a deep breath

and poured out two more. Howard Lame Deer gulped his down. He was a nasty, unpredictable son of bitch, but he had helped me. He threw back his head as he drank it. I don't think it touched his throat on the way down. From the way the bartender stared at him I don't think such a sight had ever been seen in those parts.

"I seen that woman's bank today," Howard growled. "That one on Fifty-seventh Street. Whadda they want a bank for? They own ninety percent of the money and a hundred percent of the pussy. How's about another drink?"

I ordered another one for him. I had had enough. I left enough money on the bar for the drinks and I added five bucks for the anguish the bartender had suffered and would suffer, because I was leaving.

"Good-bye, Mr. Lame Deer."

He grunted, not even turning to look at me. The bartender stood at the end of the bar, right next to the phone, his arms folded, hating me for bringing this problem to his exquisite little rendezvous. I couldn't blame him.

*   *   *

But what Indians would take the stuff? I dropped into a branch library on Seventy-ninth Street and asked to see a map showing Indian reservations. I sat down and stared at it. I had no idea there were so many. Every state except Hawaii had at least one. They ranged in size from the four-hundred-acre Shinnecock, outside Southampton, to the three-hundred-mile-wide Navajo in Arizona, so big that it spilled over into New Mexico and Utah. But maybe Canadian Indians had taken them. And what if Mexican Indians had had a hand in it? Then what about the Indians in South America? I couldn't go chasing around the whole damn Western Hemishere. I needed help. Indian help. And I knew an Indian. Well, half an Indian.

I had caught the case. It was mine. I had let Dorsey pick up the car. He needed it and he was welcome to it and its new rattle from the right rear window.

90

I phoned her from a street booth.

"Who?"

"Sergeant McQuaid."

"Well, for crissakes." She sounded annoyed. "I already told you everything. Any luck?"

"Not yet."

"You don't have to hold my hand. I'm under pretty good control. Just call me when you find the stuff." She hung up abruptly.

Bitch. I dialed again. "Sergeant McQuaid," I said politely, but with an edge in my voice.

"I told you before, you don't have to call me! An' what I want to know, is how didja get my number? It's not listed."

"I know, ma'am. I'm close by. I'd like to talk to you a bit. It's police business." She got the implied threat; after a few seconds she said she'd wait for me. I quickly walked the two blocks to her street. It was lucky I'd put on speed; her Rolls was just pulling away as I came around the corner. He had a green light at the Avenue, and he stopped only because I stepped right in front of him. He started to yell and only stopped when I held up my shield.

She rolled down the window. I was angry but managed to conceal it. "Why," she said with a grin, "it's the sergeant!" She patted the seat beside her with a hand on which there was a marquise-cut diamond big enough to choke a boa constrictor. I open the door and got in. "Goin' anywhere special later? Can I drop you?"

I said no.

"I'm real busy today. I'm all over town like horse shit, like we say around Moab. Better come with me 'n' see real live Indians. I'm goin' first to a gallery openin' 'n' then I'm open to any suggestion."

"I've just been there."

"Ah. You get around."

"I get around, yes."

"Interested in Indian art?"

"You put your finger on it. Perhaps we can talk before you go."

91

"Roy, pull over." The Rolls hissed to a stop. "Well, I dunno. I got to be in the mood. Mebbe I'll skip the gallery. I don't like that dumb Comanche's paintin's anyways. But since everyone there is dyin' to look at my turquoise necklace, I just thought I'd wear this little fucker." She sprayed out her fingers, turning her massive ring in all directions. "I'd like to see their faces when I show up, specially that scrawny bitch who owns the gallery. But mebbe I'll ride on up to Brewster 'n' see our new quarter horse. Might jus' ride around the park an' neck. Roy won't look. Right, Roy?"

"Yes, ma'am."

"What's on your mind?"

I was angry that she'd made an appointment and then skipped out a minute later. That's what was on my mind.

"Or maybe I'll jus' go downtown for a fittin'. Need a new dress. More interestin' than standin' around lookin' at some lousy paintin's an' makin' small talk. Make a choice!"

I picked the safest and chose the fitting. She gave instructions. The car hissed around the corner and drifted down Fifth. She leaned back in her corner and crossed her long legs. I noticed them with interest. She repeated her question. "What's on your mind?"

I didn't feel like telling her. Instead I said, "I'd like to get your opinion on something."

"Sure. Later. Like my shoes?"

They were made of brown snakeskin. They looked pretty good.

"Cobra. Made to order for me by Ferragamo. Two twenty-five." She unbuttoned her coat and opened it wide. "Like my dress?"

It looked to me like a nice brown dress. I said so.

"McQuaid, this cost fifteen hundred smackers at Knize. Me! Me with Ferragamo shoes an' a Knize dress! When I was a kid an' wanted to go anywheres I'd have to hitch me a ride on the back of a beatup ol' pickup an' have to put out to get the goddamn ride."

"And now you've got a Rolls."

92

"You bet your sweet ass I got a Rolls." She buttoned her coat and stared out the window. The park was dry and cold, all brown except for the gray of granite where there were rock outcrops. She had stirred up old memories and wanted to pick at them and make herself sad. It's a pleasure I deny no one, but I had work to do.

"Mrs. Sorensen."

"Yep." She dredged up her attention from whatever old ocean she had sunk it in.

"Suppose an Indian stole your stuff."

She flared up. "Now why the hell would any of 'em want to do *that*? They all know me. They ain't smart enough to keep their mouths shut while they try to peddle it, an' there's not a single goddamn Indian in these Yewnited States with enough cash in his jeans to buy *one* of those arty-facts. Not one! Jesus Christ Almighty, McQuaid, smarten up."

There was nothing to add to that.

"But just suppose—"

She leaned forward and rapped on the glass partition with her diamond ring. "Roy! Stop!" The car hissed to a halt.

She leaned across me and opened the door. I'd never been thrown out of a Rolls before. I chose to regard it as some kind of a distinction. On the other hand, I had mixed emotions, just like the man mentioned by Lincoln. Abe said the man was tarred and feathered and then ridden out of town on a rail. When he was later asked how he felt, he replied that if it weren't for the honor of the thing, he'd rather walk.

I stepped out. I knew something she didn't know, namely, that although diamonds are the hardest substance known they are also very fragile. Drop one on the floor and if it lands on a cleavage plane, you will have two diamonds. Two small diamonds are not worth as much as the one big diamond which gave birth to them. Banging with a large marquise-cut to attract your chauffeur's attention is a good way to make your one hundred-thousand-dollar diamond worth two twenty-five-thousand fragments. I turned to pass on this useful information to her, but she leaned out, grabbed the door handle, and slammed it shut with impetuous violence. Only by whisking my hand from the doorjamb did I save my fingers. Let her ruin her goddamn diamond. I took no pity on billionaires. I had other fish to fry. Her turn to sizzle would come later.

* * *

I walked into the Squad Room. Dorsey was typing up a DD5. "Look, both sides," he said proudly. Dorsey was producing one of his long, detailed DD5's for Lieutenant Slavitch; he liked to provide them. It took a long time, and that was less time he had available for ringing doorbells and climbing stairs. I was just the opposite: I wrote them as if they were telegrams.

"Yummy," I said. I hung up my coat on the cheap wire hanger I had found in a garbage can down the street two years ago. I dropped my hat on the worn oak knob on top of the official-issue clothes tree. Sitting down. I picked up a DD5 and rolled it into my typewriter. I lifted my hands—but what the hell was I going to write about the day's activities? That I had bought a Sioux three drinks, after which he took a swing at me and missed? That I then applied a nice armlock? That he had given his opinion of women and banking? That Mrs. Sorensen had thrown me out of her Rolls? It would not look good for a homicide detective.

"Look, the mad pianist!" Dorsey said. I lowered my hands. I had better go out and get some material which would look better on a DD5, especially since Slavitch's keen eyes would be scanning it.

It was 6:30. The Amerindian Museum was closed. I picked up the Manhattan directory. Someone had printed "turn to p. 781" on the inside front cover. I'm a sucker for these things. P. 781 told me to go to p. 329. P. 329 referred me to p. 11. P. 11 said, "Fuck you, Lt. Slavitch." It was worth it. I added "in spades" and signed Dorsey's name.

I looked up Dr. Shoshana Kimri's number. It rang ten times. I hung up and then did the obvious. I dialed the museum number. I got the operator. I asked for Dr. Kimri.

"Sergeant McQuaid. Dr. Kimri?"

"How deed you know I am here?"

"We have ways."

"Yes! I deed not know myself I would be here. You are seekik."

"I'm what?"

"Seekik. P-S-Y-C-H-I-C. Seekik. I know English much more better than you."

"Sure. I'd like to ask you a couple things."

"Yes, you come in on the planetarium side. It's open. I meet you."

"Half an hour?" She agreed and I hung up. I picked up three car keys from the pegboard and played roulette. I decided 39 might make it there and back. Thirty-nine had a loose connecting rod which made it sound like an insane African drummer whenever it went over forty. When I once pointed this out to the repair department they said that ours were not chase cars and that the uniformed patrol's police cruisers were more important. Well, I didn't own the Police Department. Mine but to do and die. I hung up the two other keys and went downstairs. Thirty-nine was locked in by a doubled-parked cruiser. I went in and had a harsh word with the sergeant on desk duty. Someone finally came out and moved it.

I parked near the planetarium side. Inside the entrance the lobby was filled with huge color photographs of the earth, taken from outer space. The dominant color was a pale, light blue. I stopped to stare at them and I heard her voice back of me.

"Looks like a turquoise, no?"

That's just what I was thinking. I nodded, turning around.

"The Indians were right to make it a sacred stone?"

I shrugged. "Sure. If you say so."

She frowned. Her hands were thrust deep into the pockets of her cardigan. "You follow, yes?" She turned abruptly and walked to the elevator. While we rode up she looked at me with an air of annoyance. She beckoned me out at her floor, walked quickly, stopped suddenly, and turned to me, asking sharply, "What is 'if you say so'? I don' unnerstan'. Do you think I am right or wrong?"

I chose to be cowardly. "I think you're right," I said.

"But how can you think I am right when you know nothing, nothing, *nothing* about Indians, and in your own country?"

"Yes, you're right." She smiled for the first time. "You will excuse me, please! I had trouble today. About you."

"Your fiancé."

"Yes." She opened the door to her office and motioned me to a chair. She sat behind her desk with her knees primly pressed together and doodled elaborate cubes, one on top of the other, all neatly shaded so that the three-dimensional effect was perfect. "He wanted to know if you had seen me again. He is ridiculous! He wanted to know if you have touched me. What a fool!" She drew sharp teeth inside each cube.

Maybe he was a fool. I'd watch her carefully myself if I held a mortgage on her. She was a fiery bit of property and should be protected with automatic spray warning devices. She simmered down and wanted to know what I wanted to discuss.

"Those Indian things."

"You found the robbers?"

"No. Suppose an Indian stole them. And suppose he had no intention of selling them. Or even selling them back to Sorensen."

"Yes!" She was sitting up straight now. No more doodling.

"Suppose he just wanted to keep them."

"Yes! Possible, very possible."

"Red Power?"

"Oh, yes. But they say 'Indian Power.' Never Red Power."

"So they might keep them for good medicine?"

"Yes. That is what they might do."

"Good. Now, where would the pieces be?"

"You mean, if I was Indian, and I stole them for good medicine, where would I taken them?"

"Yes."

"Why, somewhere where the power would get stronger."

I must have looked puzzled. She sighed and picked up her pen and resumed her doodling. She was giving a lecture.

"In possession of the white people, the power of the wampum belt, the carved tree god, everything, it's like torch batteries which are not used."

"Flashlight?"

"Yes, flashlight, the power leaks away. So now, after all these years, they are very weak. They have to be plugged into electricity. Then they get strong again. The electricity will have to be on old Indian land."

"A reservation."

"Maybe. Maybe not. Sometimes the tribes were tooken away—taked? Taken. Yes, taken. English is a gestapo language. Taken away to land which had never been theirs. Sometimes they were left on land which had always been Indian. That would be better, more electricty, more medicine."

"So for a full charge of juice you need your ancestral acres?"

"You think it is comical, but that is the way they think. I don't like much to waste time for someone who makes jokes. I stay late to help you and now—now I am regretting." She slapped her pen down on her drawing and stood up, her cheeks flushed through her tanned face. "Good evening, Sergeant," she said stiffly, and walking to her door, she held it open.

I unfolded myself and stood up. I don't worry if a lot of people don't like me, and a lot don't. But I was sorry about her.

"I'm sorry if I've offended you," I said, and as I turned to go I bumped into Dr. Lundberg. He glared at me and pushed me to one side in his frantic eagerness to get into her office to see if she were still a virgin. I decided not to make an issue out of the shove. I walked down the hall and pressed the button for the elevator, feeling better for the first time in two days. I no longer was like a chicken running around with its head cut off. All I had to do was head west and dig up a reservation with its battery terminals in good shape. All I had to do would be to nose around without attracting attention. And from what I had already learned about Indians, that would be as easy as pouring melted butter on a red-hot spoon up a wildcat's ass.

* * *

The next morning I typed up a DD5 which elicited cries of admiration from Dorsey. Lieutenant Slavitch took a dimmer view of it; he said it looked like a doctoral thesis on anthropology.

"Yeah," I said, "but the question is, is it good enough to win me a Police Department fellowship for Arizona and New Mexico?"

Slavitch flipped through the big pile of DD5's Dorsey and I had produced. "No other leads?" he asked with a frown. I looked at him in silence. Dorsey chewed a toothpick, his eyes glazed over with indifference. I dropped my eyes to Slavitch's chart and studied his candy stripes. Purple was overtaking orange, with green putting up a good show.

"I need everyone I can get," Slavitch finally growled. "But you better take off. Go downtown and get organized."

I nodded. Outside, Dorsey said, "Boy, oh boy, the chief of detectives must be chewing his ass for results." Sure, and Slavitch was going to bite my ass, and whose ass did I get to bite? No one's. I made my phone calls. I reserved a flight to Albuquerque. Finance said they'd have the money ready for me by two. Next I decided I needed some simple advice, such as where to go. Shoshana probably wouldn't care to talk to me any more. So I dialed Mrs. Sorensen.

"You again?"

"Yes." I strangled her mentally.

"I'm on my way out, gangbuster."

"Can we meet?"

"Whaddya got in mind?"

"I just need some advice."

She sighed. "I'm goin' to the Carlisle Gallery. Goin' try re-placin' some of my stolen pieces. 'Cause I got the feelin' I'm never gonna see 'em again. Meetcha there." She hung up without waiting for my answer.

Smug bitch. What she needed was a good kick in her beautiful half-breed ass. Or something there more persua-sive. I began to feel lustful on my way uptown, dwelling on my memory of the first sight I had of her shirt with its first top three buttons opened. It is not a good idea, theoretically, that is, to shack up with a customer, but this was a special customer. Nor did she look like the type who would gossip to the girls. I was going to have a rough time out in the Indi-an boondocks, and I needed all the help I could get on every level.

When I pushed open the door of the gallery I could see Mrs. Sorensen sitting at the desk. She must have been wear-ing the dress she was on her way to have fitted when she threw me out of the Rolls. It was so simple that it must have cost plenty. She looked like she had been poured into it hot and allowed to cool. The top part was a firm Jell-O. It was becoming clear to me that she did not approve of brassieres in any context. Her hair was coiled in a tight spiral over each ear. No rings, no necklace. High heels. We were not doing the Indian bit today; today we were old East Coast money.

Eve Carlisle was talking. Evidently, from all the theatrics, the deliberate charm carefully measured out in teaspoons and being poured over Mrs. Sorensen, she was trying to sell her something very expensive. None of the charm seemed to be sticking.

They hadn't seen me come in. There were a few people inside browsing around. I moved closer to the little office.

The desk was snowed under in a blizzard of letters, receipts, newspaper clippings of reviews, two pairs of scissors, and Scotch Tape. Eve had knocked over a little glass jar filled with paper clips and as she spoke was busy hunting them over, under, and between the mass of paper on her desk.

"Modern American Indian paintings will be the next collectibles," she said. "I foresee a trend already; within one or two years—probably the latter—anyone with a good-sized holding in this field will dominate the market. Moreover," she added, bending down to retrieve some clips from the floor, "anyone with a good collection will be able to cash in nicely in a few years, investmentwise."

"You're crazy as a shithouse rat," said Mrs. Sorensen calmly. "Tom Black Buffalo ain't bad. But he's usin' too many tricks he picked up goin' to art museums. He ain't original enough to attract good critical attention. None of his stuff has pizazz."

Eve brought her head up with a snap. The charm was instantaneously sucked within like a light rain on sandy desert soil. Mrs. Sorensen dragged a big glass ashtray to the edge of the desk and knocked her cigarette ash into it, she stuck her cigarette in a corner of her mouth and let the smoke dribble upward, half-closing her eyes. She wore an amused half-smile as she waited for Eve Carlisle to react. The woman was not fast on the uptake.

"I'm sorry you feel that way," she remarked stiffly.

Mrs. Sorensen was disappointed. She had expected a battle, I could see, and was clearly depressed at not being able to have one. She was a lady who needed red meat every day and would search for it anywhere.

"Don't feel sorry," she said encouragingly. "Fight some instead." But it wasn't any good. Eve Carlisle wasn't accustomed to being checked so abruptly. She wasn't having any of it, and resumed her paper shuffling. Mrs. Sorensen sighed and, leaning forward to knock some ash off her cigarette, saw me.

"There he is!" she called. "There's my detective! Come on in!"

I walked in. She turned to me with a wide grin. "I'm busier than a stump-tailed bull in fly-time, with evvabuddy wantin' to talk to me. You go ahead right now, Sergeant, it's your turn."

Carlisle's flush was still working; she was busily arranging her papers in neat little piles for the first time in their neglected history. I suggested we step outside. "No, honey," Mrs. Sorensen said lazily. "Eve here won't mind steppin' outside herself, wouldya, honey?"

Eve minded a real lot, but she tacked on a grim smile and left, giving me a hard little grin, which she squeezed out and then clipped off abruptly as if it had emerged from an automatic sausage-slicing machine. She left a gust of perfume as she went by us. I sniffed at it. So did Mrs. Sorensen.

"Canal Number Five," she said. "Don' unnerstan' women. Real men *want* to know what a woman smells like, as long as she's clean. You agree there?"

"I'm a real man."

"Good." She shoved aside the neat little piles and then deliberately messed them up. Then she patted the desk top. I sat on the cleared space.

"What's on your mind, buster?" she demanded, placing a brown hand on my thigh. I decided that if I were to ask her to take it off, that simple request would escalate into a shouting match or a slap. Besides, she was gently kneading my thigh as she smiled up at me. Her dress did not afford any décolleté, but I could see the firm little raspberry-sized hills of her nipples as they swelled against the fabric.

What was on my mind was to push her down onto the rug; instead, I moved the conversation around to the reservation problem.

"I have a feeling that your stuff might be somewhere west on a reservation," I said.

"Don't worry your head 'bout that," she murmured as her kneading hand moved slowly up my thigh.

"Yes. So I'd like to know what reservation they might be on."

"Now, how the hell could I answer *that?*" she demanded,

half annoyed and half lasciviously. She leaned forward and pressed her firm stomach against my knees; then she sort of squiggled around on the chair as if her ass had been a drop of water dancing on a hot frying pan. It was hard for me to concentrate. I asked her where she would look if she herself were going west.

"Blackfoot men are very tall," she murmured.

"Blackfoot Reservation? Where's that? Idaho?"

"Nope."

She took her hand off, put her elbow on the desk on Eve's little rejumbled pile of archives, put her chin on her palm, and stared at me. "Like that little massage?"

"Pretty nice."

"Lot's more where that came from. You live around here?"

"Not far."

"How 'bout questionin' me up at your place?"

I stood up, feeling like a virtuous and indignant virgin in one of those old melodramas with a villainous landlord.

"Where's the oldest reservation?" I asked, putting everything on the desk back into neat piles.

"Connecticut. Want a ride up?"

"No, thanks. I mean, where's there a reservation where there's the most medicine?"

"Where'd you pick up that word?"

"I did some homework." For the first time she looked at me seriously. "Maybe Hopi. Maybe Zuni. Maybe Santo Domingo."

"I'm going out. I hear things are rough out there for people who walk in cold."

"Yep."

"How about a letter of introduction?"

"Sure. I can arrange that. Let's go on up to your place. I'll write it out."

I eased my way out of that one by pointing out—untruthfully—that I had to be at Squad Headquarters in half an hour for a last-minute review of the case with Lieutenant Slavitch, then I had to catch a plane.

She picked up a piece of paper from the desk, and wrote out a letter for me. I thanked her and folded it away. "Keep in touch," she murmured, "and I mean on all levels."

*   *   *

All police departments are overloaded, with crime on the rise and personnel being cut back. How could I ask anyone out west to go around doing my work? For instance, suppose I were to send photos around to Gallup and Albuquerque and Santa Fe. And ask the chiefs out there to check them out. But what about the stuff stolen in Gallup that Gallup is looking for? I didn't expect them to drop their work and do mine. Maybe they would—if they loved me and if they thought that a billionaire from Gallup would run into trouble in New York someday. Now, suppose they do locate one of the artifacts in some hockshop in Albuquerque. They notify me. I then say, find out who pawned it. So they produce a name. Say it's Sam Crazy Rabbit. Will they drive around looking for Sam? Let's push the maybe a little bit. They drive around. They find out he's gone to Santa Fe. Now, they *could* drive to Santa Fe and pick him up. What about the five burglary cases that took place during the night in Gallup? Do they drop them and keep on looking for my man? If I believed that this would happen then I believed that Lieutenant Slavitch was the Sugar Plum Fairy. More. Suppose they tell me the guy's been located in Albuquerque. I call Albuquerque. They say sorry, no men available. Simplest thing to do: go myself— and chase my own tail.

Next problem: what about the gun? Solution: don't take it. Why? Too much trouble carrying it into other jurisdictions. There's a lot of respect for New York City homicide detectives around the country—and a lot of professional jealousy. I'd been arrested a couple times for carrying a gun without a permit, once in Iowa and once in Nevada. And when I started to object they responded that they'd had the same problem when they went to New York, and how did *I* like it? So the best thing to do would be to park it in my locker in the Squad Room and ask some deputy to ride shotgun if I needed help. Sure, I'd feel uneasy a couple days. I'd miss the comfortable weight of my .38 Detective Special, four in the basement and one on the front steps. None in the chamber. If I started wrestling, a good kick to the holster might get me shot in the groin, which is what happened to my good friend Brannigan in the Two Eight. Now if I ran across a bad guy I'd be naked under my left armpit, and Aramis, no matter how nice it smells, is not a good substitute.

*   *   *

I went home, had a good meal, watched TV for a couple hours, and turned in early. Former out-of-town hunts had taught me that a good night's sleep was a good idea; running around in strange towns and dealing with people you didn't know, with no reliable local informants, usually resulted in tension-filled, restless nights. Therefore, a good night's sleep first would build up a reservoir of energy I could draw on for forty-eight hours—and those frequently the most crucial. I took an early flight and I managed to add three hours' more sleep, and by the time the stewardess woke me up to fasten my seat belt for Albuquerque I was feeling ready for bear.

It was the Navajo Reservation for me. It was the biggest, so why not? It covered their ancestral home—again, why not? It had to be oozing with good medicine. And Gallup was the gateway to the reservation.

I had reserved a car in New York. When I showed up at the counter at the airport and wrote down my destination, the girl regretted that there had been a mistake, that there were no cars. I got angry; she pointed out that a Greyhound was leaving downtown Albuquerque for Gallup in fifteen minutes, and that I would be able to rent a car in Gallup. I grabbed a cab and made it to the terminal just in time. The bus made good time; I watched the land fracture into brown planes; the shadows of mountains leaned against one another, and distant mesas had fine powders of snow lodged in their crevices. The land looked as if it ran on forever, not only into distance, but into time. It was so fascinating to look at it that I couldn't sleep, even though I had fully intended to do so. I had been able to sleep on buses or trains in other parts of the country, but there was something so old and remote and harsh about the Southwest—where I had never been—that I found myself staring at it hour after hour. I could believe that gods could come out of the mesas and mountain, dance, and return.

Three hours later I was in Gallup. I checked my suitcase, went into the men's room, and immediately read "Tribal Chairman Thompson has a dirty asshole. So is his mother." I could see I might be getting involved in intra-Indian disputes as well. Another goddamn complication. Next to it was: "Native Americans United are a bunch of long-haired fagots what don't know what Indian culture is all about." More subtleties.

The office of the chief of police was located inside a modern courthouse. Whenever the town fathers decided to build a new courthouse they always seemed to come up with something that looked as if it had been stamped out of a cookie-cutter. Put me down blindfolded in rural Alabama, upstate Michigan, or way out on Long Island, take off the blindfold, and ask me where I was, and I couldn't tell unless I could get a look at some license plates. But I suppose if I'd done the same thing in the 1880s I'd have faced the same problem, only there'd have been ornate pediments, elaborate sculpture with acanthus leaves on top of all the columns, and all that Victorian junk. But without license plates. It was hard to come out ahead, but I did prefer all that mass of curves. At least a man could have something to occupy his gaze while coming up the steps for some gloomy justice.

I knocked on the chief's door. A sour voice called out for me to come in. I opened the door and walked in. A rack of

105

Winchesters stood next to the door. A few framed pictures of earlier chiefs were spaced along the walls, and a larger picture of the President, with two crossed American flags on short staffs above him, was back of the chief's desk. A six-foot length of rattlesnake skin was nailed on the side wall, and next to that was a huge pair of longhorns. Aside from that it looked like any office anywhere. It even looked like mine. A hardbitten man of about sixty was slumped down in the chair behind the desk. His hands were clasped behind his neck and he was staring at the ceiling. His hard round face was covered with a network of broken blood vessels, and from the center of that ruined area there projected a nose which had not only been struck, stomped on, and knocked sideward, but also bore purple interlacings in allegiance to the millions of drinks its owner had downed. A boozer. He had a coarse, wide mouth, and coarse white hair, trimmed to a brutally short pompadour, the kind they inflicted on me at Marine boot camp. This guy obviously considered himself a drill instructor, and I bet life was hell for everyone who worked out of his office. It's frequently dangerous to judge people from their faces, and just as frequently it's sensible. My instinct said that this particular specimen of Sheriffus Americanus was a bastard.

"Yeah?" he asked. He took his gaze from the ceiling for a moment, let it rest on me, and went back to the ceiling. I looked at it. It looked like a normal ceiling to me.

"That ceiling under arrest?" I said.

He brought his stare back to me. "What?" he asked, his forehead corrugated in suspicion. I regretted my statement. "I was making a bad joke, sir. Good morning. My name's McQuaid. I'm a homicide detective from New York. Here—"

"ID."

I put it on his desk. He dropped his gaze, looked at it indifferently, and resumed his ceiling scrutiny. "Ain't often we get the great honor of havin' a real New York City detective in here," he said, not sounding as if he thought it was

106

really and truly an honor. "As a matter of fact, Mr. McQuaid, I do believe it's the first time. Business or pleasure?"

"Business."

"Name it."

I named it. He brought his bloodshot eyes down and shoved his hands into his hip pockets. His eyes, when I could get past the mass eruptions of the tiny veins, were pale blue and hard as marbles. I would not like to be talking back to him on a lonely country road. I showed him my picture collection.

"Lessee now. You want me to figger out who I think stole 'em? Or where you might find 'em?"

"Yes."

"No idee atall. *Atall.*" He made one word out of the two. "All I handle 'round here is armed robb'ry. Drunks. Oh, Jesus, drunks. Once in a while a drunken Navajo runs over a tourist walkin' 'longside the road. Does it deliberately, too. But try 'n' prove it. Family homicides, friendly l'il things like that. But what you got here is a real sophisticated operation. Way out of my class. Nope. No one round here who coulda done it, let alone thunk it up. Couldn't help ya, McQuaid. You carryin' a gun?"

"No." That was a fair question and I was calm.

"Good. You could get in a lot of trouble. You New York people got real rough with one of my deppities once. Sure you ain't carryin'?"

Now the implication was that I was lying. I didn't like that at all, and his sharp little bloodshot eyes saw my annoyance. He smiled. This was a number-one pricko, I could see that. I would have to control myself and be very, very polite.

"You got any idea whom I could talk to?"

"Hell, no." It was clear he was bored with me and my problem. He resumed his scrutiny of the ceiling.

"What's so interesting about that ceiling?" I asked. He answered without looking at me.

107

"Hell, the painters did a lousy job. It's all full of little cracks, see? If I look hard enough sometimes I c'n see faces 'n' counties 'n' even words."

"Words?"

"Yeah. Words. They get spelled out." He sounded real interested. This was more exciting than helping a brother officer who only had something dull to offer like a homicide, and a million-dollar burglary. "I c'n see 'yes'—'n' I c'n see 'no.'"

"Very interesting."

"You wanna talk to the pawnshops round here, you're welcome."

Great suggestion. I might have thought of it all by myself.

"Any one better than the others?"

"Naw. Take your chances."

"How's about sending a man around with me to point them out."

"Aw, you're a big boy. They got more important things to do."

It all seemed like the game was called You're from New York, I Ain't Ever Gonna Need You, So Screw You.

I stood up. "Chief," I said politely, "I see a word up there. It's got two syllables."

"Yeah? Where?"

"In the far corner. I can see an A. Then there's an S. Then another S. Then there's an H. And an O. Then I see an L. Then I see—"

"I don't like wise guys," he said coldly. The blue eyes took on the glint of a blued gun barrel.

"I'm with you," I said. He stood up and came over to me with amazing speed. I wouldn't have thought him capable of moving so fast. He frisked me very quickly and expertly, even checking for an ankle holster.

"It ain't that I don't believe you, McQuaid," he said amiably. The voice was an amazing contrast to the hostility so clearly expressed in his eyes. "But a little skepticism keeps us cops healthy. You agree?"

"Damn right," I said with absolute sincerity. I had insulted him. He had frisked a brother officer. I called it an even exchange. "How about recommending a good restaurant?"

"Ain't none. Just get a can of sardines 'n' some salty crackers 'n' a bottle of whiskey."

"Whiskey? There's none left."

I bet he didn't like that remark. Screw him.

*　*　*

I found a clean, quiet motel three blocks away on a quiet street. It was too late to hit the pawnshops and Gallup wasn't the kind of town where one could take a pleasant evening's stroll. Heavy truck traffic thundered along Route 66, the next block south was full of the kind of stores every small town possessed, and there were, by a fast count, about twenty pawnshops, their windows full of concho belts, turquoise necklaces and bracelets, and small bone-carvings of deer which my very recent crash course in Indian lore told me were hunting amulets. Navajo drunks were everywhere, sitting, standing, lying, and lurching arm in arm along the sidewalks. There were plenty of women drunks, something I rarely saw in New York. It was very cold. I hoped Gallup had a Black Maria to pick them up before they froze to death in some alley. Well, that was the chief's problem, not mine.

The motel had a little restaurant. When I sat down at a small table the owner, a retired railroad engineer, was talking guns with one of the guests, a long-haired man of thirty, dressed in Levi's and wearing a magnificent concho belt. As soon as I came in they began trading stories about rattlesnakes. The owner, who still wore a railroad engineer's cap, maintained that the rattlers used in the Hopi dances had their fangs pulled.

I sipped my coffee. It was terrible. I pushed it away, and the owner caught my expression. He leaned toward me. "Listen, sonny," he said. "That's the way it's gonna be from here to the coast."

"How true that is," murmured the younger man. They resumed their discussion of whether or not the rattlers had been rendered innocuous up at the Hopi mesas.

"No," the young man said quietly.

"Sure, Jay. 'At's how they take 'em in their mouths. Stands to reason."

"No," Jay calmly repeated.

"Listen, Jay, you goes to all them dances up there at Oraibi 'n' the other mesas, 'n' you know a lot 'bout Indians, but you ain't gonna sit there 'n' tell me they don't pertect theyselves? Indians ain't dumb."

So Jay knew a lot about Indians? If the local gendarmerie wouldn't help, it certainly wouldn't hurt to talk to Jay. But now, aware I was listening, they began, without any expression on their faces, to turn the conversation toward me.

"Y' know them snow rattlers?"

"Which ones, Al? The ones up past Window Rock?"

"Yeah, them. They're actin' up again'. Guy runnin' the snowplow up at Ganado says he musta scooped up three, four hunnerd. Couldn't see 'em, 'cause they was as white as the snow. White eyes, too, on the buggers. Only spotted 'em when they started wigglin' off the blade. Chopped a lot in half. For a fact."

I was no expert on rattlers, but I knew enough to know that they hibernated in cold weather. And that there weren't any snow-colored ones, either. It was the old Western game. After a while they gave up trying to tease me. They asked me to sit at their table.

I turned to Jay and said, "You seem to know a lot about Indians."

"He sure does," said the motel owner, whose name was Al. "He's an anthropologist."

"No," Jay said. "I *was* one. For a while. But none of them ever made good money. And I wanted good stereo equipment. I switched to med school. I got a degree, then I said shit, I don't want to be a doctor, I like archaeology. So I went on digs. And since I knew anatomy it was my job to get into

110

graves and put the bones together and figure out what they had died from. Arrow? blow on the head? arthritis? bone cancer? I'd look for bone necrosis or some such happy event. I did that for a couple years, all over the Southwest. Then I realized all over again that I wasn't making money and that I was sick of looking at people long dead. I was after big money this time. So I got a job with the Civil Aeronautics Administration. Good money. My job was to fly— for free—to the scene of fatal crashes where everyone was spread out over a few acres and put them together—this leg goes with this torso, this nose belongs on that head—or does it? Good money. After a couple of years of good money and taking tranquilizers everytime I got in a plane to go to a scene, I got sick of looking at just dead people. I just didn't want anything to do with dead people, whether they were dead twelve hours or six hundred years. What I wanted was live people and pretty things where I could use my knowledge of archaeology and anthropology and money. And I found it."

I liked him. "What do you do?" I asked.

"I deal in Indian jewlery," he said. "I speak some Navajo. I buy from them, I buy out-of-pawn stuff and I own a little shop near Palo Alto. You a tourist, right?"

I could say tourist or I could level with him. But if I wasn't getting any cooperation from the chief, I didn't see any way I could go around a small New Mexican town unnoticed.

"No. I deal in dead people."

"You don't look like an undertaker."

"I'm a homicide detective from New York."

His eyebrows went up. "Business trip?"

I nodded.

"Any luck?" he asked. "But that's not my business."

"Maybe. Want to see some pictures?"

"Not if they're corpses."

He pushed aside his plate. I put the color three by fives in front of him. He went through them carefully. He put them together and squared them neatly as if they were a deck of cards. "Very good pieces. Connected with this homicide?"

"Yes. Ever see them?"

"Only in books."

"See them personally?"

"No."

"If you come across them out here, would you let me know?"

"It depends."

That was interesting. I sipped my coffee and then said carefully, "Depends on what?"

"Depends on who was killed. And why. And how."

So he had conditions.

"Taking the long view?" I said.

"I don't get you."

"Dealing in bones six hundred years old, you must take a long-range view of everything."

"I guess you could say that." He hadn't expected my remark, but I saw that he liked it.

"Law gets in the way of your ethical principles sometimes?"

"I smoke pot, too. Put me against the wall and shoot me."

He amused me. I had no power in New Mexico to force anyone to talk to me. All I was was a private citizen, since I didn't think the sheriff would be of any help. If I made an arrest it would be a citizen's arrest, and that operation was loaded with terrible possibilities of false arrest. I'd have to find willing volunteer helpers, and for that I had to be patient and long-suffering. "I'll tell you the whole story."

"Why?"

"First of all there's nothing good on television tonight. Second, I like you, Jay. Three, you might be able to help me. And four, you're a detective yourself."

"A *what?*"

"Sure you are. You look over some beat-up bones and try to figure out how come they got to be there, how he was done in, who did it, and how long ago it happened. What else do you do when you find a skull with an arrowhead in it? That's just what I do, but I have to look extra to make the indictment stick, and that's the only problem of mine you don't have to face."

"I guess you're right," he said, smiling.

I told him the whole story. He listened intently.

"Anything there which violates your integrity?"

He shrugged. "Here's some dame rich enough to buy these rarities,which were either ripped off or swindled from Indians. Then she gets ripped off. No, *that* doesn't bother me."

"What bothers you?"

"They killed that black security man. That bothers me. Forgive this pun—it's not so black and white as all that. Last year an old Apache told me his people saw a cavalry patrol heading toward their hideout near the Mogollon Rim. They took off for the hills but in the excitement they left a baby behind. A black trooper ran his bayonet through the kid and held it up in the air while the kid wriggled and screamed. Word gets around."

"Are you telling me that an Apache ran a lance through this guard to get even?"

"Let me give you some advice. You stop thinking like a white man when you're out here and start thinking Indian. You might get somewhere."

"Why do you say that?"

"You seem to think someone stole these things for resale. That's what your questions are aimed at: Where do you think I can find 'em? What pawnshop might have 'em? Now, maybe they were stolen for that reason. Maybe. But you have to understand a lot of Indians don't think that way. I'm not saying sometimes they wouldn't steal for money. But sometimes they'll do things in a very symbolic way which is very Indian."

"Now what the hell does *that* mean?"

"You're an intelligent man. I've drawn you a fast sketch-map of the Indian mind. Be careful. Keep your ears open

113

and your mouth shut as much as possible. That's the second bit of advice for Indian country and you can go pretty far with that. And here's an extra item for you: there's not a single chief of police or sheriff or marshal who understands Indian thinking. If there is I've never met any. Because all they ever think about is how to sit on them. That takes a lot of energy. And one last word: never be impatient. Never interrupt anyone, especially if he's old."

"Hot damn."

"Yes," he said calmly. "Hot damn. You ought just once to sit in council. Even the biggest asshole on the reservation can talk as much as he wants. He talks until he runs dry. No one tells him to speed it up or shut up. You'll probably see only one wristwatch on the reservation and it'll be on the tribal chairman's wrist. It's a gift from Mrs. Sorensen, it's a gold Rolex, and he's got it mounted on a silver bracelet packed with turquoises. It's more jewelry than anything else and the elders think he's somewhat of a jerk, but he's a good front man to trot out whenever a big delegation comes from Washington or from some industrial firm thinking of building a factory out here."

"Hot damn," I said again. I was getting bored with this lecture.

"The point is, McQuaid, is that he considers it jewelry and not a net to catch the time."

"Very poetic."

"Yes. One more piece of advice."

"I will not interrupt, sensible though it might be."

"You are sarcastic. Things take a long time to ripen out here. If they sense you're in a hurry, you've lost before you've begun. I'm sorry to be speaking like the Delphic Oracle."

"Your hair is long enough."

"That's a pig oinking."

"Do my eyes deceive me, or do I see a hair dryer in that bag beside you?"

"Your eyes do not deceive you."

114

"Holy Christ."

"You seem to be getting more and more hostile, McQuaid. It's a good time to say good-bye." He stood up, grinning.

"Are you for your evening shampoo?"

"As a matter of fact, yes."

"Jesus."

"It's a whole new generation. And it's passed you by."

"I don't think I've missed anything." I was annoyed and my voice showed it. I added, "What you gonna do when you hit thirty?"

"Resign from humanity and join you."

I laughed. It was hard to remain angry.

"I've met a lot worse than you, McQuaid. If we don't bump into each other on the reservation, here's my card."

"A hippie with a business card! What next, O Lord?"

He handed it to me. I sat there for a while, figuring out what my next step would be. Start at the beginning, McQuaid, I said to myself. Get close to an Indian. I got up and made a phone call.

* * *

I waited by the phone booth until it would be free. A thin powder of snow was beginning to fall. I could see by the way people were hunched up against the wind that it was very cold. Gallup was close to te Continental Divide, and so I was several thousand feet higher than New York, it was December, and all I was wearing was a thin topcoat. I was going to spend time on an Indian reservation, and my limited knowledge told me that I wasn't likely to find steam heat prevalent out there.

I watched a drunken Navajo lurching along the sidewalk. He staggered against the window of a brightly lit pawnshop packed with the silver of his people. The small Zuni bone fetishes, many carved to resemble bears, had tiny turquoise eyes. He suddenly slumped to a sitting position, leaning his head back against the window with a thump I could almost hear from across the street. Then he fell sideways. Only his sombrero saved him from a nasty scalp wound. An empty pint bottle stuck out of his hip pocket. Snow began to powder his body from the dirty silver sky. He had an hour before he would begin to freeze to death.

I dialed information. Mrs. Sorensen had given me a letter addressed to Henry Thompson, who ran the Tribal Council of the Navajo Nation. "They like 'Nation,'" she had said. "'Reservation' is a shit word these days."

"Yes?"

"I'd like the Tribal Council of the Navajo Nation, please."

"What's the number?" A shy, mumbled, badly pronounced English, as if she were eating a large baked potato.

"I don't know."

"I don't know either."

Silence.

I said, patiently and kindly, "Then find out."

I got Henry Thompson. His voice matched the weather. "My name is McQuaid. New York City Police Department. I'm out on a case."

"Yeah?" The voice implied I could take a flying fuck for all he cared.

"Yes. But it's impossible to rent a car out here."

"So I hear."

"They all said they'd have one for me, but when I get here, no car."

"Yeah. Things are rough out here all right."

I detected a note of amusement. He added, "Why not ask the chief of police for a lift?"

"We don't like each other much."

"That so?" He was silent, no doubt savoring this piece of information about white intertribal warfare.

"Yes."

"Mmmm."

God, give me patience.

He said after a while, "There's a bus at five."

"Oh."

"A.M."

"Yes."

"On Thursdays."

"And this is Tuesday," I said calmly, watching the drunken Navajo's face whiten under the snow.

"My, my," he said. "Word gets around." He was counting coup, one right after the other.

"Yes," I said, keeping my voice level and without emotion. It took some doing." At this point I would like to read a letter aloud."

"Letter?" He sounded puzzled.

"Letter." I took Mrs. Sorensen's letter out of my pocket, unfolded it, and began to read it aloud.

Dear Hank:

This note is to introduce Sergeant Damian McQuaid, a detective who is helping me recover some material stolen from me recently. He would like to spend some time in the Nation, which he is not familiar with. Anything you can suggest or assist in making his stay a pleasant experience will be greatly appreciated. I will be out soon to discuss some Indian problems with you. In the meantime may the sun shine brightly on your path.

Mrs. Elizabeth Sorensen.

There was an intense silence on Hank's end. I folded the letter. I could almost hear him thinking bad thoughts about Lizzie. I put the letter in my pocket. Never be in a hurry. Never interrupt. I looked out the window again. No one was paying any attention to the zonked-out Navajo. I could see that would become my duty as soon as I finished this phone call.

"Yeah," Hank finally said. "Where are you stayin'?"

"The Gallup Lodge."

"I'll have someone there in an hour with the Tribal pickup."

"Thanks." He grunted unhappily and hung up. I walked

117

toward the unconscious drunk, but before I reached him a paddy wagon pulled up. The chief and a deputy got out. The driver opened the back door. They walked over, the chief bent down and gave the man's face a resounding slap. I winced. The Navajo opened his eyes, mumbled something, and closed them. The driver took his head and shoulders, the chief took his legs, and with an ease born of long practice they slung the man at exactly the right moment. The Navajo slid the entire length of the wagon headfirst, and his skull banged against the steel partition at the far end with the sound of a melon dropped on a concrete pavement. Even though I was shivering in my thin topcoat, a flow of hatred surged through me, warming me up nicely. It began, as always, somewhere in my solar plexus, about four inches straight back from the skin out in front. I always felt it when I saw pointless cruelty; when I was in a patrol car I asked for another partner because the miserable son of a bitch liked to do things like that to helpless drunks.

The chief slammed the door, turned around, and saw me.

"Nice going, Chief," I said. He didn't like the tone of my voice.

"That's the way we handle 'em," he said with a sneer. "Y'oughta try it."

"When I started out as a foot patrolman," I said, "my sector was the Bowery. I never beat up on helpless drunks. I see you get a big kick out of it."

It was snowing harder now, and even though he was standing five feet from me and the air was beginning to swirl larger flakes between us, I could see the broken blood vessels in his eyes. They looked like what we kids used to call pissholes in the snow.

"You're lookin' for trouble, McQaid."

"Heavens, no, Chief. All I want to say is, if you worked for me, and if I were your sergeant, I'd tear your ass apart with my bare hands, leaving you nothing to think with."

The deputy tittered.

"You got a big mouth, Sergeant, aincha?"

118

"It's been a problem."

"Keep it shut."

"Or what?"

"Jus' keep it shut!" He gave the deputy a nasty poke in the ribs. The man winced. They got into the paddy wagon. He was so mad that when he gunned it the wheels must have burned off half an inch before they took hold.

I watched the wagon disappear in the falling snow. Boy, was I dumb. I should have cottoned up to him and proved that his first impression of me was a mistake; maybe then he would have provided wheels. I hated to be dependent on someone else for locomotion, as I would have to be, out in the Nation. That would have been intelligent. But there was something about working in thin clothes at a high altitude among a primitive people whose way of thinking was strange to me which was probably making a cold storage area of my brain. That's why it was a cosy environment for snow rattlers.

*　*　*

I went into a clothing store and bought woolen underwear, woolen shirt, woolen socks, and woolen pants. I bought a wool watch cap which would cover my ears. I bought boots. I blew one hundred sixty-seven bucks, and I couldn't collect a cent of it from the NYPD. Warm clothes aren't like a diving suit, which can't be really worn anywhere except on the bottom of the ocean. Which means they weren't tax-deductible either. Nor could I console myself with the thought that I could always use them skiing or hunting, because I don't do either one. My thing is swimming in the Caribbean when I can get away. They'd only sit in a carton in my closet, mothballed to the gills. But at least I'd be warm for now, up near the Divide.

I lugged everything to the motel and changed. I packed my city clothes in the suitcase, paid my bill, and was finishing my coffee at the motel when I saw a new pickup stop outside. Lettered on the door where the words NAVAJO TRIBE.

I went outside. A girl with long black hair and high cheekbones leaned over and opened the door.

"Mr. McQuaid?" For a second I thought she spoke English with a foreign accent until I realized the absurdity of that thought: if her first language was Navajo, could her accent while speaking English be regarded as foreign? I smiled and nodded.

"Get in, please. You can throw your suitcase in the back."

A chest with a padlock was built across the back of the pickup. I looked at her. "Just drop it in. It'll be OK." I dropped it and sat beside her. She seemed nervous about having me in the truck, and she moved as far away as she could get without standing in the street. She kept her head averted and drove expertly through the heavy traffic, obviously wishing to get this particular duty over with as soon as possible. She wore new bell-bottom Levi's and a heavy lumber jacket and a scarf over head. She made a left turn, whipped across the main line of the Southern Pacific, jolting over the eight tracks, and headed west, past wooden shacks, grocery stores, cheap restaurants, and pawnshops.

"You don't look happy," I said. She made no response. We went by shabby little houses with frozen front yards and hardly a tree. I tried out a few remarks about the weather. No response. Be patient, don't push, Jay had said. I leaned back, impassive as hell myself. But after a few miles, when we were headed north, past stubby brown hills which looked as if they had been pounded down with a gigantic sledgehammer, I reopened the conversation.

Working without informants is a sure way to put excessive mileage on the heart and brain. It's the difference between driving to a well-marked destination on a super highway and bouncing down a back-country dirt road where they've pulled up all the signposts and everyone is at home hating strangers. No numbers on the doors and unleashed Dobermans snarling at me through every fence. And every street a deadend. Except one. But which? Good luck, Damian. An awful lot of people to talk to who don't owe me a damn thing, not even the time of day. Ten thousand good-byes before I open my mouth, and not a single welcome. Not that I wanted love, but an occasional hint would do nicely to wipe away my tears. So many doors to knock on, and you never know which will be the right one. I could feel my stomach getting warm; a little gastric juice was being dumped there. Too many of these cases and I'd have a permanent tiger in residence inside. Thoughts like those put bald spots on the heart. I looked at the depressing, ugly hills which looked as if they were Rocky Mountain rejects. I tried to open up a conversation with her once more.

"Those are nice pants," I said.

"Yeah," she said, warming up slightly. Then, unable to hold back, she burst out with, "Can I ask you a question?"

I nodded.

"When famous people come here in summer, I got to drive 'em around. I used to be a nurse and I know Navajo, not like a lot of the younger kids, they don't know Navajo. So I been everywhere, from Utah down to Ramah, and from Farmington clear over to the Colorado. So last summer I had this lady from Hollywood, some movie star, I knew she was supposed to be rich and all, and she was wearin' a real old concho belt which must've cost a thousand dollars. But she was wearin' a real old faded pair of Levi's I wouldn't paint the house in. It had patches on 'em. And there she was, she come off the train in 'em, so I guess she was real poor. I felt real sorry for her. I guess they don't make as much money as people think, them movie stars."

"I don't know if you're going to believe this," I said, "so you'd better listen carefully. There are people who will go into a store and buy a secondhand pair of Levi's, all faded, with holes. They will pay more for this than they will for a brand-new pair."

The set of her jaw expressed disbelief. No one could be so crazy, she was thinking. She said nothing. I said nothing.

Indians, I was finding out, did not repeat statements for emphasis. If you missed it the first time, tough. It would teach you to listen carefully next time.

A single-track railroad went north on our left. There was a large supply of low brown hills everywhere. Some tall chimneys of a power plant were shooting pollution into the sky. This was not my idea of Indian country. But my driver's face was my idea of Indian impassivity, all right. It had the same stony indifference I found when I used to walk into a Harlem bar on business.

I heard a siren behind us. I immediately looked at the speedometer. Thirty-one. We had just passed a 30-mph sign. She pulled over, her face tightening, and waited with her hands on the wheel. The police car waited behind us.

"What did we do wrong?" I asked.

She opened the glove compartment and took out the ownership license. Then she dug in her pocketbook for her operator's.

"Speedin'," she said curtly.

"You're kidding."

She looked at me briefly. Her face was no longer impassive. It expressed vast scorn. She got out and walked back to the police car. I looked in the mirror. A black-gloved hand was beckoning me over. I got out, puzzled. At the car I saw the black gloves belonged to the chief. He wiggled his fingers at me.

"Why, if it ain't Mr. McQuaid!" he said. He turned to the deputy beside him. "Mr. McQuaid—"

"Sergeant."

"—Mr. McQuaid here," he went on, unperturbed, "is a fancy New York detective. He ain't wastin' no time, he's joyridin' with a pretty Navajo gal. Speedin', too. An' inside the city limits! Tell us how fast you were goin', gal."

She said nothing, but her face was reddening.

"Come on, gal. Talk."

122

"You got my license. My name is on it."

"Oh, I see. You want me to say your name, is that it?"

She nodded.

"OK. Seein' as how you Navajos is now citizens of the Yewnited States, I'll go along." He peered at her license. "Yeah. Here we are. Julia, how fast was you goin'?"

Her skin darkened. I'd seen faces with that expression before, and I always made sure that my jacket was open and my right hand near my gun butt.

"That's enough," I said. "You want to say she was doing thirty-one in a thirty-mile zone, OK. The rest is harassment. You push some more and I'll testify to that."

"Before a local judge, hey?" He grinned. "Boy, you sure are bellerin' outta your pasture." He wrote out a ticket and handed it to her.

We walked back to the pickup. She crumpled the ticket and threw it on the floor. She hissed something which had plenty of sibilance and droning noises, something like the cross between an angry snake and a Scotch bagpipe.

"That Navajo?"

She nodded, sulking.

"A man can really lay out some fine swearing in that language." No response. "You miss the good old scalping days?"

She flashed a wide grin.

"You know something, Mr. McQuaid? He was layin' for me around the corner from your motel. Soon's I picked you up, he follered us a block back. Just waitin' on somethin'. And I sure gave it to him. That's the chicken-shit chief for you."

I didn't think he was laying for her. Me. I could see where the chief and I were not going to develop a deep friendship. And something like that could blossom into a royal pain in the ass. It would have been smarter for me to have kept my big mouth shut. Then maybe love would have grown between us. Or some workable facsimile.

123

The Tribal Offices were in a modern building with air conditioning, gray wall-to-wall carpeting, electric typewriters, and indirect lighting. I don't know what I had expected, perhaps some beatup old red brick structure no one else wanted, something like that. Once inside, there was no way to tell you were in Indian country, except that a look through a window produced a sandstone mesa with some long-growing, scrubby pines clinging precariously to the top, all forced into a squat position by the prevailing wind.

I sat in a molded plastic chair facing Henry Thompson. He wore a gray business suit, black oxfords, and a blue button-down shirt and black tie. I could have been talking to an account executive on Madison Avenue, except for the big wall map of the reservation and his dark reddish-brown skin, and his wide face. He lit a pipe with a gold cigarette lighter, leaned back, and looked at my clothes.

"Lots of people, when they come here," he said, "they think they have to dress like that."

"I realize the Navajo country is civilized," I responded, and decided to let it go at that.

"Ummm." I was beginning to get used to the sound. It could mean, according to the context, you're wrong, you're right, keep on talking and dig yourself in deeper, you dumb bastard.

He looked at Mrs. Sorensen's letter, which I had placed on his desk, beside the four ears of corn which had been tied together with a twisted corn husk. On the wall back of him was a sign which said EAT LAMB: TEN MILLION COYOTES CAN'T BE WRONG. "So you're here on police business?"

"Yes." There was absolutely no expression on his face. It looked as intrigued as the red sandstone mesa I could see back of his head. And the mesa had more life in it.

"What do you expect from me?"

"Perhaps you might hear of some of these pieces showing up around the Reservation."

"The Nation."

"Sorry. The Nation. If you would I'd like to hear about it."

I took out the picture gallery and showed it to him.

"Ummm."

"You're in touch with the whole Res— Nation. So you'd hear."

"Umm."

I knew what that umm meant. It meant, to put it politely, go fly your kite elsewhere. I didn't see much point in hanging around the Tribal Offices, being cold-shouldered by everyone, and pussyfooting, not daring to step on anyone's toes. Detectives have to risk stepping on toes. But at any rate, her letter had gotten me a free ride from Gallup, and it was beginning to look as if that would be the end of the letter's big help.

I was looking at the big map. Holy mackerel, this Reservation—oops, Nation—extended over three states.

"How long you plan to stay out here, McQuaid?"

"Till I get pissed off."

He liked that. The red sandstone mass of his face cracked open and he slapped the desk with his open palm in amusement.

"You don't have a car." I agreed with that. "You should have picked one up in Albuquerque."

"Live and learn."

Another umm. He looked at me narrowly. I slid down in my chair and shoved my hands deep in my pockets. It was a hell of a big place to go hitching over in winter. "You strong?" he suddenly asked.

"Pretty strong."

"In condition?"

"My business requires it." I play water polo, swim a lot, work out in the police gym, do judo, box, and jog every two or three days while whoever is in my bed gets up, goes to the A & P, buys bacon and eggs and orange juice, and prepares it.

"Yeah. Let's Indian wrestle. Drag up your chair."

I pulled up my chair. We put our elbows on the desk. I was getting tired of eccentric Western characters. We locked palms together. He was very strong. His back muscles bulged against his beautifully tailored suit—fifty would get you one he didn't buy it in Gallup—until I thought for sure the seams would rip. He wore a big robin's-egg blue turquoise set in a plain wide silver ring on his right ring finger. Now that he had his arm out I could see the gold Rolex with the turquoise-studded bracelet. As he increased his pressure the ring began to cut into my palm. It hurt, and I could tell by his smile that he knew it was painful.

But, among other things I did at the police gym was lifting weights. And when I was still under twenty I used to work in construction, lifting those heavy devices which would pound concrete into ceilings. I had to stand on a ladder and suffer while my back and shoulders felt as if someone were pouring red-hot lava over them. He probably didn't play water polo, or lift heavy weights, or jog. I was banking on my endurance, which I had extracted from all that loyally conducted exercise. And he was banking on that strength of his, which was, I guessed, partly hereditary and partly based on some hard work done in his youth. My money was on me.

We had reached a point where his slightly superior strength was now matched by my ability to endure. If I could hold out a little more I was in like Flynn. From then on he would weaken. He put everything he had into it, doing some serious grunting, and I waited. When I sensed he had reached his peak I put his elbow down so quickly that his knuckles made a loud rap. I released his hand and unclenched my fingers. His ring had given me a slight cut.

He got up and went into his toilet. He came out with a small bottle of iodine and handed it to me. I doused it on and handed it back. He put it back in the medicine chest, came back, and sat down. He put fresh tobacco in his pipe, lit it, and said, "No one ever beat me Indian wrestling."

"You don't like it?"

"Nope."

"I'll keep quiet about it."

"I heard about you and the chief. Go anywhere you want."

"I appreciate it."

"You just go for a walk, take in our museum down the road. Be back in an hour. I'll have you all set up by then."

The fields were frozen. Three inches of snow lay on top. The road twisted and turned till it came to the small museum he had mentioned. I looked at the exhibits of animal life of the Nation and at native arts and crafts till they ran out of my ears. An hour passed. I turned to leave. A tall Navajo in a black sombrero came up and said, "Ain't you the feller from New York got a ride on the Tribe's pickup?" I nodded.

"You goin' anywhere special right now?"

"Back to the Tribal Offices."

"Hell, I'll give you a lift."

"No, thanks, I'd rather walk."

"*Walk?*"

He stared in amazement.

"Can I get there by cutting across the fields?" I wanted to try out my new boots.

"Sure, mister, but it's easier walkin' 'long the road. Shorter." He talked to me as if I were a village idiot.

"Yes. But I'll try the fields."

I turned. The man in the black sombrero said, "Watch out for snow rattlers."

"You bet," I said. "I know *all* about them. I'll be very careful."

127

Julia was waiting for me in the pickup. Her good humor had disappeared. She was staring at me angrily. I asked her if I had ruined her plans.

"You didn't ruin my plans," she snapped. "You just ruined my boyfriend."

"He doesn't want you driving me?"

"It's all right if you was married and had a wife along. I always drive couples. He sure don't like it. Henry Thompson said, 'What are you, male-dominated?' And I said, 'I sure as hell ain't,' and he said, 'Well, drive.' So I'm drivin' and I damn well don't like it."

"Let's go back. I can drive this thing by myself."

"Yeah, sure. And there goes my job. No, thanks."

I could see she'd be whining all day. One more cross to bear. Maybe I could scare her off, anyway. "Will there by any problems at night?" I asked.

"What you talkin' about?"

"I mean, staying in a motel. Will there by any talk which might get you in trouble with your boyfriend?"

She snorted. "Mister, for a start, there ain't any motels. There ain't *nothin'*. There's a hogan here and there and sometimes a little shack with maybe a sheepherder in them. We stop in any hogan or shack and I say it's tribal business and they put us up on the floor. Separate."

"But equal."

"Huh? Mister, if I wanna sleep with you I'll do it. But I don't wanna. I just don't wanna go on this here trip and have Ned Begay gettin' the idea he c'n go and get laid over to Flagstaff."

"I'm sorry I'm causing all this trouble."

"Oh, hell, mister, I divorced him twice."

"Divorce?"

"Navajo divorce. I just threw his saddle and clothes outside the door. When he come home he found out he was divorced. But he asked if he could come back the last time and I told him OK, and now I bet he's gonna take up with some fat Hopi gal in Oraibi or Black Mesa, and I'm gonna have to toss his goddamn saddle out the door again. Shit."

This was no time for idle conversation. I stared out at the pine-covered plateau country which was tilting upward to my left. The sun was getting low in the southwest, and long shafts of golden light pierced between the black trunks and turned the snow into long golden ingots.

Suddenly she said, "I'm thirsty."

I gave her a look which said, what the hell do you expect *me* to do? But in a minute I understood that she was not given to pointless, idle whining. A long, low building appeared on our left at the end of a long row of Lombardy poplars, evidently planted long ago as a windbreak. She made a left turn, bounced over a small log bridge spanning a narrow creek, and parked under a grove of old cottonwood trees. A sign over the door read WHITLOW'S TRADING POST.

She ordered a Coke and drank it thirstily. The room was enormous, full of piles of Navajo rugs and Coke cases stacked to the ceiling. One wall was devoted to canned groceries, with a counter in front of them. At one end of the counter was a Coke machine. Beside it, sitting cross-legged on the floor, was a Navajo woman in a long, purple, velvet skirt, working at a loom set up vertically in front of her. She kept passing a shuttle back and forth in sullen silence. She did not turn around when we entered.

Julia wandered over with the half-empty bottle in her brown hand. "Local color," she said briefly to me. "For tourists." The woman heard her voice and turned around, grinned when she saw me, and she made a remark. "No," Julia responded in English, clearly for my benefit, "this ain't my new boyfriend." The woman tittered. She wore two turquoise necklaces, two bracelets on each wrist, and three rings. The woman saw me looking at them and smiled proudly. Julia whispered in my ear, "Ask her how much they cost." I was reluctant. "Go on," Julia insisted. "Navajos

129

think that's good manners." Persuaded, I asked. The woman glowed. She told me. She was a walking jewelry store, worth close to ten thousand on the hoof. I asked if this was where the rugs were made.

"Naw," Julia remarked. "She's only here for the tourists. I don't like comin' here," she suddenly added with anger. "I don't like that ol' bastard Whitlow. I only come here 'cause there ain't no more Coke for seventy miles. An' my pop didn't like Whitlow's pop either. There's the ol' son of a bitch now." An old man with a pale yellowish face sprayed with a white stubble had silently padded from the rear of the store. He was wearing soft buckskin slippers and expensive Western-style brown gabardine trousers held up by orange suspenders. His pale-blue eyes were buried in fat. Lots of Westerners seemed to specialize in blue eyes, I had noticed.

"Ya-teh, Julia."

"Hello, Mr. Whitlow," she said. I guessed he had said hello in Navajo, and that she was stubbornly refusing to respond similarly. "I heard you had the yellow jaundice."

"Gettin' better, gettin' better. How's your pa?"

She looked at him silently for several seconds. Then she abruptly turned and walked out of the store. Whitlow grinned. I paid for the Cokes and followed her. She was sitting at the wheel, simmering. I asked her what the matter was.

"That ol' son of a bitch, he owns the tradin' post. We Navajos want to run them tradin' posts, too. We know how. So my paw goes to the bank at Winslow and asks for a loan. We got four hundred sheep an' lots of necklaces an' bracelets with good turquoise. The bank asks Whitlow 'bout my paw payin' his bills an' Whitlow says my paw don't pay. So the bank won't give him no loan."

"I'll tell you what your father ought to do."

"What?"

"How does he buy things?"

"When he wants somethin' he jus' saves till he gets enough money, then he buys it."

"He doesn't buy on installments?"

"Hell, no. It cost more that way."

"He should. And then pay promptly."

"What for?"

"To establish a good credit rating. Let him do that in a few places. And in two, three years he'll have a good credit rating and then when he asks for a loan the bank will be willing to listen."

She looked at me in boundless contempt. "That's the way a white man thinks," she said slowly. "Indians don't think that way." She was right, of course. It was a conniving way to behave, when you thought about it, and if they didn't want to do it, they would never get to own a trading post. I was certainly learning more about Indians, and that would be fine if I were working on my PhD thesis about economics and the modern Navajo. But I wasn't getting anywhere. I decided to work out a round with old Mr. Whitlow. I got out of the pickup and told her I was going to talk to him. I asked her if Whitlow had lived there for a long time. She said he was born there and his father had come out west in the 1870s.

"Does he speak Navajo?"

"Bettern' me. You wanna talk, you go, I'm not gettin' out."

Whitlow was standing amid his piles of rugs with a clipboard in his hand. He was busily and absentmindedly scratching his scrawny ass with a pencil. Then he bent down, flipped up the corner of a rug, and made a notation. He scratched his ass once more, yawning.

"Mr. Whitlow."

He turned around slowly. There was nothing to fear anymore from Indians except an economic attack, and he had that well under control. The military post had been replaced by the local banks. He had a pompous smug air that made me want to kick him just to see if I could dislocate it, but he was so smug that I had the feeling that the man, well-lacquered by generations of monopoly, wouldn't even know there was a pointed toe in his rear. Sorensen had that look a little bit, and so did Slavitch, but they faced some opposition, and opposition is what prevents lacquer. No one ever disagreed with Whitlow, I could see that. I would like to be the first, but my heart belonged to Lieutenant Slavitch. Easy does it, McQuaid. Think of Slavitch's fitness report. Whitlow's face resembled a sour-lemon drop shaped to human features. He scotch-taped a Dale Carnegie smile on it. Two could play that game. I rummaged in my smile box and dug out an eager, friendly one.

"Got the best rugs on the Reservation," he said. "That gal drivin' you around, she's an awful liar, that one. Know her since she no biggern' a horned toad."

"She seems all right," I said doubtfully. That implied I could be persuaded I was wrong.

"She's no good and so is her pa. Raises sheep up to Chaco Canyon. Brings in the wool weighted down with sand. Old trick, don't fool me."

Now who the hell was lying? Goddamnit, just as soon as I line up on one side, the other brings in some evidence which cancels out my favorite. Best thing to do is stay out of these neighborhood brawls unless I *have* to get in the middle. Julia, you bitch, were you lying to me?

"How much is that top one?" I asked, keeping my smile attached with strong effort.

"Four twenty-five."

"Ummm." A man like Whitlow, who knew the Reservation well, who spoke Navajo, and who didn't automatically distrust me on the grounds of my skin color, might be very well able to help me.

"Mr. Whitlow." I ran my hand back and forth across the rug. It was straw color, with a black and red geometric pattern around the border. I liked it. I smiled. This smile was not removed from the box. It emerged naturally.

"Yep. I might lower the price a bit, seein' it's off season. How's four hundred strike you?" It struck me hard. I liked the rug, but I had never paid more than seventy-five for one.

"Mr. Whitlow—I'm not a tourist."

"You buyin' rugs for a store back east, that it? Buyin' Navajo jewelry, openin' up a place? We get lots of people like that these days. I c'n make wholesale prices. Though you don't look like no dealer."

I flipped open the wallet with my gold detective shield.

"Ain't no marshal's badge," he said, scratching away again. I told him the whole story. He listened. It was clear that if there was no money to be made on me, he saw no reason to waste time. When I had finished he asked, "Why you come to me?"

"Maybe you've heard something."

"Naw." He began to turn over rugs and make notations.

"Maybe you will."

"Mebbe. I hear a lot. Ev'ry Navajo for sixty, seventy miles is gotta come here. Sardines, flashlights, fresh meat, tomatoes, out-of-pawn concho belts, rugs, gas, kerosene, gossip—you want it, I got it. Or I c'n get it, give me a couple days. This Reservation is like a big funnel, and whatever gets dumped in at the top is gotta come down to the spout, and that's Whitlow's Trading Post. There's not a single white man on the Reservation c'n say as much."

"I heard they like the word 'Nation.' "

"Fuck 'em. I always said Reservation an' so did my paw before me. Yeah, I might help you. Where you stayin'?"

"No special place. I'm moving around. But I suppose I can get messages care of Henry Thompson."

"Nothin' but a windbag. They all are up there at Window Rock."

"Thanks a lot." I started to leave.

"Wait a minute, young feller."

I turned.

"I'm helpin' you, right?"

"Sure. I appreciate it."

He waved an impatient hand at that remark, as if it were a horsefly buzzing around him. "Forget any bullshit 'bout my duty as a citizen."

"I've forgotten it," I said with a sinking feeling.

"Good, good. So why am I gonna do this for you?"

"Let me guess. There's going to be something in it for you?"

"Right! An' what's gonna be in it for me?"

"This is a beautiful rug," I said, putting my smile back in the smile box. I had a powerful urge to kick him in the ass. In New York I'd have a warrant for his arrest within twenty minutes and I'd dump his ass in the slammer in another ten, where he could reconsider his un-American behavior. But here I was as helpless as a newborn kitten and he damn well knew it.

"So you like that rug! I knowed you was smart, soon's I laid eyes on you, mister."

"I can't carry it around."

"No, no. We'll jus' ship it. How'll that be?"

"Fine." It *wasn't* fine, you crummy thief bastard. I pulled out my checkbook.

"Can't ship till it clears."

"I don't blame you," I said. I pulled out another smile. "You must get lots of crooks here. And it must come as a terrible blow." He didn't quite know how to take that remark. I shouldn't have made it. It was not wise.

"Well, it ain't that. An' then I got to add shippin' charges."

"Fair enough. So what do I owe you?"

"Five twenty-five."

I put down my pen. "One hundred twenty-five for *shipping?*

"No. Five hundred for the rug, twenty-five for the shippin'."

"What happened to the out-of-season price?"

"Yeah. Well, that was supposin' you was a dealer."

I looked at him for five seconds. I had trouble restraining my natural impulse: with the usual informant I would hint at this point the terrible things which would happen to him unless his information turned out to be useful. That would work because I had something on him which I was refraining from using. And all I had on this Continental Divide thief was that he screwed up Julia's paw's application for a loan. I was sorry that I had doubted her story. I would now believe anything about that fart Whitlow.

I bent my head and wrote out the check. He had himself a rare sucker here—Sergeant McQuaid, New York City Police Department. Homicide Squad 3. It would make a good story to tell on cold winter nights to the other thieves at the other trading posts. "This dumb cop from New York, he come in once. An' I took offen him five hundred." Oh, boy. Not only that, if I tried to slip in the invoice for the rug as payment to an informant, forget it. I could see Slavitch's face when he picked it up. I wouldn't even try. But there was one consolation, I thought, running my fingers over the rug, with that goddamn rug used as a blanket I'd never be cold again in New York whenever the goddamn boiler would bust.

* * *

Julia started the engine. She pulled out into the road and headed west in silence. She was still burned up about Whitlow. The sun was over a ridge to the west, poised on the edge like a huge Sunkist orange. I lifted my palm, shielding my eyes against the glare. A sign in the road said SNAKE VALLEY. "Why do they call it that?" I asked.

She looked at me as if I were the village idiot. "They got plenty there," she said crisply. She stared at the road again, letting the silence wash over me with contempt. I should have remembered Jay's advice. *Keep your mouth shut,* he had said. She said suddenly, "You bought a rug."

I looked at her in surprise. The pickup had been parked at least fifty feet away from the door of the trading post. Only a small window opened onto the rug area. She understood my puzzled look. "I saw him lift up a corner of the top rug. Then he talked. Then you took somethin' outta your pocket. Why'd you buy a rug from him? He charges too much. You shoulda tole me you was lookin' for a rug. My aunt woulda sold you one for a lot less." Her hands were squeezing the steering wheel tightly. Was it my neck or Whitlow's she was strangling? How could I tell her that I wasn't looking for a rug? Whitlow was of value to me only if no one knew he was searching for information. Remarks dropped carelessly in his hearing by people who'd forgotten he understood Navajo, people speaking English about a strange carving they had seen on the Reservation, or a strange Iroquois wampum belt—that's the kind of thing he might pick up. The chance he might was enough for me to spring five twenty-five for a rug. And enough for me to drop in every couple days, like a lobsterman on his rounds, pulling up his cages to see if any lobsters had crawled inside. So Julia had to be kept in the dark about all this. She drove, despising me.

The sun went down behind the ridge. We hadn't seen anyone for miles. The road looked as if it would go on forever. It was winter on the Divide, and the road stretched for three hundred miles. I saw decaying fence posts, suspended by rusting barbed wire. The land tilted upward towards a cold, deep-blue sky. The tip of a mesa behind us was opalescent from the last reflected light. A crescent moon and a bright star nearby slowly slid above the pine forest on our left. I put my palm on my window. Christ, it was cold. Once I saw a woman in a long Navajo dress sitting on a horse on a small bluff looking down at us impassively.

The dusk was getting deeper and more silkily black, and I was with a hostile Indian girl who was convinced that I was solid marble between the ears.

"Where you wanna go?" she demanded abruptly.

"Eat."

"OK."

She drove forty miles in dead silence and parked next to a shack with a crudely lettered sign saying EATS above a door which was fronted, in turn, by a rusted screen door full of holes. The shack was full of Navajos in Levi's and sombreros, eating mutton stew out of soup plates. A juke box blared in a corner. No one was listening. Several men lifted their heads. Julia said, "Ya-teh," they said "Ya-teh," stared at me, some impassive, some with faint hostility. Two drunks with their heads pillowed on their arms slept at the next table. Everytime the door opened a fine powder of snow whipped inside. I had never felt such cold since the retreat from the reservoir in Korea. It seemed to have the intelligence of a rat as it sought for the nape of my neck. It was getting colder. The wind blew so hard that our entrance brought in a thin layer of snow just inside the door.

She ate hungrily. Mutton stew was not my speed. I toyed with my food until she had finished. I paid. "They got a cabin in back with a couple rooms," she said. "Nothin' else for seventy-five miles. You wanna go back to Window Rock or you wanna stay or you wanna keep on goin'?"

"Stay." I was tired.

"Yes. I got an uncle near. I'll go sleep there. What time you want me?"

"Seven."

"OK." She got up. The two doors slammed, one a fraction of a second later than the other. The engine of the pickup started, and I was alone in Indian country. I figured someone would pick a fight with the only white man available for forty miles and then dispose of me in some unknown canyon, but no one did. They acted as if I weren't there. I drank a cup of vile coffee. The cabin had a room with a washbasin, a narrow bed with a thin mattress, and clean, coarse, well-worn sheets. There were two woolen blankets. In the middle of the night I got up and dressed completely and lay down again. If I ever saw Henry Thompson again I would damn well tell him why people dressed the way I did when they came west. Because we were smart. And I would also point out that Navajo blankets might be a sensible idea for Navajo rooms. I fell asleep planning some sarcastic dialogue, just in case someone would ask me, with a grin, how I had slept.

Next morning I felt rotten. I had a headache and there was no aspirin closer than Whitlow's. The watery coffee did not improve it, nor did the mutton stew for breakfast. I got into the pickup.

"You wanna see some very interestin' cliff dwellings?"

"For crissakes, *no.*"

A Navajo staggered out of the café. Over one shoulder he carried a pickax and a shovel. He lifted a thumb.

"Let's give him a lift," I said.

"He's not lookin' for a lift."

The man came around to her side. She had the window up and the heater going full blast. He put down the two tools and motioned for her to roll down her window. She did so, but reluctantly. I wondered what he wanted. He leaned inside the cab and talked in Navajo. After ten seconds she flushed angrily and tried to roll up the window. He put his head and shoulders further inside and added two big arms. She couldn't roll the window against that kind of weight.

"Friend of yours?" I asked.

"No. He said somethin' dirty about me an' you." She tried to push him away but couldn't. I could see he was too drunk to be spoken to politely.

"Excuse me," I said to Julia and, reaching across, I lifted both his arms and gave him a hard shove. He staggered back and fell.

"Let's go!" I said, but she was leaning out the window, screaming in Navajo. He got up surprisingly quickly, grabbed the pickax, and swung it at the windshield. I saw it coming and forced her head and shoulders down toward me. The sharp end sliced through the glass and showered us with particles of powdered glass. The rest of the windshield looked like a dirty white spider web. He lifted the pickax for another swing. I pushed her down and said,

138

"Stay there!" By the time I was standing beside him he had smashed another hole and was lifting it for a third try. I grabbed his right wrist with both hands and as he swung I pulled down hard, using his own strength, but trying to deflect the blow and take him off balance at the same time. It's nice when it works, but all I accomplished was to make him sink the pickax into the left fender instead of the window. It stuck there. He let it stay sunk five inches into the fender and just touching the tire.

He swung in a wild roundhouse at me. His eyes were wild. I ducked it easily, saying soothingly, "Now, calm down, buddy. Calm down. Let's talk it over."

He was in no mood to talk it over. I didn't want to hit him and get marked lousy all over the Reservation for slugging a drunk, but when he reached out and grabbed the shovel by the handle, and I caught sight of the heavy, sharp steel edge, I knew it would be all right for me to get myself marked lousy, and that real fast. The shovel soared up in the air, reflecting the morning light off its polished surface. He really kept it nice and clean. He had it gripped in both fists. As it reached the apex of its flight I stepped in and hit him in the pit of the stomach as hard as I could. He barked out an agonized *woof,* dropped the shovel, and sank to the ground, holding his stomach with both hands. He began to vomit what looked like blood but what was probably cheap red wine, as I could tell by the smell. There would be no permanent damage and he would be partially paralyzed for several minutes. Time enough to leave in dignity. I refrained from hitting his jaw. It looked very hard and I would probably have broken a couple of knuckles.

I jerked the pickax out of the fender. She was busily brushing glass particles from her hair and swearing in English. I was very interested in her language. "Shame on you," I said, getting back in. There was a hole in the windshield six inches in diameter right in front of the driver's seat.

"Let's go," I said.

"I'm gonna kill that son of a bitch as soon as I get this god-damn glass outta my hair," she said conversationally.

"Not when I'm here, you're not." I got out, walked around the front of the pickup, passing the Navajo. His face was gray and he was still gagging. He tried to grab one foot by the ankle, the stubborn bastard. I shook his hand off easily, eased around him, opened the door on the driver's side, and pushed her over. She was digging in her pocketbook for a comb and muttering in Navajo. I turned the ignition on. She turned it off.

"We ain't leavin' till I finish climbin' all over that shit-head," she said.

"Save it." I pulled her hand away, turned on the ignition, slapped her hand away again, and pulled out. I kept her at arm's length until we were five miles south. It wasn't easy driving with one hand, peering through six inches of wind-shield facing an icy wind, and keeping a strong woman away from the ignition.

"It's cold," she said, wrapping both arms around her body.

I stopped. "Where's the jack?" I asked.

"In the chest. There's a key to the padlock on the key ring." I opened the locked trunk on the back and took out the jack handle. She got out. I smashed out what was left of the windshield. I found an old napkin in my coat pocket and brushed the glass fragments from the inside with it. I gave her my spare woolen undershirt and my spare socks to wear, but even with those and the heater going full blast we were both half frozen when we pulled into the Tribal Offices an hour and a half later. Julia spent all that time cursing and trying to remove all the tiny glass fragments from her wool jacket. It was very difficult. She thought she had removed all of them, but when the sun came up high enough to clear the eastern ridges and struck us full force, the jacket looked as if someone had scattered tiny diamonds all over it.

While I waited to see Thompson I phoned Dorsey. I got him in the Squad Room, typing, which was no surprise.

"Hey, it's Mr. McQuaid! How you doin', Damian? Gettin' any of that Indian pussy?"

Oh, for crissakes. His voice carried and he talked very loud. That's all I needed, for someone to hear it near me.

"Hi, Dorsey. No luck so far. How's it coming at your end?"

"Checked out five art galleries, checked out the jewelry district, both Forty-Seventh Street and Canal. No one recognized anything. Said they'd call if they were offered for sale. You droppin' your pants on Indian pussy?"

"It's snowing here, Dorsey."

"Yeah—I get it. You can't talk. Mrs. Sorensen called. I bet *she's* got an educated ass. She wanted to know how you were makin' out. I said just fine. Also a dame named Kimri called. She's got some kind of an accent. She wants you to get in touch."

"Thanks. How's your old lady?"

"Very sarcastic. She said I'd jump anything with hair, even the floor around a barber's chair."

"She's perceptive."

"Yeah. Maybe. Slavitch wants you to keep in touch."

In good time, in good time. I hung up and walked down the hall to see Henry Thompson.

*　*　*

Today he was wearing a pink shirt with blue stripes. He was standing and looking at the big map of the Reservation.

"I think it would be better if I drove myself around," I said. "I don't need a driver. All I need is a decent car. If I had been alone in that pickup it would still have a windshield and a fender in one piece."

He grunted.

"As it is," I went on, "I'll pay for them."

"No. It's not your fault."

"If it hadn't been for me, that guy wouldn't have gone ape. Right?"

"You're right there."

"So I insist."

He yielded. Why not? He had no insurance, and a hundred and fifty, two hundred bucks, was too much for the tribe to shell out, even for doing a favor for a good friend of Mrs. Sorensen's. Besides, I might get the money back as a legitimate business expense. Might. Suppose they said downtown it was a normal business hazard? He was feeling pretty good about that, so I pushed my luck. I asked him if I could rent a car from someone in the Tribal Offices.

"I think I can dig up someone on the Tribal Council who could use the money. How about coming around here in an hour?"

"Sure." He stood there at the map, poking it here and there absentmindedly. I asked him where he was born. "Out here in the sticks," he said, pointing to the extreme western end of the Reservation. "In some crummy hogan. But you ought to come out in April out there. Everything starts moving in April in the desert."

"Except the snow rattlers."

"Yeah," he said, smiling. "Those little buggers work all winter. Got to watch your step."

"So I hear." The Tribe owned a beautiful new motel half a mile down the road. I trudged down there, taking long steps for the exercise. The land had a hard, tough, unfriendly appearance. I didn't know how much I was reading into it because of my experiences, or how much rose out of the land itself, but it certainly had none of the rolling friendliness of the Connecticut or Westchester countryside. An occasional rocky outcrop, some scrubby, thorn-filled bushes, and stones, everywhere, with small gullies slicing up the landscape. As if all the good soil and lush grass had packed up and moved away in disgust. A good land for snow rattlers. You bet.

I sat down and ordered a steak with french fries, apple pie, and coffee. Not the best food in the world, but on an In-

142

dian reservation it was ambrosia. The coffee was the usual rotten junk, but I sipped it. The waitress had long black hair and the kind of a sullen, deadpan expression you are surprised to find outside New York. She wanted to know if I was a lumberjack working the pines up in the mountains. I said yes. If anyone wanted to hand me a good cover story I would take it. I was halfway through the cardboard-crust apple pie with its canned apples floating in a thin watery syrup when Whitlow walked in.

"Heard you was here."

"Sit down, Mr. Whitlow." I was glad to see him. "Coffee?"

"Don't mind if I do. You buyin'?"

"Don't I always?"

He chuckled. He lifted the cup to his lips and stared at me. "Business pretty slow wintertime. Heard this mornin' what happened to the pickup. Figured you'd come back here to fix it."

"That's fast hearing."

He shrugged. "My daddy called it moccasin telegraph. No great mystery. You hadn't been gone two minutes from that restaurant up there when Nachodise phoned me."

"Who?"

"Nachodise. He's the guy who busted your windshield. He figured you was carryin' on with Julia. She's an old girlfriend of his."

"Yep."

"They better arrest him fast and keep him locked up till you leave. He don't give up easy."

"I'm not worried."

"You oughta be. Indians don't care if they die. Jus' thought I'd pass on that piece of information."

"Thanks. How about that other matter?"

"Ain't heard a thing yet. But I will. How 'bout throwin' in a piece of pie?"

I nodded. Here was a man who could buy and sell me ten times over grabbing freebies. He had a wide mouth like a grouper, and he ate silently and at full speed, like a human vacuum cleaner. I got up. He said he would keep me posted. Maybe. I picked up the check. The Navajo girl at the cash register looked at him. Her expression showed distaste. I refrained from telling her that I did not pick possible informants on the basis of personal charm.

When I reached the Tribal Offices I found a car parked outside, owned by a man named Simpson Bekis. It was a six-year-old Chevrolet, and it looked well taken care of. Thirty dollars a day plus gas. I held out three tens. Bekis hitched up his concho belt a few inches and maneuvered his thick fingers around till he found the thin slit of his watch pocket. His fingers looked like miniature boa constrictors. He held the belt out, crumpled up the bills, and pile-drived them into place. Then he let the belt snap back into place, above the loom of his belly. His somber face suddenly split into two. Why not? I was being screwed.

"You the feller from New York?" I nodded. He wanted to know how many Navajos there were in New York. I couldn't help him there, but I said, "Maybe three, and when you come out there'll be five." He quivered in amusement, like a two-hundred-and-eighty-pound Jell-O statue. "You're a cop, aincha, mister?" I nodded again. Useless to deny it.

"Listen, Mr. McQuaid. Be careful, is all I c'n say. You treat me all right. I heard 'bout you an' Julia an' the chief back in Gallup. You just be careful walkin' the roads round here. Specially at night. You'll get yourself run over an' they'll say it was a drunk Navajo. It'll be a Navajo, all right, but he ain't gonna be drunk. He'll *say* he was drunk."

"How about driving at night?"

"Oh, my goodness!" Thompson had said that Bekis was a devout Baptist as well as a leader in the peyote ceremony. Peyote ceremony leaders are not supposed to have bad thoughts. "Drivin' at night is special bad. Please don't do no night drivin', Mr. McQuaid! My old car runs good. That's because I don't drive on night's time or weekends. I hear

144

some people might be awful innarested in makin' you wish you was back home."

What was all this? A volunteer informant suddenly deciding the only way to protect his well-kept jalopy was to issue dark hints of evil by night? Even though his first loyalty should be to his people? "Who might want to run me over?" I asked, faking skepticism.

He combed his hair with his big fingers and put on his wide-brimmed hat. "Lots of dumb young squirts around," he said. "Sayin' nasty 'bout tribal chairman an' me. I ain't sayin' no one in particular, mind you, now. All I want is for you to be careful. Then you'll go away with a good impression of the Nation."

"And tell my friends to come out for their vacation?"

"Yep. Sure!"

So the motivation was classical: economic. And political. It hung together. He didn't consider himself a traitor, he didn't name names, he just wanted me to be extra special careful. A healthy approach. I would operate on that level. Rarely did I get such specific warnings for a triple sawbuck.

I phoned Mrs. Sorensen. No answer. I phoned Shoshana Kimri. Ditto. I tossed my suitcase in the back and drove to Gallup. To Lieutenant Slavitch I would then be able to say that I had driven to Gallup to check out the pawnshops. To myself I would deliver no such lies. The only reason why I was going there was that a rolling stone might gather some valuable moss.

The first person I saw in the first pawnshop was Jay. He was sitting on a tall stool in the back of the store with a tray in front of him crammed with turquoise necklaces. In his right hand he held a magnifying glass. As he put one necklace back in the tray and picked up another one he caught sight of me. He motioned me over. "Any luck? Been using my advice?"

"Yep. Kept my mouth shut and someone smashed in my windshield with a pickax. Got better advice?"

"That doesn't count," he said calmly. "Any general statement has its exceptions, and it was just your rotten luck to meet one sooner than later."

"Sure. You remind me of the statistician who drowned in a creek where the average depth was four inches. He just stepped in a twelve-foot hole."

"I thought detectives from New York were much smarter, that's all."

"I'm an exception to the general rule," I said, poking a finger in the gorgeous blue mass.

"Careful. That tray is worth about a hundred thousand on the hoof, and the owner is getting nervous watching you."

I shoved my hands in my pockets. "Jay," I said moodily, "I wish to God I had some juicy informants who were scared to death of me. That's what I wish."

"Feeling homesick?"

"In spades, buddy."

"No luck?"

"Nope. But I might pick up something. Do you think I look like a detective in this outfit? I told a waitress in Window Rock that I was a lumberjack. I mean, *she* thought I was."

"McQuaid—buddy—if you told anyone in the Tribal Offices what you are really out here for, believe me, the word is out all over. I mean *all over.* A stranger could whip through New York and no one would notice, but not here. Never." He looked at the owner, who was edging closer. "Let's go out and talk."

We stepped out. I leaned against my rented car. "What's *that?*" he demanded. I told him. "It's OK," I said defensively. "Sure it's OK," he said. "It's OK on a good road. But what'll happen when you hit a dirt road with big rocks in the middle? That thing will blow a fanbelt, bust a spring, bust the oil pan. No traction in snow, you might get a bad storm any hour out here. You better ditch it. Park it at my motel. It'll be safe. I rent a jeep from a garage owner here. It's the only safe way to travel. I'm driving out right away to Acoma and Santo Domingo. I won't attract attention because I'm on a regular buying trip, and you won't attract any either."

"How come I won't? You just told me that they'll spot me with blinding speed. Remember?"

He sighed. "Yeah, on the Navajo land. But we can be pretty sure word hasn't gotten out yet to the pueblos. Besides, I'll tell them you're a friend of mine from California who's come along to see the Indian country. I've taken friends along before. I'll call you George."

"After Washington?"

"No, after Custer. But that'll be our private joke. Besides picking up jewelery we might pick up some information."

I looked at him. It must have been the old suspicious stare I find so hard to break away from whenever I work with people whom I don't know well. He caught the look right away.

"Want to know why I'm taking this trouble?" he asked.

"Yeah."

"Because it isn't trouble. I get awful tired of listening to country music on the radio in these long stretches. I'd like very much to have someone interesting to talk with. I'd really appreciate it if you'd come along."

It sounded fine. He added, "We can drop off your car up at Window Rock before we start. It'll save you a hundred and twenty bucks at least." I vetoed that. I pointed out that *everyone* would know I was with him then, whereas, if I left the car hidden in the motel garage, we might get away with our little deception. He agreed. I put the car in the garage. I said it would be a good idea if I scrunched down in the back of the jeep until we were well out of Gallup. He agreed enthusiastically. Four miles out of town I climbed into the front seat. "This is great!" he said, "I haven't had so much fun since I was in high school."

"Where's our first stop?"

"Acoma. I have to play it very cool there. Especially when I bring someone."

"Why?"

"I went there once with a girlfriend—you know Acoma?"

"No."

"Acoma is a flat-topped mesa three hundred feet high. They live up there and farm the valley below. They make beautiful clay pots. Some very expensive. The people may look small and peaceful, but they're rough. In 1680 they revolted and threw their priests off the rock. I went there once for a dance with this girl. They put on costumes, just like those kachina dolls you see everywhere around Gallup. Then they become gods. Listen carefully now: they do *not* impersonate the gods, they *are* the gods. The spirits of the gods come down and enter their bodies. They are living gods, and every Indian believes it. So I brought this girl. Dumb bitch! She had too much to drink when we were in Albuquerque, anyway, and then she brought along a thermos full of martinis. Big mistake. Well, here we are sitting on the edge of the plaza watching them dance. One of them passed us real close. 'Ooooo, he's cute!' she said, and before I could stop her she reached out and stroked his leg."

"What happened?"

"The dance stopped. *Boom!*—just like that. Dead silence. About eighty men, in costume. Faces and bodies all gorgeously painted, buckskin leggings, little silver bells, branches of spruce, headresses with white feathers blowing in the wind up there, all immobile. I tell you I panicked. Then they moved toward her. I knew what they had in mind, 1680 all over again. I kid you not. And Acoma is an Indian republic, like all of those pueblos, Santo Domingo, Taos, Zuni. They exercise real sovereignty. And their laws hold. They grabbed her. I begged for her life in Spanish, I didn't trust my knowledge of their language. She kept giggling. Finally the governor said, 'All right. Take her away. *Now.*' I said, 'Thank you,' grabbed her by the elbow, and the stupid bitch refused to go! I had to get an armlock on her to get her in the car and she spat at me and scratched my face in the bargain. So there might be some coolness when they see me."

Half an hour later we turned right onto a road going

148

straight south. It ran between fields full of sheep, and low ranges on each side. Small mesas jutted up from the desert floor. Far off to the left was an isolated mesa with tiny flat-topped buildings on the top. We parked below the summit. The Indian in charge of the parking lot put his hand inside for the money, saw it was Jay, and withdrew it. "OK," he said. Jay let out a breath. We got out of the car and walked up the steep road. A small plaza opened out at the top of the road. It was warmer than it had been, and many of the door-ways in the low adobe houses were open. The first room had a bath mat hanging from one wall with a badly printed color image of John Kennedy; beside it were three pictures of an-gels and one of Jesus, two sets of antelope horns, one chair, and one TV set under the pictures. There were three calen-dars on the opposite wall, two of which were out-of-date, two drumsticks, and a large lithograph of Jesus. Feathers were tacked up all around the walls, and one wood stove and one table completed the furniture. In the rear two iron kettles simmered over a small iron stove. An old woman came out of the back and calmly disregarded us with that closed, impassive look I was getting used to. She placed a plain brown bowl on the table, opened a drawer, took out paints and brushes and began to work. She had that bland, bored disregard of us you could see in leopards in a zoo.

"That's Antonia," Jay said. "She's the best potter in Aco-ma. I'd buy from her but there's not enough people where I live who know good pottery."

At the sound of his voice she looked up, and her closed face burst open with a radiant smile. It was the first relaxed, impetuous, friendly expression I had seen on an Indian's face since I had stepped off the plane at Albuquerque. She held out her arms. Jay looked at me, blushed, and, moving close to her, bent down. She put a palm on either side of his face, pulled his head down to her bosom, and squeezed. Then she released him, stood up, and said, beaming at the both of us, "I go make coffee." She went to the stove. Jay was still embarrassed.

149

"Two months ago I was up here looking for pots," he said. "Lots of excitement. Antonia's four-year-old granddaughter was choking and turning blue. I took a look. The kid had diphtheria and would die pretty quickly. I took out my jacknife and opened up her windpipe. Someone found a piece of copper tubing, and I stuck it in her throat. I gave the kid a fast ride to the hospital in Albuquerque. She pulled through OK."

Antonia came back with the coffee. She set it down and beamed at us some more. "Is he your friend?" she asked Jay, who nodded. "Jay is good man," she said.

He cleared his throat nervously and pointed to the pot she was working on.

"Two hunnerd for you. Buyin' this here time?"

"No, Antonia. You're too good for my dumb customers."

Oh, it was nice to be liked in Indian country. But the chances of finding another kid with diphtheria in the next few days were small. Would it be a good idea to work on other angles than a warm interpersonal relationship with native informants? You bet it would, buster! Well, what, for instance? In this business no one gets A for effort. I would have to follow any kind of scent that I could pick up, even if my nose got badly scraped.

She painted quickly and expertly. There was no design sketched first. She painted directly onto the bowl. Black, orange, and red went on without hesitation. She was making a Gila monster.

"That's beautiful," I said.

"Sure. There's one thing I can't get used to. They live here, surrounded by such lousy taste, and yet they're natural superb artists when it comes to clay and turquoise. I just can't figure it out."

"It's one of those Indian mysteries."

"Yeah. I guess so."

We watched her unerring hands. Two women tourists peered over our shoulders. We moved out of the way.

"My," one said, "they sure are pretty!"

One bowl was my favorite. It was colored a pale-brownish white, and a frieze of leaping deer ran around its greatest diameter. They liked that one too.

"I wonder if she'll sell it."

"Sure she will, Myra. They're all for sale."

Myra asked the price.

Jay whispered in my ear, "Wrong way to ask. She thinks she's in Woolworth's with a dumb little clerk buying lipstick. Wait."

Antonia did not look up.

"I said, how much is that?" Myra demanded sharply.

"Worse and worse," Jay whispered in my ear.

Antonia looked up. She examined the woman casually. "Six hundred dollars," she said without expression.

The women stalked away furiously.

"What should the price be, really?" Jay asked.

Antonia held up four fingers.

"If she *likes* you," Jay said. "Don't look surprised. That's a fair price. But I have a friend with a little farm down at Los Lunas. He comes up sometimes with a bushel of tomatoes. If she's in the mood, she'll trade one of those bowls for the bushel."

I looked again at Antonia. She sat there painting placidly away at her vicious Gila monster. "Where's that crazy drunk lady?" she asked.

"I don't see her anymore."

"Umm." She looked at me. "Is *he* coming to the next dance?"

"Probably not," Jay said.

"If he does, he better be very careful."

I nodded. Damn right I would. Falling off a mesa was not my idea of the end of a perfect day. I watched her put the finishing stroke on the Gila monster and hold up the bowl, turning it around critically, cocking her head. The orange, black, and red flowed in massive, sinuous force around the bowl's equator. Jay was staring at it in admiration.

"You like it?" she suddenly demanded.

151

I kept looking at the bowl.

"She's talking to you," Jay said sharply.

"Oh, yes," I said. I never collected pottery. I mean, an Irish cop collecting pottery? I'd never hear the end of it. I could hear Dorsey saying, "Hey, fellas, we got a fag on the squad!" I owned a three-shelf bookcase with the standard works—Sutherland, Soderman, Kirk. Grim works on fingerprints, bloodstains, tire marks on corpses, charts showing the pattern of buckshot on bodies relative to the distance of the muzzle, all sorts of household items like that. A few novels. Ah, what the hell would I do with it? Keep loose buttons and paper clips in it?

She spoke quickly in Spanish. Jay looked surprised. Then she held both hands palm upward, at waist level, moving them alternately up and down, till they both stopped at the same level.

"She wants you to take it as a gift."

"My God, how can I?"

"Take it. Indians don't make empty gestures."

"But—"

"Take it, McQuaid. She means it."

She held out the bowl. I took it, embarrassed.

"Thank you very much, ma'am," I said. I looked around for something to buy, anything. Jay poked me in the back. "We better be going," he said. I thanked her again. She sat placidly in her chair, her hands in her lap, as if they were dozing in the shaft of the warm afternoon light which was flowing in the door.

I wrapped the bowl carefully in my extra woolen underwear and stowed it in my suitcase. Jay pulled out of the parking space and drove down the hill. "That's an A-number-one present," he said, jealous. "She never gave me any. Boy, you rate."

"Sex appeal," I said. But I was thinking very hard. Why me? I'm no great friend of the Indians. Christ, I never even met any until this case started. Mrs. Sorensen was only half an Indian, and doing what I was doing for her was my duty and deserved no recognition. And I hadn't done a damn thing yet.

Jay went past the big isolated cylinder of Enchanted Mesa. He was talking about its history. I pretended to listen; he was sure I was fascinated with his lecture and I did not want to burst the illusion. Why did she give me a six-hundred-dollar bowl? Jay said these things went up in value very quickly because they were one of a kind, and the demand was growing every year. In twenty minutes, therefore, it was worth six hundred dollars and eleven cents. Why me? I didn't get it. The thought nagged at me. It was an unsolved mystery, and I had been trained, very expensively, to solve unsolved mysteries. Then that gesture she made—moving her opened palms up and down, up and down, what the hell did *that* mean? I interrupted Jay's talk on the geology of the mesa to ask him what that meant in Indian sign language.

He said there was no such gesture in sign talk. So that left me with the theory that it was her personal sign. What did it stand for? Jay was now on Upper Pleistocene.

But there was a diner ahead. "I have to make a phone call, Jay," I said. We pulled in and drank some of that discolored hot water while I sat in the booth with a handful of quarters. Mrs. Sorensen was out.

"When will she be back?"

"I really couldn't say, sir."

"No idea when's a good time to try again?"

"No, sir. Impossible to say."

"Tell her that Detective McQuaid returned her call."

I phoned Lieutenant Slavitch. He was in and jumping around like a drop of water on a hot stove.

"Jesus, McQuaid, what the hell's going on? You got to produce! I'm short-handed enough, what with vacations and guys out sick!"

I told him what was happening. He didn't care for any of it. "You haven't come up with a goddamn thing to sink your teeth into, for crissakes. We've had four homicides since

153

you left, and they wcn't pay for overtime. I'm falling behind, goddamnit!"

No one forced you to be a lieutenant, Slavitch, you dumb
hunky, is what I thought, but had sense enough not to say.

"Yes, sir."

This was not a good time to mention the bill I was going
to submit for the windshield and fender.

"You'll have to do better. Corinto's going on vacation on
Tuesday. If you don't get hold of a real good lead in five
days I'm going to pull you off the case."

"But—"

"But nothing! Five days!" He hung up.

For a while I toyed with the idea of a puce-colored crayon
for Slavitch, gift-wrapped, to play number of detectives out
sick against the new homicides. I didn't know what color
puce was, but the word expressed my feelings nicely.

I got back in the car.

"How are things back east?"

"Couldn't be better," I said. "That is, if you define 'better'
as 'rotten.'" I slumped down. Palms going up and down.
Up and down. I asked Jay for some new thoughts on that.

"Probably she was weighing a bushel of tomatoes," he said.

I didn't need jokes. I sank back in the seat and closed my
eyes. The sun was shining pale and weak across the frozen
fields. It was so thin that not even a feeble glow penetrated
my eyelids. Up and down, up and down, her hands had
gone. Suddenly I sat bolt upright. I had it!

She was balancing something on a pair of scales—and
what could she be balancing except the stolen pieces? And,
in an attempt to redress the Indian artifacts taken away by
her people, why not try to replace them—if only symboli-
cally—with another one? As a kind of thank you to Jay's
saving her granddaughter?

And that in turn had to mean (a) she knew me and (b) she
knew who had stolen them.

"Turn around," I said.

154

*　*　*

The old lady was scared. She slid her brush along the bowl in her hands. She refused to tell me why she had given me my bowl. She said it was because I had a nice face, but I wouldn't buy that. When I mentioned that I could only come up with one reasonable theory explaining that balancing gesture and that I was willing to listen to her explanation, she clammed up. When I produced my theory, she froze solid. I know what the fear of a reluctant witness looks like when see it, and the only thing her face resembled at that point was that of an old lady in Little Italy who'd accidentally been a witness to a mob rubout. They *never* talk. And they never talk because they know if they do they'll suddenly become very dead. But who would kill this nice, placid, harmless old lady?

I asked her that question. The brush she was holding trembled. In her kind of work there was no way to start over, or to cover up a mistake. She had ruined the bowl. Or, really, I had ruined the bowl. She looked at it with an annoyed expression. It was clear she wished to her gods that she'd never given the damn bowl to me. I sat on the ruined easy chair, trying to look quietly menacing; trying to look as if I'd never leave; that way she'd have to choose between being silent or telling me something just to get me off her back. I slid down in the chair and shoved my hands in my pockets, feeling like a bully. That putting the hands in the pockets is a small tactic in psychological warfare to make people believe you'd be there for hours.

She suddenly put down the bowl and turned. "Lots of young fellers live in Albuquerque. Go Indian school. Go university. Talk very bad 'bout whites."

I had the feeling that she was on the verge of breaking in my direction. I nodded gently. She had been nibbling at my hook and had taken it a little bit into her mouth. Too en-

155

thusiastic a reaction on my part might make her reconsider. Gentle and encouraging would work better. And gentle and encouraging I was, but it wasn't any good. Not a word more would she say. I bought a tiny clay deer for ten dollars. Maybe people would think I had liked the bowl so much that I had come back half an hour later to get something else. Maybe. You had to get up awful early in the morning to move something past an Indian. To put it in Western terms, I had as much chance of not being noticed as daylight had of sneaking past a rooster. I made sure that I carried the deer in my hand when I left. Let the word go out on moccasin telegraph that McQuaid's only interest in coming to Acoma was to buy Indian artifacts, a regular practice with New York City homicide detectives, as is well known. I ran this theory up the flagpole. One would get you fifty that I would find it next morning nailed to the flagpole by a bunch of arrows.

* * *

On the way to Albuquerque once more, I cheered Jay up by telling him that the first thing I'd be doing as soon as we got there would be to rent a car of my own. He brightened and listened to rock and roll all the way to the car rental, snapping his fingers and drumming them on the wheel. Being pals with a homicide detective was OK, but only in a limited way. "Remember," he said, when he dropped me off at a car rental, "tell 'em you're going to Santa Fe!"

I thanked him for everything. He waved happily at me and drove off. I rented a nice, dark green Pinto without any trouble, and then drove to Police Headquarters. The chief was pleasant and helpful. He told me that the best-informed man on young Indian militants was Stanley Millman, a reporter on the Albuquerque *Star*. He phoned the paper, got Millman right away, and told him he had a New York City detective who'd like to talk to him. "I'd appreciate it, Stan," he said. "Five minutes. OK?"

156

"Tell him I'll buy him supper," I said. The chief passed it on. "That all?" he asked. I nodded.

"Well, for gosh sakes."

I left. Meet a bastard cop, meet a nice one. I drove over to the paper. Millman had said he'd be waiting downstairs. I spotted him right away; he was the young, serious, dedicated type who were coming into the profession because they thought they would be able to turn the country around. He was slender, had a sandy unkempt mustache which looked like a dead mouse strapped under his nose. He wore a business suit with motorcyclist's boots which were badly in need of a cleaning. He immediately offered me a marijuana cigarette. I declined.

"Mind if I light up?"

"Hell, no."

"The locals seem to take it personally. I figure you New York detectives are more sophisticated."

"We are. We are." I let him smoke it awhile. Some people need alcohol to unwind, this group did it on pot. He took several long drags, packing the smoke deep in his lungs. I opened the door and he jumped in nervously.

"You a pearl diver?" I asked.

"A what?"

"You act like you're getting ready to stay on the bottom for five minutes."

"Oh, no. No, no. I'm just a little tense. Nothing serious."

"I see." I didn't like the idea of nervous reporters. They affect me like nervous doctors. People who take the pulse of society should not be jittery. It affects their judgment.

"Make a right. We're going across the river to Corrales. Very nice out there, not like the disgusting extended suburb that's Albuquerque these days."

I drove. He seemed to relax as we moved, the tension leaking out of him.

"You seemed pretty nervous when I picked you up."

"Damn right. I thought you'd be waiting for me on the

sidewalk, so when I saw someone leaning out of the car I thought you were going to shoot me."

I looked at him.

"Go left," he said. "I don't mean *you* personally, you know. Pull in there, at that restaurant. I'll tell you why I come here to eat," he said as we got out of the car. "It's very elegant. Elegant for Albuquerque, that is. And very expensive. And the people who've expressed a sincere interest in my demise can't afford places like this. So I can relax. I hope you didn't think I'd bring you here just to take advantage of your supper offer."

I reassured him that the thought hadn't passed through my mind. He had a thin, reedy, strangely pleasant voice, something like an oboe with a broken reed. We took a table against the back wall. He wanted to be able to scan anyone coming in. There was a candle on each table. It was dark between the candles, but the drinks were big and cold. He swallowed half of his bourbon and water right away.

"Who's after you?" I asked.

"Indians."

I burst into laughter.

He looked at me angrily.

"I didn't mean to laugh," I said contritely, "but this dialogue belongs in one of those cowboy movies set a hundred years out in Sioux country."

"I suppose. But it's not funny to me. You want to listen? Because it affects what you want to find out, I think."

"Sure."

"I majored in anthropology. Specialization, American Indian languages. I speak Comanche and Zuni. Pretty stupid, I used to think. Six thousand people speak Zuni. Hell, that's pretty good, there's some Colorado River tribe with only three hundred people, and their own language not like any other language in the world—let's not get on Indian languages now. In order to study these languages I used to spend my summers on their reservations. By the way, Zunis don't have a reservation. Zuni has always owned its own

158

land; it's been confirmed by treaty. See, the academic mind! I can't even stick to the topic!"

He speared some steak and chewed it for a while.

"Well, two years passed. Then my father died, I dropped out in order to support my mother. Just then the *Star* was looking for someone to cover the pueblos, the Navajos, and police news. The managing editor remembered from the college paper when I used to do book reviews for the *Star* because I got to keep the books and sell them for some extra money. So I got the job. My mother's sick now, I'm still on the paper—seven years now. I've got excellent contacts."

"Your steak's cold."

"Yeah, thanks." He swallowed it. He didn't look as if he were enjoying it. "OK, you've got my background. Now, many of the Indians I met when I was living at Zuni or with the Navajos have shown up here in Albuquerque. Some in the Indian school, some at the university on scholarship. And most of them in police court."

"D and D?"

"Drunk and disorderly? Most of them. But some wind up being shot. And some wind up stealing the better concho belts and turquoise necklaces."

"From pawnshops?"

"Too risky. They're too well protected, alarm systems tied in with Police Headquarters, stuff like that. Nope. They burglarize expensive houses. Most well-to-do people here collect the better Navajo jewelry. That's all they take. The stuff can't be traced. When the Indians sell it, they say it's been in their family a long time, they just need the money. It's a natural. And with the big demand back east and in California for the older stuff they can go to any dealer here and get three, four hundred for a concho, and as much as two, three thousand for the exceptional necklaces."

"What has this to do with you?"

"Coming to it. This new Red Pride movement is all splintered into lots of little factions. Some model themselves on Black Power, and go for big, splashy PR techniques to grab media attention. Indian clothes, long hair, scalp locks, all that kind of stuff which looks good on TV. Other groups aim at the electoral process. No glamor there, no money. Others go for coalitions with all the other minorities. An awful lot of pushing and shoving for whatever crumbs there are. And some go for violent, terroristic actions. This was just bullshit till a couple months ago when NAU—*Native Americans Unite!*—killed a wealthy rancher up in southwest Colorado because he was saying that Indians ought to die out like the buffalo and make the West profitable for decent, hardworking whites.

"I know NAU gets their money through burglarizing homes here and in Santa Fe. So I wrote an article a couple months ago, without naming names, in which I pointed out that it was terrible that this was happening, pointed out that it would keep on happening unless the white power structure corrected the old injustices, blah blah blah, and two nights later someone fired a rifle at my house when I was sitting at my desk at the front window. See this?"

He put a finger to his right cheek. I saw a faint horizontal red mark, as if it had been made by a pale pink lipstick.

"I mean I *felt* the wind as it went by. *Close.*"

"Close is right."

"But the problem is, there are people out there who say I'm too favorable to the Indians. And they've threatened me too. So I don't know who the hell took a shot at me."

"And that's why you jumped when you saw me lean out of the car?"

"Yep. I'm just about getting over it now."

"Don't worry too much about it. Everyone in public life gets threats all the time. It doesn't mean anything."

"Sure. Martin Luther King. Bobby Kennedy. It doesn't mean a thing. To hell with winning the Pulitzer Prize for journalism, McQuaid, if I could get a good job selling desert lots to suckers from New York I'd grab it."

"Better a live dog than a dead lion?"

"Damn right. But I get union scale here, and that takes care of my mother. I'm locked into this job and I'm scared to death."

I was sorry for him. I ordered another round. As the liquor worked he talked about the physical beauty of the Indian country and his experiences in the field when he worked as a linguist. I was wondering how to steer the conversation around to my problem without making him shy like a nervous horse; he still didn't know why I was in New Mexico. The chief of police hadn't told him. I hadn't told him, and he'd been sitting so tense or so full of talk that he hadn't thought to ask what had brought me west.

"Oh, Christ," he said wearily, "I don't want to go home."

"Nothing will happen," I said soothingly.

"You know it won't. I know it won't. But do *they* know it?"

I sipped my drink. I had been put in my Pollyanna-ish place. I had an idea. I asked if he worked the next day.

"Yeah."

"What would happen if you took a day off?"

"Nothing much."

"Suppose you take off, head for Santa Fe, and sort of bum around with me? You could show me around, and you'd feel better if you could get away awhile. I guess your mother would be all right if you were gone a day or two."

"Say, that's a great idea! My mother'd be all right, no problem. I could phone in tomorrow and say I'm tracking down a story. I might even pick one up on the way."

"Fine. Let's head on up to Santa Fe right now. I'll loan you some fresh underwear and a pair of socks."

"Hey, McQuaid, you're cookin'! I'll give her a call first."

We made Santa Fe in little over an hour. We had a drink and then to bed in a little motel. In the morning Millman had a mild hangover but no nervousness. He crunched his two aspirins like peanuts before he swallowed them with coffee. I asked him why he did it that way. "To distribute

161

them all over the stomach lining instead of letting two big lumps sit there, dissolving slowly. I get faster action. Why do you ask?"

"I like original thinking even if it's disgusting," I said. "I think we'll get along, Stan."

"Yeah, maybe. I'm not used to classy detectives like you You don't look like a detective, like the ones around Albuquerque. And anyone who doesn't look like a detective is my idea of a detective."

"What do I look like?"

"Well, not like a real estate salesman. Tell you what, if you had a tan and walked bowlegged, I'd put you down for a rancher come to town to raise a little hell."

We were strolling around the plaza looking at the Indians sitting cross-legged, selling pottery and bowls.

"Seriously, Stan, what *do* I look like?"

"Like a tow-truck driver but with clean fingernails."

"Thanks a lot."

"But the kind of a driver I'd trust not to screw me. There's something kind and trustworthy about your face."

"And loyal and reverent."

"Yep." His headache had disappeared and he was feeling good. We had toured the plaza and he had his hands in his pockets. One of the old Indians, swathed in a white blanket, called out, "Hello, Stan."

"Hello, Juanito."

"Goin' to the dance?"

"What dance?"

"The mountain spirit dance. At Santo Domingo."

"Jesus, I forgot. It's today, isn't it?"

"Sure is."

"Thanks for reminding me." He turned. "Great," he said, "I can tell the paper I came up here to cover the dance. Interviews with local celebrities, with the dumb governor of Santo Domingo—God, he's dumb—and so forth. It's like covering a St. Patrick's Day parade every four days. Every pueblo has lots of dances. That or digging up a road-paving

162

scandal involving a county commissioner—and you get better pictures."

"Where's your camera?"

"If they see a camera at any dance they'll take out the film if they're in a good mood, and if they're not they'll smash the camera."

"So how do you get pictures?"

"Ohho. Years ago when the Army was still doing heavy cavalry patrols people would come with those heavy cameras with a hood they had to duck under. The Indians were afraid to object. I just dig up one of those old ones and run it. The Indians know I don't carry cameras and they know about the old ones. They don't object to those."

We were walking along a wooden colonnade when suddenly, out of the corner of my eye, something in a shop window caught my eye. I stopped. It was a very expensive Indian jewelry shop, and in the center of the display was Mrs. Sorensen's carved walrus-ivory bird.

*　*　*

"It's a nice piece, isn't it?" Millman said. I had not mentioned anything about the Sorensen case except that there had been a murder committed during a robbery.

"Yes. What do you know about the owner of the store?"

"A very knowledgeable screaming faggot named—honest—Devereux de Brissac. Works the Key West, Southampton, Santa Fe circuit. Blood brother to the Zunis, believe it or not. Speaks their language, for which all honor to him."

"That's *very* interesting. I'm sure he cooks divinely and does his hair in a daring fashion, but what I want to know is—is he honest?"

Millman looked annoyed at my sarcasm. "I haven't heard any complaints," he said stiffly. "There he is now, in the back." I saw a thin man, in his early forties, with long blond hair in a ponytail that was held in a silver clasp studded with turquoises. He was bent over a box of turquoise fragments, examining them with a jeweler's loupe. He wore very tight, very old Levi's. He looked as if his buttocks had been planted in them years ago when he was small.

"His ass looks rootbound," I said.

"Very good, McQuaid," Millman said, grinning. "I'll mention that line to him."

"Not now. He'll take it unkindly."

"No, he won't. He'll take it as an indecent and interesting proposal."

"You say he's a blood brother? I didn't know Indians went for that type."

"Faggots don't bother them. You going to buy some jewelry? Wow, that's a fantastic piece in the middle! It doesn't look Navajo. Could be Hohokam. Ancestors of the tribes. At any rate, if you've got your eye on it, forget it. That's gotta run twenty, thirty thousand."

"Really?"

"That's museum quality. I wish I knew where it came from. Looks like southern Arizona. Before cliff dwellings. Wow."

I could tell him but I preferred not to.

"You sure got good taste," he said, staring at the bird.

"You think he's honest?"

"In a store, yes. I wouldn't let him get back of me in a crowded elevator unless I had both hands clapped firmly over my ass."

"Would he knowingly buy stolen property?"

"Ohho! That's what you're driving at! You mean, supposing that piece is stolen, would you get into some sort of trouble if you went in and bought it?"

If that was his way to explain to himself my interest in the ivory bird, let him. I could always straighten him out later.

"This is an academic discussion, right? You're really not going to buy it?"

He was a nice kid, but he was also a newspaperman. I saw no reason to tell him anything more than he needed to know to help me along. He was doing all right up to now. If he managed to dig up more from me, he would be able to latch onto a very nice story, since Mrs. Sorensen was probably very well known around here. A billionaire Indian jewelry robbery! A smash scoop for the Albuquerque *Star*! An exclusive by Stanley Millman! Uh uh. No.

"Not me. But I know a rich collector who I think would be very interested."

"I prefer for you to make your own judgment on these matters. Come in and I'll introduce you."

The shop was very narrow. It was almost like being in the barrel of a telescope. The back wall was crammed with massive turquoise necklaces. Hundreds of concho belts hung from nails in the back wall. The showcase running along one side wall was filled with thick silver bracelets set with huge blue stones.

"Look at those conchos," Stan said. "Big as soup plates. All done before 1900. He won't handle anything made after 1920. Best collection in the country. Better than anything in Gallup. Since he's a blood brother, he's got the best contacts. That ought to give you some kind of a hint about him. Indians don't make blood brothers out of crooks."

It made sense. But what was the bird doing in his window? Best to keep mouth shut and ears open. "What's his background?"

"He came out here twenty years ago to spend a week. Rich Chicago family. Young broker. Big future in stock exchange lined up for him with the family firm. He fell in love with the art, the tribes, the mountains. It's a common phenomenon. And Indians don't make fun of faggots. So he stayed. Had a couple thousand bucks saved up, told his family to shove it, opened this little store. I admire him."

De Brissac approached us. The loupe hung around his neck on a long black cord, banging gently against the huge turquoise chunks of his necklace. Sure, he liked it here. If virile Indians wore necklaces and bracelets, he could do it also, and no one would make fun of him. I could see the appeal of Santa Fe.

165

"Stan. Hi. Let me guess what brings you here—the dance at Santo Domingo. Right?" He had a rich, pleasant voice, frank and open. Not self-conscious, not prissy; his mouth didn't work over each juicy syllable, as did so many of the type back east in creative fields.

"Right, Dev. I'd like you to meet a friend of mine from the east, Danny Sullivan. He's a newspaperman out here on a vacation."

We shook hands. He had a firm grip, which I didn't expect.

"I noticed that piece in the middle of your window," I said calmly. I was playing the shrewd buyer, never enthusiastic. "What would it be going for?"

"Forty thousand. But you're not going to buy it."

I was annoyed. He was right, of course, but no one likes to be told that he's a time-wasting pain in the ass. I concealed my emotions and continued on blandly.

"What is it?"

He sighed. Not too much. Not too offensive. Just about the amount a very good headwaiter would do in a very good restaurant. This man was a very careful player; he dealt in minute subtleties; he was not careless or reckless; he was not given to spontaneities. I made that judgment from that tiny sigh. Was he the kind of a man, therefore, who would knowingly buy stolen property? I wasn't sure yet.

"I think it's pre-pueblo. I wouldn't want to authenticate it until I get some expert opinion, plus some carbon-dating. I think it's prehistoric, maybe the earliest piece I've ever seen from this area. I won't want to sell it till I'm positive. It's one of the most beautiful pre-Columbian pieces I've ever seen. It should be in a museum collection."

It was, I wanted to say. But all I said was, "Of course, I understand. I know someone, however, who might very well be interested, once you finish all the tests." My next question was the crucial one; all the others had been camouflage.

"Did it come out of an excavation?"

"Yes."

166

"Suppose someone had slipped it into the excavation so that it would be found?"

De Brissac stared at me. He didn't like interruptions. He hadn't expected my remark. I had made it, not because I wanted him to think he was dealing with a man who wanted him to realize he was facing someone with some shrewdness, but because I wanted him to come up with an answer so precise that I wouldn't have to bark around him until he disgorged a response which would yield good results.

"That would complicate matters, of course." The expression on his face announced I was a stupid jerk, busily engaged in wasting his time. "That's why I want to wait for carbon-fourteen dating."

It was clear to me that De Brissac was honest. I didn't like him, but I thought he was honest. Time for the next question.

"You have no doubts about the man who sold it to you? I only ask because my friend would be very concerned about provenance."

"Of course. Imagine the difficulty in buying a Rembrandt which had been stolen, say, from a French chateau in World War II. Title, to put it mildly would be blurred. And it is the same with rare pieces like this, only there are tremendous difficulties about providing provenances. It would have to go like this: 'Found on unknown skeleton, circa A.D. 200, accidental discovery by sheepherder from Santo Domingo sometime in March of this year. Acquired by Devereux de Brissac.' Not a very impressive genealogy. Still, it is one which satisfies many knowledgeable buyers in the entire Southwest."

"That's true, Danny," Stan said.

"What box canyon?" I turned to Millman. "Shouldn't your Archaeology Department at the university latch onto that?"

"Yeah," he said. "Not a bad—"

De Brissac interrupted, more annoyed than ever. "But you see, Mr. Sullivan, there are problems!" He was beginning to simmer, but he was handling himself very well, only little bits of irritation were beginning to leak from his eyes. "Once *that* happens I'll get no more pieces from there. The university will put a hold on it. No one will be able to touch the digging, and all the pieces found will go to the museum down in Albuquerque. Although I admire the museum and what it has done for archaeology, I must think of myself and my business, and of the profits I must make to keep going. It's the old dilemma between dealers and scholars and I haven't been able to solve it. If I pass the location on to the university, my supplier will drop me. And I'll never get any more such magnificent pieces."

All through his explanation he had been getting angrier. He had greeted me pleasantly in the beginning, but from then on I was a prize ball-breaker, an East Coast wise guy know-it-all, wanting to show off a few odds and ends of art gallery gossip. I was giving him the impression that I was a Big Man in Town laying down the law to some hillbilly hicks. At the end of his little talk his voice had risen considerably and it was clear to both me and Millman that he was restraining himself only with difficulty. I was a son of a bitch and I knew it, poor Millman would get his ass chewed later for bringing me into the shop, but I had a homicide and a big robbery and I had an ugly lieutenant to placate. My ass had been chewed the afternoon before and I didn't mind passing it along the line.

I decided to stir up a little war. I turned to Millman. "Stan," I said, "if you could only interview whoever found it at that box canyon you'd have a good story."

"You bet!" he said enthusiastically.

"With pictures this time."

De Brissac thought it was a lousy idea.

"And," I added, "although I say this without any personal implication, you could tie up this story with dealers' tendencies—present company excepted—to suppress news of important archaeological discoveries in the prehistoric Southwest."

You couldn't beat *that* for being a pain in the ass.

De Brissac came to a rolling boil. "And nothing personal either," he said, his face reddening, "but do you mind getting the hell out of my shop?"

"Why, not at all," I said pleasantly, and walked out. Through the window, above my ivory bird, I could see the two of them arguing in a very heated manner. De Brissac jerked his thumb at me a couple times. They got more and more excited and finally Millman emerged, slamming the door behind him.. His face was flushed.

"Oh, that son of a bitch!" he muttered. "That faggotty son of a bitch!"

"What's up?" I asked, falling into step beside him as we walked toward the car.

"First he accused me of bringing you there deliberately so that I could be amused while you tried to put him down. Then he said *I* had put you up to asking those questions, sounding him out on that piece in the window, and the whole archaeology bit as well."

"Why did I sound him out?" I asked.

"So that I could determine by his reaction whether or not he'd go along with that idea you had of a series of articles," Stan replied. "If he liked the idea, he said, then the plan was for me to take over the discussion. If he didn't go for it, on the other hand, you'd take the blame and I'd come out as a friend to all mankind. Shit!"

He mooned along. "This makes my day," he said. "Night before last, someone shoots at me. Last night, hangover. Today I lose a good friend. What the hell's next?"

"Bad things come in threes," I said. "From now on it's downhill for you. But I've got an idea for you. Why not do the series anyway? It could bring you national attenton, and with everyone interested these days in American Indian art, and with New York interested in art and Indian wrongs, the New York *Times* might pick it up. And when you want to crack the big city, you might find that series a very nice in to a job on the *Times*."

He perked up a bit. "Maybe. Worth thinking about."

"De Brissac said something about a box canyon near Santo Domingo. Isn't that where we're going anyway?"

"I'm not going into *any* box canyon on Indian land unless I'm invited," he said firmly. "You can get killed there very easily and they'd never find you."

"I don't care about box canyons as box canyons, Stan. One box canyon is supposed to have produced one Hohokam bird. The finder of this bird is in Santo Domingo. All I want is to talk to the finder. You're not going to catch me clumping up a box canyon with snow rattlers underfoot."

"Step on a snow rattler," he said, "and you get a deadly invisible bite. Your head falls off and neither you nor your friends notice. You look and talk like the person you used to be, but there's been a serious change. Most people never find out they've been bitten until it's too late."

"Dig it," I said, wishing I was back in New York, chasing a nice simple heroin murder.

*   *   *

Santo Domingo was about thirty miles south of Santa Fe. We stopped for the usual coffee. I took my suitcase into the men's room and changed back to my city clothes. When I came back to my stool Stan eyed me oddly, but said nothing, since he had the good newspaperman's instinct—which was not to ask questions unless he felt a compliant mood in the air. He was not feeling it because I was not giving it. He tried for conversation. "When we get closer to the pueblo," he said, "I want you to notice the big breasts on the women and the small ones on the cows."

"Very funny," I said politely. He dropped into silence, which we both maintained the rest of the way to Santo Domingo. At the pueblo cars were pulling into the parking lot. A long line stretched in front of us. "Stan," I said, "I'm getting out here. You park the car. If you see me, act as if you don't know me. I'll talk to you when I want to."

170

"Sure. As long as you give me an exclusive if you come across something good."

"For New Mexico you've got an exclusive."

I opened the door and stepped out. He slid into place and I walked ahead. Other passengers were getting out and walking down the road to the dance plaza, which, like in most pueblos, was situated in the midst of the low, rambling adobe structures. I was pretty sure I hadn't been noticed, but that's something you only find out later. I walked past a big, low, wooden building which was the trading post, then into an area which looked familiar. Square adobe houses, piled on top of each other, all cubes. Cubes everywhere. My consciousness kept tugging at my memory. It didn't want to let go. And suddenly I had it: the doodlings made by Shoshana Kimri in her office. She had been building pueblos. I could understand why now. There was something so solid, so calm, about the broad bases and the cubes piled on top, all the same height. In the distance the heavy shoulders of the flat-topped mesas repeated the pattern. The houses looked as old as the mountains. Sometimes you thought that the houses had been there first. It was hard to figure out what was imitating what. The brown flat dirt floor of the plaza continued on in narrow alleys between the houses, blended into the fields, which, in turn, merged imperceptibly into the lower slopes of the mountains. It was as if the land had decided to give birth to the houses.

Several people were sitting on a porch, extracting whatever warmth they could get from the pale, watery sun. A piercing wind was whistling down from the mountains. I buttoned the top button of my thin topcoat and shivered. The edges of the plaza were crowded with spectators. Tourists composed about a third of the crowd. The Indians sat, immersed in their blanket almost as stolid as the mountains. The cold wind knew exactly where to attack the back of my neck. I took long deep breaths. A Japanese cop, when I was once on leave in Tokyo, had told me that if you took several very deep breaths, that you would feel warmer in a minute or so. He explained that the heart, having to pump harder to deal with the sudden demand on it, gave you the illusion of warmth. I tried it. It worked a little bit, but then what did my lungs want with big amounts of icy air? Win one, lose one.

Millman had told me to watch the circular structure in the middle of the plaza. It had a ladder sticking out of it. The dancers would emerge from it, as if they were gods emerging from the underworld. I told him he could see that any night in New York.

"*What?*" he said, astonished.

"Sure. Watch any good Italian restaurant in Little Italy when the Mafia dons come out."

"Why, Sergeant," a voice said in my ear, with a light mocking quality. "I'm sure glad you're workin'. I bet you could track a bear in runnin' water. This is your case DD7432 talkin'."

As if I needed to know. DD7432 was the Detective Division case number for the Sorensen matter. I knew automatically she had been talking to Dorsey, who, in his drive to climb into her pants was probably keeping her filled with all sorts of interesting data better left unsaid. I couldn't see her extracting that kind of information from Slavitch. I would have myself a little chat with Dorsey soon.

I turned around. I wished she hadn't spoken so loudly. It's like yelling "fire!" in a crowded theater, only worse.

"How do you do, Mrs. Sorensen?"

"Jus' fine, jus' fine!" She flung her arms wide open to embrace the sky. Her voice carried far, and she was not mousily dressed. Several people had turned around to stare at her. And at me, too, goddamn her. About seven or eight little Indian children were clustered around her, like bees around a honeycomb, clinging to her skirt and pressing against her.

"Ain't it a great day! The air is shinin' like a bathroom in a big Paris hotel."

"What brings you here?"

"I'm havin' me a war with the nuns here."

"Nuns?"

"The church runs a school here. I was talkin' a couple days ago on the phone to Joselito—he's the governor—an' he happened to mention that he wasn't goin' to insist that the kids take today off to go to the dance. Said the dance wasn't very important nohow, jus' a l'il ol' midwinter dance. Well, I *slammed* that phone down so hard I bet I broke his eardrum, an' I took the next plane. I walked into the mission school with a big box fulla crayons an' colored paper an' I gave them to the kids. An' Sister Teresa jus' glared me, an' I gave her a big l'il ol' smile. An' I asked, 'What's today?' An' the kids said 'Wednesday.' An' I said, 'NO IT AIN'T. It's the dance when the ground is frozen hard. An' you know what we're fixin' to do? We're goin' to the dance *right now*. You put on your coats, all you kids.' An' they did. An' I walked right up to Sister Teresa an' I put my hands on my hips, like this"—here she stuck out her jaw and narrowed her eyes—"an' then I said, 'You try to stop me an' I'll climb all over you like honeysuckle on a front porch.' Well, I declare I bet Sister Teresa was forgettin' all her vows 'bout lovin' her enemy, 'cause she looked like she wanted to kill me. Then I went an' chewed out the governor. He was tryin' to hide in his office, but I rooted him out. Then I took the kids here to watch, an' who do I find here playin' tourist but my favorite lil ol' homicide detective!"

Sister Teresa, move over.

Several Indians nearby were watching us with deep interest. She had blown my cover. Nothing to do now but enjoy the dance. I wished I had on my woolen socks.

"Any luck on my case?" she asked, having shushed the children. Like all Indian children, they were well-behaved and were quiet immediately. The wind came down the mountain and picked up speed as it entered the narrow spaces between the houses. I shoved my hands in my pockets and squirmed my toes around to heat them up.

"Some." For crissakes, someone might be listening.

"Such as?"

"I'd rather not say."

"Why the hell not? You workin' for me, it's *my* case."

I didn't care for her commanding attitude. Name, rank, and serial number, that's all she'd get out of me. Goddamn-it, I would never even have given her her case number.

"No, I don't. I work for the people of the State of New York."

"It doesn't matter, it's still my case."

"It's the State's case." It sounded like a schoolyard squabble. I was getting embarrassed with the silliness of it all.

"It's my jewelry, Jesus Christ!"

I spoke calmly, but I was beginning to heat up. "It's the State's body that's dead, not yours. You don't understand something else. In a burglary *you* are not the plaintiff—the *State* is. You got this all confused with a civil case. That ought to be the end of the civic lesson."

"I don't know what the hell all this bullshit is about, McQuaid," she said impatiently. "All I want to know is, what the hell did you find out so far?"

Typical female logic. Going right to the heart of the matter. Completely bypassing everything I had told her. I had dealt with this kind of thing before. It's more common with women. There's only one way to handle it: *Never* lose your temper, just calmly repeat your points until they finally understand, or give up and stop talking, or just walk away, screaming you're a goddamn stupid no-good thick-skulled cop. I couldn't tell what she might do. I could predict, however, that it would be totally unexpected. The whole situation was all right with me: the arguing was keeping me warm.

"Well? Speak up!"

That's all I needed: an order. "You're used to having people jump, aren't you? I want you to understand something: I jump badly. Next point: when I determine that you can be told something, I'll tell you. Not before, If you want someone to jump through a hoop and answer all your questions when you snap them out, hire a private detective. Only there are problems there: they don't like to fool around with homicides. They don't get paid enough when the murderer is loose. I don't either, but then I asked for homicide duty. So be a good girl and lay off!"

I had thought she would explode. But she just smiled and put her arms around as many of the kids she could reach, bent down, and said, "Now, every one of you kids look at the man with the red face. He's a sheriff but he don't dress like one. That's 'cause he's from New York City, the biggest town in the U.S. and A. He's a friend of mine though he don't talk like it, and his name's Sergeant McQuaid. Everybody say, 'Hello, Sergeant McQuaid!'"

Everyone did, goddamn the little bastards. And goddamn her. Their shrill voices chorused across the plaza. Never, *never* had my cover been blown like that. I could see Millman's sandy mustache across the plaza, with his mouth half open in astonishment. I suppose mine was open too. One consolation: this wa s a better way to warm up than taking several deep breaths. Hear that, Inspector Yoshida?

*   *   *

McQuaid never gives up. Although he feels like it. I gloomily hiked back to the parking lot. There were a couple hundred Pintos there of exactly the same make and year and color, and it took me half an hour to find the goddamn heap, and me getting angrier by the second. There was no point in hanging around the lady with her penchant for screaming out my name in public. I had thought it might be useful to change back into my lumber jacket and boots. At least I'd be warm. Maybe people wouldn't tend to recognize me in that outfit, as compared to the magnificent introduction made by Mrs. Sorensen. At least they'd be looking for some jerk in a thin topcoat.

I still had not understood that Indians, visually, were much too sharp for silly little games like that. But my mind wasn't working very well. Millman had parked the car after

175

I had left it. We hadn't been near each other. Ergo: he still had the goddamn key. Maybe the cold had frozen my mind. Maybe it was Mrs. Sorensen's comments which had done the trick.

When I stepped onto the road from the parking lot on my way back to the plaza I saw de Brissac. He had parked much closer to the pueblo than we had and he was walking briskly. He wore a sheepskin-lined long overcoat and a fur hat. The dance had begun, as I could tell by the drumming and a line of jagged spruce branches joggling up and down above the massed heads of the viewers surrounding the plaza. I stayed fifty feet back of de Brissac. He never turned around.

At the plaza edge one of the Indians, sitting on the flat roof on top of one of the houses, called down to him. De Brissac looked up, smiling. The Indian beckoned him up. De Brissac went through the crowd, climbed a ladder against the side of the building, and sat down beside the Indian, who shook hands with him. They began talking. I moved close to the porch and maneuvered my way through the crowd, little by little, till I judged I was directly underneath him. There was no way he could know I was there, and I would be able to tell, from any Indian's face—if he were close enough, that is—if he were looking up at de Brissac. I looked around. I couldn't see Millman. My position was too good to risk losing it in a search for him and the key to the car. I would just have to go on freezing. Besides, if I moved, de Brissac might see me and then play it too cool.

The line of dancers shuffled past. They were naked to the waist, painted with violent diagonal yellow slashes, with spruce branches tied to their wrists and ankles; their headdress made from more spruce branches, with plumes of white feathers quivering above the green mass.

It was a shame I didn't have Millman beside me explaining the meaning of all that. An all-expense tour—well, almost all—to the Southwest, with a nice tour guide nearby, and me not able to ask questions. White feathers for rainclouds, green for growing things? Therefore, dance for rain next summer? They wore buckskin kilts, leather moccasins to their knees, and buckskin fringes tied all around their waists so that the ends of the fringes just cleared the ground. Why? More men were climbing up the ladder sticking up out of the kiva. This dance was reeking with meaning and I didn't have the faintest idea what it all meant.

Suddenly I felt a piece of paper being slipped into my hand. I made no sign, and after a minute I read it, as if I were looking into my notebook. It was signed "Stan," and it read:

> At last I've found you. I'll be opposite you, directly across the plaza. If you see our friend making any interesting moves, remember the person he's interested in. Raise your hat then. I'll join you right away. In the meantime make careful notes on this dance. You will be given a written test. This is the midwinter dance. It is to make sure that the sun will have sense enough to come back next spring. The spruce is to remind him to keep things green, the long strips of buckskin is to remind him that rain is what this is all about, the yellow is to attract his feeble attention. Professor Millman, Anthropology 101.

I bet I could pass.

The dance was a slow hop, from one foot to the other, constantly repeated, but in synchronization with my heartbeat. Hundreds of feet coming down at the precisely same split second made the bare ground vibrate; the beat of all those feet was reinforced by the throbbing of the hard-packed soil. The vibration was transferred to the porch of the house I was leaning against. I put my hand out and felt the wooden upright. It, too, was vibrating, ever so slightly. After five minutes the effect of the strong, heartbeat rhythm became hypnotic. My heart began to beat faster.

I looked hard at the dancers' eyes as they filed past. They were only five feet from me. They all looked ahead, or to one side, looking for relatives or friends. One of the dancers now nearing me attracted my attention. He was much bigger than the others, and his right shoulder was scarred. It looked like the entrance made by a .45 bullet. I made sure to get a good look at his back as he passed. Sure enough, he had the usual big whirlpool-shaped scar of the exit wound. The bullet had tumbled right after impact and had gone out broadside. From the way the man moved his arms it was clear that the damage done to his shoulder blade by the bullet was minimal. He was lucky, usually the bullet takes a good part of the bone with it in its travels in that area. He interested me. I watched him closely.

When he had gone around the plaza and was near me once more he looked up, grinned, and made a thumbs up sign at someone directly above my head. It had to be de Brissac. The gesture would have passed by unnoticed had anyone been looking at the dancer casually; it would have been passed off as a meaningless little erratic movement due to the excitement of the dance.

It may not have meant a thing. On the other hand, I now had a little something to sink my teeth into. I raised my hat. In about three minutes I heard Millman's voice in my ear. "Point him out," he was saying. The dancers came around again. When the man with the scarred shoulder was in front again, grinning upward at de Brissac, I said, "That one."

"Oh, oh," said Millman quietly. "We're in trouble."

* * *

We had split up again. Millman walked through the parking lot and toward the road, which by now was heavy with traffic heading back to Santa Fe. I drove out and he pretended to be a hitchhiker. I stopped and picked him up.

"Isn't all this childish?"

"Probably," he said. "But since there's so many strangers here today we won't be getting any special scrutiny. What the hell, it won't hurt to take a chance. I just don't want to be seen associating with you. Do you *mind*?" He was getting nervous again.

"No."

"Where do you want to go?"

"Santa Fe," I said. "I might want to talk again to de Brissac. Tell me about Scar."

"Oh, boy. His name is Pete Kills Twice. He's half Comanche. His mother is a Santo Domingan. His brother-in-law is a Zuni and dancing in Shalako. Pete has been asked to help him get ready. A big honor. All this gives him plenty of opportunity to get around and make contacts. His great-grandfather was a famous Comanche war chief named Kills Twice. He got the name because he once thought he had killed a white soldier with his lance. He turned away and the soldier shot at him. Kills Twice lanced him again and this time the soldier died. Hence the name. Pete was in Vietnam sharpening his ancestral skills. Green Beret, naturally. He took scalps and mailed them home."

"You're kidding."

"I kid you not. Santo Domingans never took scalps, but in honor of Pete they held a scalp dance. His mother kicked the scalp all over the floor, the way they used to, spitting on it. Pete came home a sergeant. Parachuting, mountain climbing, killing with piano wire, eating snakes, living off the country. You name it, he did it. Then he got interested in political activity. Old-line Indian politicians, old-line ranchers, people like that, they don't want any crazy young kid around who mails scalps home. Too impulsive. Too quick to insult Federal officials come down from Washington to OK Indian-country projects: roads, bridges, reforestation, soil-erosion prevention. Lots of money there, lots of jobs. Lots of votes. Pete speaks his mind. He could blow it for the whole state of New Mexico. So they sat on him. They wouldn't come near Pete in the primaries. The guy's broke. He gathered the young ones around him. The ones who want money, power."

"So he's the one who started NAU?"

"Right. There they are without influence, without money, with about twenty-eight supporters. I think they've bombed a few county courthouses. I think they killed that rancher

179

down south. They're always broke. No one gives them any money, no one gives them any attention. But they need money. How do they get it?"

"Burglaries."

"Right. Up to now they've stayed away from banks. They don't want the FBI on their ass. No Federal raps. They've seen that massive power let loose in Nam and they don't want any part of it."

Makes sense. Rob a rich New York lady with top-quality stuff. Even if they took it interstate the Feds wouldn't care much. Big market in New Mexico for good Indian material. Just about impossible to prove it's been stolen. Could come from a ruin. Prove it didn't. Oh, smart, *smart*.

"This Pete is tough. A little crazy, too. For all I know he's the one who took a shot at me."

"Did he see you today?"

"Maybe. Gee, he makes me nervous."

Christ, I'd have to play nursemaid. He wanted to stop at a diner for a leak, there were too many cars on the road.

I pulled in at the next one. While I waited for him I decided to eat a piece of pie. I sat in a booth and gave my order. De Brissac and Pete Kills Twice came in. I had the menu in my hands. I held it up in front of my face as if I wasn't sure what to order. They gave me a casual glance and sat down in the next booth. The waitress came with my order. I hoped Millman wouldn't come and sit down. He'd certainly attract their attention. They ordered coffee, and Pete Kills Twice said, "Buy me a sandwich?" De Brissac said OK. They talked quietly.

I heard de Brissac say something ending with the word "more?"

Pete Kills Twice laughed and then said something which sounded like Shah Lah Koe. I wished Stan were beside me listening. Pete then asked, "What about that price?" The waitress brought their coffee. They waited till she had left. De Brissac said, "Some jerk nibbled, but he was a phony."

The jerk grinned. The two men got up and walked out. A

180

few seconds later Millman slid into the booth. "Jesus," he said. "I saw 'em. I ducked back inside the toilet and went into a stall and locked the door. Oh, boy."

"Don't look so nervous. I don't think he's so much of a menace."

"You've been West less than a week and you're an expert? I've been here so long I know all the lizards by their first names except the younger set, and I *feel* like being nervous whenever I see Pete. He gives me the creeps. I don't know what your plans are, but I've shown you around, it's getting late, and I'd like a ride to Albuquerque right now, if you don't mind."

"You're wearing my socks," I said, trying for a light touch. "Please be more respectful."

He gave me a sullen look. "See that little piece of wood Pete had around his neck? The one on a leather thong?" I had noticed it, but I had thought it was some kind of necklace.

"That's his medicine. It's a piece of wood from a tree that's been struck by lightning. It's a fetish of the twin war gods. Some of the crazier ones believe him when he tells them it's powerful, medicine from his warrior-chief grandfather, who'd never been hit by a bullet in his life. Which is true. It's supposed to make the bullets circle around him and keep on going. I mean, some of those guys *believe* it."

"I can use one myself."

"Albuquerque, please. Once you drop me, you can go chase Indians till you get saddle sores."

We rode in silence for about half an hour. He gave me directions till I arrived at his house.

"Sure you don't want supper? I'm buying."

"No, thanks. I want to see if my house is in one piece."

"It looks OK to me. Reconsider supper."

"Nope."

"Care to invite me in for a cup of coffee?"

"Not especially."

He was becoming more and more tense. I gave up.

181

"Sure, Stan. I'll give you a call at the paper if I hear anything interesting."

"Do that." His faint hostility puzzled me. He opened the door and got out, looking around both sides of the street first.

"Millman."

"Yeah."

"What's the trouble?"

"Listen. I'm the nervous type. I'm not a hero. I'm a newspaperman. I get nervous when people threaten me. I don't know about you, but I shit in my pants when people *shoot* at me. Jesus! Tell the truth, were you ever shot at?"

"A couple times."

"Well?"

"I maintained good sphincter control."

"Yeah? Well, I'm different. I'm a civilian. Christ, you go around carrying a gun and all, no wonder you aren't chewing your nails."

I unbuttoned my coat. I flung open my jacket. "Look," I said, a little sharply, "No shoulder holster!" I hooked my thumbs in my belt and pulled it away from my stomach. "No belt gun!" I pulled up my pants legs. "No ankle gun! And I'd even open my fly and prove I don't have a crotch piece, only we'd never get out of the slammer if a patrol car saw us."

"Wow! No gun?"

"Nope."

"I'm sorry."

"I'm a little nervous myself, if you must know." This wasn't exactly true, what made me nervous was the thought of Slavitch waiting to bite my ass each time I called.

"Yeah. Well—" He stood there indecisively.

"Stan, what is Shah Lah Koe?"

"Shalako. That's the big midwinter dance at Zuni. Most important dance of the year. Not a two-bit affair like the one you saw today. Indians come from all over the country for Shalako. It lasts three days. Why do you want to know?"

"Just curious."

"As long as you're out here you ought to see it. Of all the Indian dances, if I had to choose one to see, that would be the one." He was leaning on the door. "Going?"

"Maybe."

"Chasing Pete?"

"Maybe."

"He'll be there to mend his political fences, believe me. He'll have to show how tough he is whenever he comes up against a white, so you better watch your step out there. Every Indian you can think of will be there. There's an awful lot of bootleg liquor floating around at Shalako. I'm supposed to cover it this year, but I have the feeling I wouldn't be happy there. I'll think up a good story to cover down at White Sands."

"Other end of the state?"

"You got it."

He turned around. Then he turned back. "A word of warning, McQuaid." He opened the car door and leaned inside.

"Let's have it."

"Try not to cross those Red Power guys. They're rough. Especially when they know you don't carry a gun. Nothing gets respect around here like a gun, and a shotgun especially. Get one. When you haul it out they'll all take off like gutshot wolves. When I was a kid I was stealing watermelons once from one of those Hispano farms along the river, and the farmer came out and pointed a shotgun at me. I threw my hands up so high that when they came down they were clutching wild-goose feathers between the fingers. So long, thanks for your socks, thanks for the food, thanks for your great ideas on how to be famous in the world of journalism. I'm going to embroider your name on the shorts."

"Do that."

He closed the car door. I waited till he had unlocked his front door, like a New York cabdriver waiting till a nervous lady lets herself inside. I didn't know what I would have

183

done had someone let off a rifle in my ear just then. Probably suffer a massive loss of sphincter control.

* * *

Route 66 in and out of Albuquerque, when you hit it at night and when you're tired, is a large sample of hell. A wild, savage, hysterical blitzkrieg of neon smashing your eyes and filling your numbed skull with short, hot spurts of information which you might want: GAS EAT SLEEP. But there are so many neon scalpels carving away at you, handing you data you're not interested in: LAMPS VOLVO PIZZA TOPLESS BEDDING. Just half a mile of this, especially when you're moving fast with lots of other cars, when the area is strange, and when you've been moving all day, is more than enough.

I pulled in at a motel three blocks north of 66. Who could take the roar of the tractor-trailers and the constant horn-blowing? It was owned by an old couple who were happy to see anybody because business was bad and they were bored with talking just to each other. I said I was going to Shalako and they became envious. They had lived in Albuquerque forty-five years and they were always meaning to see it. They were like New Yorkers who had never gone to see the Statue of Liberty. I said I was a tow-truck operator on vacation and they had no trouble believing me. Score one for Millman. They settled happily down in their chairs in the lobby for a long, comfortable chat, but I had to cut them short. I was tired and a long day was coming up. I got up and said goodnight and their faces fell, like children when they find out that the circus is bypassing their town.

I took a shower, washed my underwear and socks, and went to bed. The bed was lumpy and the sheets were coarse, with the ripe smell of crude disinfectant. I slept well enough. The gas heater hissed away during the night. There were enough blankets. I got up at 5, dressed in my warm clothes, ate breakfast in an all-night diner, and by 5:30 I was

184

on my way to Zuni. I was entering it at 8. It didn't have the compact, intense, locked-in appearance of Santo Domingo. Zuni rambled, went across the road, covered fields, had a river. Lanes ambled absentmindedly, horses stood in small fenced-in pastures, looking cold and miserable. Small barns, usually dilapidated, stood in the fields, looking just like barns anywhere in the American countryside. East of Zuni was a massive, brooding mesa; others stood to the north and west. There were no motels. I stopped at Sam's Chile Parlor for coffee and a feel of the place. Across the front was a cluster of red, yellow, and white bulbs. It looked like a very lousy piece of costume jewlery laid on its side. I opened the door and a blast of Mexican music on the radio came out and struck me. I sat at a clean little table with paper doilies embroidered around the edges with small kachina dolls. At the next table sat an Indian in a black sombrero, a thick pigtail wound around with eight round turns of dirty white ribbon, and black pants. He wore dark glasses, Western boots colored olive, an insulated jacket, and a huge turquoise and silver ring on his left hand.

Two little children sat beside him. One bent over and whispered to the other, "One time some of the kachinas chased me on Second Mesa. Chased us on top. We got away," he finished proudly. The other nodded. "You know the Yeibichai?" The first one nodded, scared at the mention. "They whip little children and put you in a bag." The two of them considered each other's information gravely and somewhat scared. I sipped my coffee and stared out the window. It looked just like a shabby, beat-up Western town. Alleys with pools of water, a dog scuttling across the road. Daylight was not very kind to Zuni. I paid my check, opened the door, and Shoshana Kimri and Dr. Lundberg stepped inside.

"Thank you," she said, not noticing me, and they sat at a table. He picked up a menu. I stood beside the table.

"Here for Shalako?"

She looked up, startled, then smiled. He glowered, looked

at his wristwatch, and resumed his study of the menu as if it had been a badly written paper submitted to him for approval.

"Yes," she said. "I come always when I can. It is very interesting. Do you know about it?"

"No."

He looked at me over the top of the menu with intense dislike; when he caught me looking at him he dropped his eyes. I thought he was a childish jerk. He looked at his watch again. "Where the hell's the waiter?" he demanded.

"To be brief, there are six gods," Shoshana said. It looked as if just about everyone in the state of New Mexico was determined to give lectures. "These gods are personated—"

"*Im*personated!"

His angry correction did not seem to bother her. "By six very big birds. Yes. They are very tall. They are Shalako. They come down from those mountains at dask—"

"Dusk, dusk!"

"Dusk, They talk. They talk to the Zuni, they tell them good things for the next year. They go '*eee-eeee-eee*' and their beaks go *clackety-clackety clack.* It is a happy festival. The mythology is so rich, very complicated. Other gods dance. A great many."

"Don't bother telling him. Waiter!"

"He's not the waiter," I said. "He's the owner."

"Who gives a good goddamn? He's not a Zuni, I don't have to be nice to him. He's too goddamn slow. Waiter!"

"I will tell him if he wants," she said stubbornly. Dr. Lundberg was not my favorite person.

"No, no," I said, trying to placate him. "I'm not here to learn anything. Just on business. And I'd appreciate if it you wouldn't mention why I'm here."

"Yes," she said. He grunted reluctantly. She wanted to know if I had managed to find a place to stay in Zuni.

"I haven't looked."

"Yes. There's nowhere. Nowhere. We are staying with an anthropologist. But everyone else has to drive back to Gallup for the night. But it is important to be here day and night, because dances go on, stop, people eat, maybe sleep a couple hours, dances start. There is nothing like it. Every year they say the Zunis will not let any more white people come to the dances. So I must go each time, just in case. Just in case? That's a funny idiom, did I say it right?"

He didn't respond.

"You said it right," I said.

She gave me a warm smile. He did not like that at all. He stared out the window at Zuni as if he would like to give it a D.

"Why do they want to keep the whites out?"

"Oh, they say it is because the NAU want it. Some say it is because the very conservative old men want it. That is why I come. To feel out the underwaves."

"Undercurrents."

"Yes! Undercurrents!" She gave me another warm smile.

He stood up abruptly. "I'll meet you outside," he said curtly. "Don't you two lovebirds stop! This dull little lecture in Beginning Anthropology bores me." He walked out, slamming the door behind him. I could next see him pacing up and down in front of the restaurant, his jaw hard set, looking at his wristwatch.

I had startling news for the world: women are a little nuts. And in many ways they are like Indians. That is, they play brilliant chess all around me while I stumble amid my checker pieces, wondering how they can zap on a long diagonal across the board while all I do is plod grimly from one square to the next. I can't figure them out. Maybe that's why I never married, and that's why my two young nephews are stand-ins for the sons I never had. I looked at Shoshana as she sat across from me busily crumpling her napkin. Her face was pink with embarrassment and annoyance. I leaned over and asked, "Why do you put up with it?"

Typical checker move. I wouldn't put up with it, so why should she? She didn't look up at me, she just tore the napkin into small pieces and said, "I love him, he needs me."

Same reaction as an Irish longshoreman's wife in a red-brick tenement on York Avenue. I'd see her and plenty like her on uniform patrol after they'd been handed six kids, a year apart, receiving a regular bonus of two black eyes and sometimes a nose fracture thrown in for a little added excitement. There'd be the kids bawling under a four-color lithograph of the Pope on the kitchen wall, the wife washing the blood off under the cold water faucet and telling me, "Don't be after takin' him away, he's a good man." I'd look at the nose, pushed to one side of her face. I'd like to kill the bastard as he sat glowering at me in the kitchen chair. And she'd never file a complaint. Then maybe the same night I'd have another beat-up wife in a duplex on Park, usually without kids, but with a Yorkshire terrier yapping in excitement, and maybe a genuine Cezanne on the wall. And what would this product of an expensive finishing school in Virginia say? I will spare any suspense. She would say exactly the same goddamn thing, but with better grammar. When I'm ninety I'll figure it all out. In the meantime I decided to drop the whole thing. I needed my brain for simpler things like figuring out how to solve the problem of passing the lieutenant's exam, and also, if any time was left over, how to find the Declaration.

"You people wanna eat?"

"No," she said, looking at Dr. Lundberg. She got up, smiled at me, and walked out.

"He's been here before," the owner said. "He's like a sheepherder, always nursin' a grouch and a watch, and when he ain't busy with one, he's lookin' at the other. You here for Shalako too?"

I nodded.

"Ever seen it?"

When I said no, he went on, "It's really somethin'. You better watch your drivin' round here. Specially at night. When them Navajos get hold of a car and whiskey, they go crazy. Hey, Pete! Pete! 'Scuse me, mister."

He ran outside. A beat-up jeep had screeched to a stop. It backed up, spraying gravel generously. Pete got out and shook hands. I walked out on the porch and turned my back to Pete, pretending to read the menu that was scotch-taped to a window.

"Where ya been, Pete?"

"Around. New York."

My ears must have pricked backward at that answer.

"Glad to be back?"

"You betcha. Came for Shalako."

"You better. I hear your brother-in-law's dancin' this year."

"Yeah. How 'bout *that*?"

"That's his jeep, aint' it?"

"Yeah. Look how he banged it up! Well, boy, I'm shovin off for the mesa. Gotta kill a couple sheep for Shalako. You come by tomorra night an' eat *good* food for a change, hear?"

The jeep pulled away. I waited a second, then turned around, just in time to see the jeep reversing violently. It stopped two feet from me. Pete Kills Twice leaned out and examined me with a wide grin. I cursed myself silently for not continuing to stare at the menu until he was out of sight.

"Hi, Officer McQuaid."

I nodded.

"You wanna know somethin?" he asked. He leaned across the front seat. I could see the butt of a Winchester carbine sticking out of a leather scabbard resting on the dirt floor of the jeep, amid a debris of empty oil cans and crumpled cigarette packs. One massive paw gripped the edge of the door. It looked as big as a grizzly's to me, except that there was less hair on it.

"Yep," I said.

"McQuaid—"

"Mr. Kills Twice—"

"Yeah?"

"I wanna know somethin'," I said. "But wait till I get closer. If we're going to have an intimate discussion let's keep it private." I moved close. "Go ahead," I said, leaning on the door. "I got all day."

"You got a big mouth," he said.

"Is that all? I expected more."

His smugness lessened. "This is Indian country, man. This is an *Indian* republic. It ain't United States. Wanna know somethin' else?"

A red flush was deepening on his high cheekbones. Get people mad and they don't plan things too carefully. Even if they have planned them, you can break their logical approaches. They make mistakes.

"I wanna give you some good advice. Whatever you're here for, *drop it.* Go buy a pretty Zuni necklace at the Hawikuh Tradin' Post down the road. Or even buy a Navajo one up in Gallup—I ain't particular. An' then blow."

"Blow?" I said, pretending incomprehension.

"Fuck off, man. Don't hang around for Shalako."

"Funny. I was thinking how amusing it sounded. All you Indians jumping up and down in those colorful costumes."

He didn't like that either.

"I'm warnin' you, McQuaid. You don't rate here. You don't rate nowheres. 'Cause why? 'Cause this is *all* Indian country, from way up at the end of Alaska clear on down to Tierra del Fuego, an' you sons of bitches stole it all, an' you ain't got any kick comin', no matter what we do!"

He was breathing faster. I hadn't expected this kind of a speech so soon. He had that .30-.30 in the back seat. I moved closer. If he went for it I would have a chance to tumble in on top of him and try for a spoiling action.

He took one long last look at me. He was now in control. "Hang around here," he said softly, "an' you're gonna lose all your tail feathers."

"What a colorful metaphor!" I said, with my voice full of admiration. I wanted to steam him up some more; maybe the head of Native Americans Unite might say something the assistant district attorney could go to town with.

He gave me so tight a smile that I couldn't have driven a nail between his lips with a sixteen-pound sledgehammer. Another colorful metaphor, yes, but I was beginning to get the gut feeling that he would be moving soon from metaphor to motion. I wished to God I had a gun.

Pete Kills Twice had promised de Brissac that something very interesting would happen at Shalako. Shalako was next day. And it went on for three days more. I would need an exceptional night's sleep, and there was noplace to stay in Zuni. No motels, no tourist homes, no nothing. I went into the Hawikuh Trading Post and asked if they knew of a place. No, There was nothing. Zuni was jammed for Shalako. Navajos had come, Hopis, Blackfoot, even some Iroquois. They were staying with Indian friends. The whites who worked for the Indian Service had all *their* friends staying with them. No. Absolutely no.

It would have to be Gallup, forty miles north on a winding mountain road.

"An' watch out, mister, specially if you drive it by night. Plenty drunken Indians drivin' back an' forth. More'n ever now 'cause of Shalako."

It was getting toward late afternoon. I wandered for a while around the older parts of the pueblo, staring at the round clay ovens where the plump Zuni women were baking bread for Shalako. Some averted their gaze. Zuni wasn't for strangers; they hated just about all whites since Coronado had come through. Dusk was coming quickly now, partly because it was winter and partly because the mesa to the west cut the sun relatively early. It was very cold and would get colder, although there was no snow on the ground. Everyone's breath hung in plumes. Every available space was jammed with cars. I saw plates from every Western state, and some from the Midwest, and even a few from Pennsylvania and New York. By the Red Power stickers in their windows I deduced that most of them were Indian owned. Several Arizona cars were nosed in together, and Navajos squatted in a circle inside the ring of their radiators, brewing coffee over a small fire. Dusk settled quickly on the old, old adobe houses. The few streetlights came on. It was time to be inside a warm place, take a hot shower, eat decently,

191

and get a long, comfortable night's sleep. I thought of the motel in Gallup. It could supply all of those things. People were laughing in the houses behind the warm yellow windows. I suddenly felt sorry for myself. There was no one I could laugh with in Gallup. I would even settle for Dorsey. I sighed and got in my car. I warmed up the engine, and when it was hot I switched on the heater. I moved slowly through town, cars passing me wildly on the narrow road, or barreling straight at me, dazzling me with their up beams. I shielded my eyes and watched the right edge of the road in order to avoid the glare. A sign with an arrow: GAL⁼ LUP. I turned north.

The driving was better. Hardly any cars seemed to be coming south, facing me. The road climbed and twisted, skirting nasty canyons. Sometimes there was simply a wide shoulder in lieu of a stone wall or guardrail. I was not used to these kinds of roads: the roads I had driven up to Santa Fe and from Albuquerque to Zuni had been on long, easy, level stretches. I drove slowly and carefully, clinging to the middle of the road whenever there was a drop and no guardrail—as long as no car was facing me. I drove into canyons and out of them. Steep cliffs fell away to the right for sickening distances. Far below in the darkness there were the tiny yellow blotches of scattered ranchhouses. My headlights picked up decaying fence posts with the usual snapped strands of barbed wire Snow lay in crevices and pockets in the rocks. It was much colder at this altitude than Zuni, and because of the narrow canyons the sun could only penetrate here briefly, unlike Zuni, which spread itself over a broad valley.

A pickup truck with a man in a black sombrero whipped past me with only inches to spare; only by great effort did I restrain myself from pulling hard to the right to give the crazy bastard plenty of room. And the reason why I didn't move over was that, after the six feet of shoulder, I then would have about a thousand feet to cover. All of it vertical. I had caught a glimpse of a bottle being upended by the driver. If I were back in New York, I'd make him pull over. Even if I were on homicide duty. But this was a country where not only the Indians, but also the cops didn't like me. Three miles farther, a car shot out of a side road to my left. It made a sharp right turn and headed very fast straight for me. The only way to avoid a head-on collision was to risk a swerve to the shoulder on my right. I cut over, and I might have made it all right, except that his left front fender gave me a hard boost. The front wheels went into space.

* * *

I hadn't buckled on the seat belt. I slid off the seat and tumbled onto the floor in order to be as low forward as far as I could get. I didn't want to be bounced around like a Ping-Pong ball. I had no time to feel scared. Everything moved in slow motion, as it always does when the adrenalin is being pumped into the bloodstream.

The car went straight out into space. Then gravity took over. It started to nose downward. It hit the steep slope front wheels first. They snapped off with a brittle crunching sound, like someone eating a carrot. I felt the car squat down on the axles, then the back wheels landed. The broken front wheels acted as a brake, and after plowing downhill through the sagebrush for about a hundred feet, the car slid to a jarring halt against a piñon.

I heard the sound of liquids gurgling out. Either the gas tank or the radiator was ruptured. Maybe both. It would be a good idea to get out first and figure out later which was making those repulsive noises. I reached out a hand and pulled the door handle down. The door was jammed shut by the impact. I smelled gas now. My inducement to leave became stronger. I hauled myself up to my knees, rolled down the window, and heaved myself up and over the edge of the window. I slid down and landed on my palms on gravel, fell in a heap, and scrambled away on all fours till I had built enough momentum to straighten up. I had once

193

seen some tankers burn to death in Korea. Fifty feet away, after stumbling over low-growing sagebrush a couple times, I came to a halt. I would be safe enough there if she blew.

She blew.

I had plenty of light for a change. I backed away, shielding my eyes. There was a slope leading down from the road at a 45-degree angle. I had landed on that. Had I been a hundred feet farther when I went over, or fifty feet further to the rear, I would have gone four hundred feet straight down to a boulder-strewn dry riverbed. God was good.

I looked at my car again. It was very hot. There went my nice leather suitcase, and a good suit, good shoes, and a good overcoat, even if it was too light for this altitude. No wonder they wouldn't rent cars in Gallup. I wouldn't rent them either if I owned an agency. I could just see myself explaining to the car rental people in Albuquerque just what the hell I was doing thirty miles south of Gallup when I was supposed to be one hundred and twenty miles east of there, and seventy-five miles north. Then I would have to put in a claim for my destroyed property. I could just see another great battle looming up with Lieutenant Slavitch.

Oh, the hell with it! I was lucky. There was a dull ache in the small of my back where I had bounced against the gear-selector lever on my way down the slope, but I was so pleased with myself for surviving this meeting with a drunken driver that I began whistling as I started climbing. I stopped that right away. I had to grab sagebrush for handholds as I climbed up; all my breath was needed for that. When I reached the road I stood there getting my breath back. There was still plenty of light. It even warmed me as I stood on the edge of the road. I had gone over at a place where they had dumped the rock when they blasted the mountain. That vast rock pile had formed itself into a 45-degree slope. Finer material was dumped on top, and eventually sagebrush lodged in the crevices. If I had taken off before or past the rock pile I would now be looking like a butcher shop. I suddenly felt so weak that I just sat down on the road. I could feel sweat pumping itself all over. The snow rattler will getcha if you don't watch out.

"Oh, Jesus," I muttered. "Holy Jumping Jesus." I was trembling. It was the delayed reaction, and a damn fine specimen.

I was aware of headlights. I lifted my head. A car had stopped and two Navajos got out. They looked down at the wreck and then looked at me.

"You all right?"

"Yes."

"You sure?"

"Yeah."

"You want a ride to Gallup?"

"Yes, thanks."

I sat between them. A shy little boy of four kept staring at me, except when he crawled across his father's lap, across mine, and then onto the floor. There he ducked his head under the steering wheel and then slid his head upward to the dashboard. "That's my son," said the proud father. "He wants to know how fast we're goin'."

Plenty fast.

They were drinking cheap wine from a bottle and offered me a drink. I took a long one. The driver was lousy and was weaving all over the road. I didn't care. Two in a row wouldn't happen. God wouldn't dare. They dropped me off at my motel. I thanked them.

I got my old room. The hot shower felt very good. I felt various aches and pains which were beginning to declare themselves. I had no complaints. I knew I was a very, very lucky son of a bitch.

*   *   *

Both palms bled a little in the morning from the gravel. I bought iodine and Band-Aids, shaving material, and all the other necessities, and a little plastic flight bag to keep them in. Then I waited till nine and called the car rental people back in Albuquerque. When I told them I had been forced off the road between Gallup and Zuni they began yelling. They wouldn't let me finish talking.

"You told us you were going to Santa Fe!"

"And so I did tell you, and I did go there."

"But you had this accident between Gallup and Zuni!"

"After I went to Santa Fe, my business required me to go to Zuni." I was very patient, although I do not relish being bawled out.

"Now, look here, Mr. McQuaid, we—"

"I'm getting very bored with this conversation, buddy. You want your car, it's about thirty miles south of Gallup. What's left of it. You have my home address. Good-bye."

I bet the next person who rented from them would have to fill in a road map and then sign an affidavit swearing he would not depart from that, no matter what. I got out of the phone booth, wondered what the hell to do next, and remembered I had a car in the garage, the one I had rented from Simpson Bekis. I threw in my bag, had a good breakfast, and drove south. The steering was very stiff and painful to my raw palms, and I drove it by hooking my fingers around the wheel rim.

Half an hour later I stopped. I pulled far over to the right, even running the car up the bank. I didn't want another car to face the same accident I had faced last night; I figured if my car were to force another one into the center of the road, it might smack into one coming up the hill from Zuni. I wouldn't want that on my conscience. My ex-car was down the slope, not looking healthy. It didn't look like a car anymore. I scrambled down the slope. The suitcase and its contents were a charred mess. The car had almost a full tank of gas to play with; the heat had been so great that some of the lighter metal members were twisted. Thank God I hadn't been knocked unconscious. All my ID would have been burned, I would been unrecognizable, but eventually I would have been identified through the car plates and my dental work. That was some sort of a consolation.

196

I shoved my hands in my pockets. It was cold on the slope, with currents of icy air sweeping over the ridge way up across the road and sliding down toward the narrow rocky riverbed far below. I stared at the front wheels. Both had snapped at the end of their axles. The car looked like a kneeling camel. I sighed and turned to make my aching, painful scramble up the hill. But after I had gone only a few feet I stopped. Something was unusual about the car. I went back, sliding and slipping on the frozen ground, thanking God it wasn't summer when all sorts of life would be crawling around. I stood beside the car, frowning. A message was in the air and I was not receiving. It was comig from the car. I slowly circled it. Nothing. I stood there a few minutes, my ears beginning to get numb. And then I got the message.

An area an inch in diameter had been painted black in the center of each headlight. Someone had then scraped most of it off, but there were a few tiny hairlines of paint still clinging to the glass, enough for me to determine the general shape and extent of the paint job. I scraped off one of the hairlines and held it close. Ordinary house paint. Still somewhat wet; the air was too damp for it to have dried completely. My guess was that it wasn't more than twelve hours old.

I climbed again to the road, thinking hard. Twelve hours old meant that the paint had been slapped on when I had been in Zuni. I got in my car, baffled. I got out again and walked up to that place in the road where I had first seen that car come barreling down at me, blinding me with its glare. I walked up to that point where I had first seen it entering the road. There was a little dirt track there winding up the mountain. I walked up the road and looked around. I saw fresh impressions in a herringbone pattern pressed into the thin powder of fresh snow. The pattern was sharp, the kind you'd get from new tires There were skid marks. Well, not skid, but what you'd get if you were at rest and then decided to leave at about ninety miles an hour without waiting to build up your speed gradually. There was no reason for those marks at that place. If you were there and wanted to go down at the paved road, several yards below, all you had to do was release the brakes. You'd make it all right. The tire tracks did not go farther up the mountain. Someone had backed into that area and stayed there. Not long, not long at all; there were no oil drips whatsoever. A close search on my knees and painful palms proved that. I stood up and shoved my hands in my pockets, looking across the road and into the valley opposite.

No reason for the skid marks. Unless someone had backed in, keeping his motor running, and waited for me to appear. When I showed up, coming up the hill from Zuni, he gunned the motor—much too hard, being nervous or impulsive. The rear wheels spun till they finally gripped on the slippery surface. Then he shot into the road and came straight at me with his headlights aimed straight at my eyes.

He would be wearing polaroid lenses. Because they would cut the glare from the headlights, and they would let him see the round black paint marks and know, without the shadow of a doubt, that it was me coming up from Zuni with freshly painted headlights not an hour old. Done while I was eating supper. I wouldn't know about it. I'd get into the car, turn on the lights, and the little spots wouldn't affect the way the bulbs would light up the road. How would I know?

He knew the road well. He'd back in at a good place, where he wouldn't be seen from the road, wait till he saw me coming, fat, dumb and happy, and he'd know just where to drop me into the canyon. Like a good pool player dropping the ball into the side pocket. That should have been the end of me, except that he misjudged by fifty feet. Sometime afterward, probably after sunrise, and before there was any traffic on the road, he had gone back and tried to remove the paint.

So I knew he was smart. Not too lucky. But smart.

Oh, yes. It was an ideal country for snow rattlers.

* * *

I slid down the slope once more. I used the blade of my small pocketknife as a screwdriver and took out the two headlights. I climbed again, and by the time I reached the road I was panting. I was out of condition, damn it. No good. I carefully packed the headlights at the bottom of the airlines bag, just then realizing my Acoma bowl was ruined in the fire. Great.

I thought another minute. I now had the headlights. They were evidence of attempted homicide. But where could I keep them in Zuni? In the car? Forget it. With a friend? I had no friends in Zuni, although I did have an acquaintance—Shoshana. But I didn't want to tangle with her boyfriend who, for all I knew, might have been the guy who was laying for me.

I opened the bag, removed the headlights, and walked up the road to the dirt track. No car was anywhere in sight, nor was there anyone in view. It was just too cold to be out strolling around a mountain. I walked in and out of the chaparral for fifty feet. I found a small hollow, put the headlights at the bottom, and tossed several dead piñon branches on them. Now it looked like an ordinary pile of brushwood. I would be able to find it without any trouble.

"Detective McQuaid, I call to your attention People's Exhibit Number One. Describe it to the jury, please."

"A pair of automobile headlights."

"Are those your initials scratched on the reverse side?"

"Yes."

"Describe for jury the situation in which you discovered the headlights."

That's how it might go if all went well. That question would give me free rein. I would describe the glare in my eyes, the impact, the jetting into space, the terror when my car shot into the air, the explosion. And then my eventual

199

discovery of the still-damp paint. I would glare at the defendant—but who was he?—and then the jury, emotionally and logically swayed, would look at the son of a bitch, hating him. I relished my dream.

Only I hadn't cuffed the man who'd be sitting with his lawyer at the left-hand table. But he'd damn well be sitting there, sometime in the late spring.

I drove into Zuni. There was a state police roadblock on the outskirts. The trooper poked his head in, his eyes roaming everywhere. "Good morning, sir. Are you carrying any liquor?"

"No." He waved me on. The road was packed for cars arriving for Shalako. Traffic was crawling.

I parked at the restaurant. It was there that the paint must have been slapped on. It was very easy to do; all it would take would be two quick dabs with a small brush from a small can, say the pint size. With a lot of cars double-parked, he would have gotten away with it unnoticed.

I walked into the restaurant and sat in a booth and ordered coffee. The next booth held two Zuni policemen, with fat shoulders and dark sunglasses. They were listening to an Indian with a dark-brown face and a slipknot string tie. He had just begun to talk when the two cops noticed a third Zuni policeman come in. "Hey, hold it, Paul," one said. "I want Joe Ortiz to hear your story." Paul waited calmly, slowly twisting an enormous silver ring about his finger.

"Joe," the first cop said, "I want you to meet Paul Many Goats. He's a Hopi."

They shook hands. Paul asked, "I talk now?" They nodded. Paul put his gnarled hands on the table, where they rested, looking like a pile of cracked lobster claws. "Two carloads of NAU people come up to Old Oraibi a couple days ago. They told us we should kick all the whites off the mesa and keep 'em away from all the dances. The old men said they would consider it." He paused and sipped some coffee out of a saucer. "After we said we would think it over, the leader—it was Pete Kills Twice—he said, 'we're here now.'" A thin smile seeped over Paul Many Goats' lips. "I said we would consider it. So we all walked away. In a little while eleven ogre kachinas all painted up, they come out of a kiva and chased those sons a bitches the hell off the mesa. They ain't comin' back. There's Pete Kills Twice."

I turned. Pete Kills Twice was standing in the doorway. No wonder he had been brooding when I last saw him. A man running a revolutionary movement having his ass run off a mesa by the tribal elders is not a happy contented being. He stepped inside and let the door bang behind him. He watched me with no emotion on his face. I stood up and walked toward him.

"Excuse me," I said when I reached him. He stepped aside. I walked across the parking lot to his jeep. I didn't see any paint pot in the back. He wouldn't be that dumb, of course. The tires had a herringbone pattern. But so did lots of others. The tires were new. I walked around the jeep slowly, my hands in my pockets. Pete Kills Twice had come outside and was staring at me from the restaurant porch.

I stopped my circling at the left front fender. There was a fresh scratch on it. And, buried deep in the scratch, were a few minute paint flakes.

I scraped a couple off with my thumbnail. The color was a deep green. I should say it matched the paint of my dead car. Holding my hand in such a way that if the scrapings fell out they would land on my upright palm, I walked to the door. Pete hadn't moved. "Excuse me," I said politely. He stood aside. I opened the door, went inside, scooped up a paper napkin from the dispenser, turned around, said "Excuse me," for the third time to Pete Kills Twice, and stepped out again, half amused at my politeness while I was gathering evidence against the object of my good manners. I walked to the jeep. I opened the napkin, spread it on the fender, and scraped out my thumbnail, depositing the tiny flakes on the napkin. I took out my pen and wrote down,

"Zuni, New Mexico. Paint flakes removed by me from left front fender of jeep driven by Pete Kills Twice." I added the plate number of the jeep. I estimated the length of the scratch at 14 inches. I wrote that down. Then I carefully folded the napkin, put it in my pocket, put the pen away, and turned into a looping overhand right coming at me from Pete Kills Twice.

* * *

I was fast but not fast enough. I caught it on the side of my jaw, staggered back, and tripped. My head hit the corner of the bumper. I was dazed. I felt his hand ripping the pocket where I had stashed away the napkin.

I clamped onto the hand with both of mine and hung on grimly. I needed a few seconds for my head to clear and then we could do business. He broke my grip as if I had been a sick kitten and went on digging for the napkin. But I had shoved it well down and he was having trouble. I felt my blurred mind slowly clearing. Ten seconds more and I could start selling tickets. I clamped both hands once more on his wrist. It felt as big around as a sewer pipe. This time I hung a little more weight on him. He had trouble working on me, and when he managed to break my grip once more I decided it was time to go to work.

I pushed him away from me as hard as I could. He tried his best to force my arms backward. I pushed some more, and he fell for it, he pushed back even harder. I suddenly grabbed both sleeves at the elbows and pulled him toward me as hard as I could. Since he was pushing as hard as he could, I simply took his energy and directed it. As he came down I stretched my right leg, put it between his legs, and swung it upward. His head and shoulders came down and he sailed over me in a lovely arc and came down on his back. Thank you, old Mr. Imamoto of the Sokol Hall Dojo, on East Seventy-first Street. You said once I was big and stu-

202

pid, but I practiced hard, like you said I should, bearing you no resentment.

Before I could move, several people had run up, including the four Zuni cops from the booth in back of me. Pete was sitting up, a bit groggy, and as someone whom Mr. Imamoto, who weighed one hundred fifteen and was seventy-three years old, threw the same way, I could testify feelingly that he was thoughtful. He may have been hating me, but a throw like that shuts down the throttle for a while. He was holding his balls. Good. That would give the master painter something to think about the next time he took a leak for the coming week. He was yelling that I was trying to steal his jeep.

"That true, mister?"

"Hell, no."

"How we know that? We saw you walkin' around it."

"Jesus Christ, I got a car of my own, that's why."

They stood there, indecisive.

"He's a goddamn thief!" Pete Kills Twice yelled. "I want him arrested!" He bent over, favoring his tender testicles.

The crowd parted. A very old Zuni, with each brown gnarled hand hooked arthritically on a cane, was approaching very slowly. He wore the biggest turquoise necklace I had ever seen since I started to become an unwilling expert in the Indian jewelry business. It looked like a blue coalpile in a blue coalyard. His white hair hung down to his shoulders. He moved very slowly toward Pete Kills Twice who, seeing him coming, sat up and removed his hands from his balls, sitting at respectful attention, if that was possible if you'd just been violently kicked in the family jewels. I almost became sympathetic toward Pete. Just almost. I was leaning against the jeep, aching more than ever because of the strain all this activity had put on my bruised muscles. Shoshana Kimri's voice spoke in my ear.

"Are you in trouble?"

"I doubt it." I was watching the old man, who seemed to

203

be giving Pete a nasty little lecture. Pete looked half angry, half embarrassed. The old man ended. The Zunis around them all seemed concerned and disturbed. The old man turned and walked slowly and painfully away. I remembered that Shoshana knew Zuni.

"What did the old man say?" I asked.

"He said Pete was supposed to be helping his brother-in-law dance. He said he should be ashamed, fighting today. It will bring bad luck."

Pete walked sullenly away, with a long glance at me.

"Where is the son of a bitch going?"

"Up to the mountains back there." She waved a hand to the west. "The Shalako come from underneath. Then they come to Zuni." She warmed up to her story. "Once I was driving up there in jeep, and I see them getting into their uniforms? No, costumes. I turned around quick, so quick! I didn't want them to get mad with me. They have secret places up there for hundreds of years. They kill people who come across their caves and secret places. Places with trees planted right in front of caves so that you would not know they were there. No one knows what happened to many whites who went up there for maybe to hunt deer and never came back, I think they came across some ceremony. Bodies they never find. And nothing happens, it is all Indian country, you see."

"I didn't ask for a lecture," I said sourly. "All I want to know is where is he going, based upon the conversation you heard."

"I answer you!" she said angrily. She turned and walked away. There went my only friend in Zuni. I was sorry I had spoken so harshly.

The Zuni sergeant came up to me. "You hang around here, mister," he said. "We want to talk to you after the dance."

"Yeah, sure. You can be damn sure I'm not leaving. And I want to talk to *him*. I'm going to charge him with attempted homicide—what do you think of *that?*"

"Not much." The voice came from back of me. I turned. It was Mrs. Sorensen.

"You get around," I said.

"What about you?" she retorted. "Anyway, McQuaid, Shalako is my favorite dance. I come here every year for it. That wasn't much of a fight just now. I seen better in the schoolyard back in Santo Domingo a couple days ago with a couple eight-year-olds."

"I bet," I said. "They don't make 'em like they used to."

"Wasn't you talkin' just now to that an-thro-polo-gist from the Amerindian Museum?" Her voice crackled with scorn as she made fun of the word.

I nodded.

"She came up once suckin' round for some of those pieces," she said, grinning. "I tole her to go peddle her papers. It done took me five minutes to explain to that damn furriner what I was talkin' 'bout. You here on business or pleasure?"

"Both."

"Both," she repeated slowly. She smiled. She was wearing a long camel's-hair overcoat with a hood. She knocked the hood back and unbuttoned the coat and held it wide open. "What do you see?"

I saw a very nice bust, but she didn't mean that. "A red wool dress."

"Right. Look familiar?"

"You wore it the night of the burglary."

"Right! You've got a good memory. I always thought it was my good-luck dress till that night. The old man likes it. The old man who stopped your l'il kid fight. He's a hunnerd an' four. I wear it to please him. He says when he sees me in it it makes him feel seventy again. He says it makes him feel as crazy as a parrot eatin' sticky candy. How does it make you feel?"

I looked at her for a long time. I had been lonely and celibate long enough, and the chances of Slavitch or her husband hearing about our activity out here would be small.

"Like a member of the parrot family, Mrs. Sorensen."

She chuckled with pleasure. "Where you spendin' the night?"

"In my car, I guess."

"Hell, no need for that. I got a place three miles from here out to Black Rock. Friend of mine's a doctor in the Health Service. Got a nice modern house. He's away in Washington and give me the key. Shalako don't start till sundown. Three hours to go. Nothin' to do in town. Come on out 'n' have a drink."

The more she talked the closer she got. It was a very good idea.

"Let's go," she said. "We'll use my car."

I felt a faint warning glow on my distant early warning radar, and a very interesting idea popped into my head. I had no intention to threw it open to public debate.

"I'd like that very much," I said, "but I have to make a few phone calls to New York."

"Girlfriend?"

"Official reports.

"Well, come on out. You'll get privacy."

"Not only phone calls," I said. "After that I'll have to write a couple reports and mail them by four thirty—that's when they send out the mail to the airport. Tell you what, I'll just write them out here. It'll take me an hour or so. Then I'll drive out. How about that?"

She stared at me. If she wanted my car gone over to look for the headlights, that wouldn't create much of a problem. Someone could look at it during Shalako or during the night. If she pressed it might look too suspicious. Yet I couldn't figure out why she'd want to get the evidence. I decided it was probably because she didn't want to get her Indian friends in trouble.

"Sure," she said. "You jus' drive east, three, four miles. You'll see a big yellow water tower sign says ZUNI. Make a left till you come to a fork. Take the left-hand road. Fifth house on left. Sign says DR. HARRIS."

"Got it."

She got into her pickup and drove off. I watched till she disappeared. I went into a jewelry shop and spoke to the owner. He didn't have any. I tried another. The third one was more modern. He was willing to rent me his five-inch-diameter, twenty-power, hand magnifying glass overnight for five bucks if I'd give him a fifty-buck deposit. I handed him the fifty.

I was finally prepared for an afternoon of love.

*　*　*

I went to the trading post and bought a small plastic bag and a large envelope. I put my gloriously battle-worn napkin in the bag and mailed the envelope to myself. It was easy, the entire post office consisted of a desk at one side of the trading post. I walked out. Pete Kills Twice was sprawled across the front seat of his jeep.

"Hi," he said lazily, lifting a hand. "You're lookin' surprised."

"I sure am. I thought you were supposed to be up on the mysterious mesa."

He didn't like that. But he was calm. "Wanna make sure you're goin' to Shalako. I came in to tell the local flatfeet I'm withdrawin' my charges. Don't want you sittin' in the pokey while Shalako is goin' on."

"I appreciate that. I hear you're featured."

"Yeah. Somethin' you should know, McQuaid."

"What is it, Kills Twice?"

"We put on that outfit, we're gods."

"I'm impressed."

"Ain't tellin' you that to impress you. I'm tellin' you that in case you feel like tryin' for a Federal warrant. Which you ain't gonna get. 'Cause the charge you're bringin' up ain't Federal."

"You mean don't make a Federal case out of it."

He crossed his hands behind his neck and stared at me. "I bet you're a scream back at Headquarters, McQuaid."

"I don't work out of Headquarters, Kills Twice. Homicide

Zone Three is home to me. You ever come to New York I'd like to show you my stamp collection and make you some hot chocolate and maybe kill you."

He let out a deep sigh. "Ho, ho," he said, without mirth. "The point I'm tryin' to make is that if you feel like clappin' on the cuffs at the dance, don't bother. They'll kill you."

"And you like me too much for that to happen, of course."

"Just catch our performance."

"OK, Kills Twice."

I got a perverse pleasure out of saying his name.

"Be lookin' forward to havin' you in the audience."

"I'll bet."

He uncoiled and settled himself behind the wheel. He started the jeep and took off in one of those dramatic spurts so beloved around Zuni. I watched him weave in and out of the heavy traffic, heading for the mesa out of which the Shalako would come at dusk.

I got in my car and drove east against the traffic flow. I couldn't see where they would park. But I left that problem to the inscrutable and ancient wisdom of the Zunis. It was cold again. Some Zunis were plodding to town, encased in blankets. They seemed much heavier than Navajos. McQuaid, the Department's expert on the American Indian.

Four miles east I saw the water tower. I made a left, then took the left at the fork. I found the little bungalow right away. It all looked like a miniature Levittown, with the neat lawns, the asphalt driveways, the cement sidewalks. I parked behind her car and rang the bell.

The door opened almost immediately. She was carrying two tall glasses. She was wearing a negligee. "Here!" she said, without preliminary. I took my glass and stepped inside. "Good bourbon an' hardly no water. Here's to Shalako an' to hell with Christmas!"

Why not? It's their midwinter festival. I drank, eyeing her above the rim. I was standing in a small hallway which opened out into a slightly larger living room with a convertible sofa and two chairs. A rug, a small table, three framed prints on the wall showing Monument Valley, Canyon de Chelly, and a Navajo on a horse. I could see a small kitchen beyond. I was looking for her dress. I was very interested in that dress. Where was it? In a closet? Where was the god-damn closet?

"What you think of this place?"

"Better than having a gearshift sticking in my ear."

She smiled and took three big swallows. "Drink up!" she commanded. I drank. It was good bourbon, all right. I could not drink too much. I had an empty stomach, and too much liquor made me inefficient when I had to move fast, surrep-titiously, illegally, and to peer with great intensity at her red dress—through my rental lens. I set the glass down. "It's awful hot in here," I observed.

"Yes," she said lazily. She was naked under her negligee. She moved closer, swishing the liquor around in her glass. The only sound was the tinkle of the ice cubes. "Take off your coat," she said slowly.

I took it off. I moved into the room. There was no bed-room. But I saw a closet door. I opened it. No dress. I took out a hanger and hung my coat on it slowly. Where was the goddamn dress?

"First time I ever saw anyone puttin' a lumber jacket on a coat hanger," she observed with amusement. First time for me too.

"I'm obsessively neat."

"You look it. Especially with that torn pocket. There's a needle an' thread here. Take it off."

I hesitated.

"Shy? There's a robe in the bathroom. You look awful hot."

"You bet. I'm wearing woolen underwear and woolen socks."

"Better strip an' take a hot bath. Bet you haven't had one for a while."

"Right."

It *had* to be in the bathroom. I opened the door. I couldn't see anything for a while because of the steam. She had filled the bathtub with hot water. "I'm steamin' the wrinkles outta my dress," she called out.

God bless you. There it was, draped from a hanger on the shower ring.

I stripped, feeling better. I added cold water until the water was just right, stepped in, and soaked away the aches I had acquired when I went over the mountain in my car. I felt that sense of exhilarated tension which I always did when I felt I was coming close to a solution of a problem that had been baffling me for some time. There was a slight hitch. I sat up suddenly, muffling my curse. I had forgotten to bring in the magnifying glass without her knowing about it. Then I shrugged. I ought to be able to do it sometime during the busy afternoon she had lined up for me. And I didn't mind soaking in the tub. She could sew up my torn pocket. She wouldn't mind doing that either. She could go through my jacket looking for the paint samples I had taken from Pete Kills Twice's fender. Everyone was getting a fair shake on this deal.

I soaked. When the water had cooled, I got up, toweled myself vigorously, even though it hurt a little in a few tender places, put on the bathrobe and slippers I had found under the sink, and padded out.

I heard the roar of a car outside, followed by the squeal of brakes. Then the slamming of a car door. A few seconds later someone was alternately ringing the bell and banging the brass door knocker as hard as he could. It had all the distinctive earmarks of Pete Kills Twice's charming style.

"Oh, for crissakes," she muttered, and walked to the front door. She bent down, opened the mail slot in the bottom half of the door, and asked, "What the hell's the matter?"

"Hey, Lizzie," came Pete's voice. "I gotta talk."

"Talk."

"Yeah, but lemme in."

"I'm not dressed, Pete! What is it?"

"McQuaid there?"

"Sergeant McQuaid has just taken a bath. He was smellin' like a load of goat manure. What's got you so steamed up?"

"Yeah. Lizzie, there's a couple French TV reporters showed up on the plaza an' we took their cameras away. They're real pissed off an' we figured you'd be good to talk to 'em an' make 'em feel good."

She turned to me and shrugged. She turned again, bent down, and said, "Sure. You tell 'em I'll be right along."

"You bet, Lizzie. I'll be waitin'."

"I said I'll be right along, Pete!"

"Sure, Lizzie. I'll be waitin' an' that's what *I* said."

His footsteps died away. She turned to me with a smile of relief, but a loud burst of noise came from the car. He had turned on the radio full blast and alternated that with pumping away on the accelerator. It made a nice counterpoint for anyone interested in music, which I was not at that point. I could have gone out and politely asked him to cut it out, but he was looking for trouble and I was not. And even if I had been nosing for it diligently I couldn't afford it, especially in enemy country.

I would have given a week's salary to have Pete in New York, even to nail him on a parking meter overtime violation. I could really work that up into something glorious. I could move the bastard from precinct to precinct so fast that his lawyer would have his tongue hanging out trying to locate him. I could piss into his coffee container before I handed it to him in his cell. He'd never know the difference anyway. I could do lots of things, all of them very interesting from a cultural relativity angle. I could even do sand paintings in his hamburger. I become aware that she was staring at me, with her amused, knotted, faintly mocking smile. I was beginning to hate that smile, and if it went on some more I would like to wipe it off with a good strong backhand. There's something very insulting about being slapped with a backhand.

"I suppose you could say that's life," I said, jerking my head towards Pete Kills Twice's jeep.

"Yep."

211

"I think I'll shave."

"Always a good way to pass an afternoon."

"If nothing better offers. Right. I wonder if I could ask you for a cup of coffee."

She shrugged and got up. As soon as I heard her puttering around the kitchen I opened the closet door, bent down, and dug out the glass from my boot. No reason for her to look there if she wanted to search for the napkin. I slid the glass into my pocket and walked into the bathroom. I closed the door, took her dress off the hanger, turned on the extra light above the medicine chest, and proceeded to go over her dress, square inch by square inch.

In twenty seconds I found what I was looking for. Plenty of them. I hung up the dress carefully. I put the glass in my pocket, opened my shaving kit, and shaved quickly. Then I went back into the bedroom and dressed, thinking hard. It all fitted in. The problem for me was how to get the dress and keep it. It was out of the question for me to get any kind of a warrant in Zuni. If I could get a warrant to be served on state land, however . . . I suddenly laughed. It was easy, easy. All I had to do was wait till she came back to New York, get a warrant, and pick up the dress. But before she sent it out to be cleaned. That would blow everything. If she were to go back before I did I could get Dorsey to swear out a warrant and pick up the dress. He could handle that without complaining too much. That should wrap it all up. I let out a long, low breath.

The engine racing hand stopped outside. He was contenting himself with very loud rock and roll. She came in with a cup of coffee." You better drink it in the livin' room," she said. "I don't wanna shock you by dressin' in front of you." OK by me. I sat down on the sofa while she spoke to me through the door. "You better figger on spendin' the night here. You won't be able to find a place anywheres, an' you better not risk drivin' up to Gallup. How's that strike you?"

I said fine. Maybe there'd be no serenade later. "An' there's no reason for you to drag your car out to Zuni an' back. You jus' ride to town in mine."

Sure. Great hospitable broad. Have someone go through Simpson's car looking for a couple of paint-smeared headlights and an interesting crumpled napkin. Then you can always tell me someone just broke in during the night and stole everything out of it, the dirty bastard. Take the spare tire and jack to make it look good. I only hoped they wouldn't bust the door lock too badly. Paying the Chevrolet agency in Gallup twenty-five bucks to repair the busted lock before I returned the jalopy to Simpson Bekis would result in another invoice guaranteed to send up Lieutenant Slavitch's blood pressure another five points. I thought for a second of just giving Simpson twenty-five bucks cash and getting a receipt from him, but I dropped that idea fast. Much more convincing to get a formal, itemized receipt from a large firm. That's the kind of stuff to give the accounting troops.

I was sure I could get the DA to present all this to the grand jury. But would there be enough to persuade the good twenty-one citizens to issue a true bill? It might be a good idea for me to get an assistant DA on the phone back in New York to see if he could get an indictment on what I'd scraped together so far. A felony murder rap could scare some people into talking fast. It might work on her. Might.

She stepped into the living room wearing State's Exhibit Number Five or Six. Seldom had I seen a more attractive accessory before, during, and after the fact.

*   *   *

It was still cold. It seemed as if it would always be cold. We drove to the far side of Zuni, past the last houses. Here were dirt roads, pastures which would be green in the spring, but now were flat, snow-powdered areas of dried brown grass. There were sheds and barns of weatherbeaten gray boards, and goats tethered to stake pins, idly chewing the dried grass and staring at us with their usual look of supercilious boredom. It was beginning to get dark; the sun had slid down behind the western mesa. People clustered

213

against the fences or sat on the hoods of their cars, staring expectantly at the top of the mesa. There was a mood in the air, just like there exists in the theater before the curtain goes up on what everyone is sure will be a stunning performance.

The smarter ones had brought thermos bottles full of hot coffee. When they unscrewed the top the cold made the coffee steam like an old locomotive working its way up a difficult grade. Others were doing little shuffles to keep their feet warm.

I was about the only white there who wore no turquoise. One young white couple was snugly buried in Afghan sheepherder's coats. Minute by minute the sky darkened, as if a blue mist were sliding down off the mesa.

She was wearing her red wool dress, the one in which I had developed such a large proprietary and legal interest. She had hung two tremendous heavy turquoise necklaces around her neck; the only bigger one I had ever seen was that around the neck of the very old Zuni elder who had stopped my fight with Pete Kills Twice. Over her dress she wore her camel's-hair overcoat. She had thrust her heavily ringed hands deep in her pocket, and she was frequently removing them to shake hands with the many Indians who saw her and came to greet her.

"This is a big deal, isn't it?" I asked.

"It's the Fourth of July an' Christmas an' Genesis all rolled into one. An' what makes it extra special A to bull frog is that this is Zuni land. It's been theirs forever. No one *made* 'em come here, sayin', 'OK, this land is yours now, you asshole redskins, no white man wants it, it's too lousy for farmin' an' too dry for crops or for stock-raisin', so you c'n have it, kiss my ass.' Nope. Big difference. Indians *feel* it. Look!"

She pointed to the mesa. Six monstrous figures were towering against the sky.

"The Shalakos," she said.

I judged they were twelve feet tall. Their beaks stuck out

214

two feet. Horns protruded from the sides of their massive heads, which were covered with long black hair. They stood motionless, staring down at the pastures. A high-tension tower stood near them. Strangely enough, the juxtaposition did not make them look ridiculous, the way the contrast of cultures frequently is: Geronimo wearing a silk top hat as he sits in an open touring car. Here the tall Shalakos and the pylon reinforced each other as if the invisible power of which the pylon was a symbol was repeated in the far older and just as invisible power symbolized by the six Shalakos.

The figures seemed to stare down at us. Then, as if satisfied that Zuni was still there after their year underground, the Shalakos moved closer, one by one. As they neared I could hear their beaks snapping shut and opening again, *clack clack clack!* Eagle feathers sprayed upward at the backs of their heads. Each great bird was draped with beautifully ornamented blankets. They filed down the mesa.

"Can't we move up for a closer look?"

"Not allowed. We got to wait here till they pass us. They'll pass within a couple feet of us," she said, grinning, "an' you'll get a *good* look. An' lemme tell you, it's somethin' to write your lieutenant about."

That seemed to be a weird way of putting it, but I let the remark pass, as if I didn't think it important enough to react to.

They moved now across the pastures. The closer they came the more impressive they looked. The beaks clattered away; then an occasional high-pitched whine came from them.

"They're tellin' the people how much they love them," she said, "that they've been thinkin' about 'em, that they'll send rain and good luck for the next year."

They came closer and closer. She looked at me expectantly. I was impressed. But did she have to stare at me with that anticipatory grin? I felt uneasy.

Thirty feet. Then twenty. Then ten.

The first great bird paused for a fraction of a second in

front of me. The long, painted beak swiveled in my direction, clacking. His two hands reached out, grabbed the edges of the blanket covering his breast, and pulled it slightly aside. Just a little bit. Enough to reveal to me the carved ivory bird I had last seen in de Brissac's window.

I stared at it, feeling my face flushing. I turned for a quick stare at Mrs. Sorensen. She was smiling at me. The Shalako pirouetted in front of me, clacking and making the tiny, birdlike cries which meant he was talking to the Zuni and telling them he had good news.

But not for me.

*   *   *

It was all bad news. The second Shalako wore the wampum belt. The third the forest god. And so on, goddamnit. And the sixth and last, last but not least, gave me a fine sighting of the Declaration of Independence, first printing, last auction record, five hundred and seventy-five thousand bucks.

She leaned over and whispered in my ear, "It's a great honor when a Shalako stops in front of anyone. A great honor."

Bitch.

People turned around to stare at me. Many smiled enviously. The Shalako with the Declaration pirouetted, clacking. He was trying to tell me something, and I knew very well what it was. It was a two-word, terse, Anglo-Saxon phrase. Pete Kills Twice and Mrs. Sorensen had me up the creek and they knew it. If I touched any of the Shalakos I'd be dead. The Zuni police would not help. If I waited till I could get to a Federal judge, I'd never get a warrant for Indian land. And if, by a miracle, I did succeed in getting one, how could I find anything hidden on Indian land?

In a way, it was beautiful. It was more than that—it was flawless.

I watched the six Shalakos with all that Indian treasure

and the Declaration file through the dirt lanes on their way to the plaza.

Dirty bastards.

* * *

I got McCullough, the assistant DA on night duty, on the phone.

"How do you know she was in on it?" he asked

"Do you know anything about the behavior of glass under compression?"

"No."

"OK. When glass is forced outwards from one side, tension accumulates on the other side. Say you're using a glass cutter to make a ring around a window from the outside. You will push or tap on that circular piece. It will pop out, with no apparant slivers of glass on the floor. But what happens is this: the compression on the glass causes great tension all over the glass surface on the other side. At a certain point, tiny, unnoticeable pieces of glass spray out into the air from the inner surface, along the cut line. You can't even see them. But these microscopic pieces cling to certain fabrics."

"Such as a red wool dress?"

"Right. It's proof that whoever wore that dress was standing in front of a piece of glass under great compression."

"Makes sense. What else?"

"She went downstairs and turned off the alarm. Pete Kills Twice, in the meantime, had gone next door. He used a plastic card or something like that to force the spring latch on the downstairs door when the elevator operator was taking a tenant up. He used the card to get into the locked door at the bottom of the stairs. He walked up to the eighth floor, opened the window leading to the fire escape. He stepped out and made scratches on the railing, the kind of scratches a metal hook might leave. He went back, closed the window, went down the stairs, and waited till the elevator man was taking another tenant upstairs. Now he's out in the street. It's raining hard, no one sees him. She lets him in. There's no reason for the guard to go into the gallery. He makes the rounds once an hour. He's already done it, and so no one thinks he'll be any problem. Pete Kills Twice is not clumsy.

"Now she takes him up to the roof on the elevator. He makes scratches on the coping directly above the window, just where a steel hook would rest. They go down into the gallery. Her husband is busy with the guests. He puts on gloves, opens the window. He leans out and makes a big circle with the glass cutter, to make it look as if this had been done by burglar. She stands in front of the window, ready to catch the glass when it falls out. And when he taps it, she catches it with her gloves. And her red wool dress catches a nice spray of tiny glass particles. She doesn't have the faintest idea that this has happened. She puts the glass cutout on the floor. So far so good. But then the guard steps in. No one knows why. He carries a gun. He sees the both of them. There's no way to talk themselves out of it. No time. Pete Kills Twice grabs his weapon of opportunity—the old lance—and kills the guard. His tribal instincts take over. He grabs another lance and jams it deep into the floor in front of the dead guard. It's an old traditional Indian way of declaring war. They then decide what to take—probably it had all been decided long ago. She takes a look—it's safe. She takes him down in the elevator, lets him out, and then turns on the alarm system again. She goes back to the party, and a couple hours later her husband suggests they all go and look at the Indian art. Pete Kills Twice by then is probably in the plane on his way to Albuquerque and Santa Fe; he figures he can sell that Hohokam piece, using de Brissac as an agent. De Brissac buys his story about his finding it in a cave on Santo Domingo land. But when Shalako time comes, de Brissac hasn't sold it. So Pete Kills Twice decides to take it back for Shalako. He thinks the display by the big birds will gain many adherents to his cause. Maybe later, if he needs money badly, he will take it out of one of those hidden caves up in Zuni and let de Brissac handle it for a commission."

"Got the dress?"

"No. But when she goes back to New York I think I'll pick it up fast with a warrant."

"Suppose she gets it cleaned when she gets back to New York?"

"I thought of that. Dorsey will pick up the warrant from you tonight or tomorrow so he'll be ready when she gets back. He'll get the dress when she comes home. But if he misses her and she's sent it out to be cleaned, you'll have another warrant ready with the name of the dry-cleaning joint left open. It'll take a second to write in the name and Dorsey'll pick it up easy."

"Sounds OK. What about the stolen stuff?"

I was silent. I had seen it. Could I swear to an absolute knowledge they *were* the pieces that had been stolen from the Sorensen house? No. Could I swear that it was the real Declaration I was looking at? Could it have been a facsimile? Yes.

And suppose I *could* prove it. I couldn't, but just suppose. What chance would I have of going up on the mesa and finding them? One in a million? Let alone coming out alive? Zero.

After a minute McCullough said patiently, "Sergeant?"

"I'm thinking."

"OK. No rush."

What about the felony murder rap? I might be able to place Pete Kills Twice in New York at the time of the murder. But who saw him there? Fingerprints? None. Confession of a coconspirator? No good without independent corroboration, and she'd never talk, anyway.

So what did I have? I might be able to prove that Pete Kills Twice had been driving the jeep that dumped me off

219

the road. But all a good lawyer had to do was to say that accidents were so common on that road why didn't I think it was an accident?

Then again, how about another defense? Why couldn't Pete Kills Twice have scraped another car colored green just like mine in a parking lot? Could happen. Plenty of green cars in Gallup.

"McQuaid?"

"Mr. McCullough, let me call you back."

"Sure, Sergeant, I'm on till midnight."

I hung up and stared out the window of the restaurant. Suppose I produced my headlights? Suppose I hung around and tried to dig up someone who'd sold some black paint to Pete Kills Twice? So what? People used black paint for all sorts of things. And I couldn't see that chief up in Gallup being interested in following up my complaint. And I was alive, right? Go away, McQuaid, don't bother us. That was the message from the mesa.

I called McCullough.

"McCullough here."

"Sergeant McQuaid again. I've been thinking it over. I don't think I've got enough to make an indictment stick."

"You're damn well right. You don't even have enough to make an arrest, Sergeant. What do you want to do?"

I'll tell you, McCullough. I want Pete Kills Twice taken to a motel in New York with Mrs. Sorensen. I want him to bring all those stolen artifacts with him and the Declaration. I want them to be screwing away. In the meantime I would have secured a perfectly legal warrant, specifically listing the five items I had reason to believe would be in that room. I want to break into the room with some good photographers and several witnesses, including Mr. Sorensen. I also want a permit for a wiretap and the phone conversation they had unwittingly recorded in which they discuss their plans, at length, for the theft. Then I want their recorded conversations in which they discuss the completed theft and the accidental murder. Yes. That would be a nice present, McCullough.

"Sergeant?"

"McCullough. I'm dropping the whole goddamn thing."

He laughed. "We can't win them all, Sergeant. Come back."

I walked outside. She was sitting there, behind the wheel of Pete Kills Twice's jeep.

"Howja like Shalako, Sergeant?"

My stomach was churning like a washing machine, but in instead of dirty clothes it was dealing in bad thoughts about her and Pete Kills Twice. I also threw in the chief of police up at Gallup, and the brief, intense conversation I'd be having with Lieutenant Slavitch as soon as I got back to New York.

Pete leaned out out of the back seat. "Colorful dance, don't you think?" he asked.

"Especially the accessories," I said. I would kill him last. "They showed taste, I think," I added. "Did you have a hand in their selection?"

He grinned.

"And I liked the Declaration of Independence bringing up the rear. Very good touch. But the symbolism escapes me. And I hear that everything in the dance symbolizes something."

"An' you want us to help you?"

"If you'll be so kind."

I had myself under much better control. I had just about accepted the fact that I had lost. And now I wanted to analyze why. I also wanted to work out their motivations so as to be absolutely sure.

"You writin' a book for anthropology students?"

"I got one waiting for me in the Squad Room."

"Yeah, OK. You know what good medicine is?"

"Yes."

"All them Indian things—they come from a time when

221

we was strong. So that's good medicine for us. An' what's good medicine for you?"

"I get it, Kills Twice."

"Right. The Declaration. It was good medicine for you, an' I figure we can use it. Simple, right?"

"Yeah." I felt better. Now I understood everything.

"Well, "I said, "I'll be going. I'll be driving up to Gallup, and if you take the same road, I do hope you'll be more careful."

He looked at me with a funny little smile and shrugged. I turned away, feeling very hot, although it was colder than ever.

"McQuaid," she said.

"Yes, ma'am," I said, turning back.

"Pete wasn't anywhere near your car that evenin'."

"Bullshit!" I shouted, starting to lose control.

She started the motor, put the jeep in first gear, pulled her hood over her head, smiled, and said very quietly, "*I* drove." She let out the clutch and made one of those Indian departures, leaving me standing there with my dumb mouth half-open.

When I got into Simpson Bekis' car my two headlights were resting on the front seat. Indians have a colorful way of saying fuck you.

I gave them to Bekis when I arrived outside his house two hours later. He folded away the money I gave him with a pleased smile. He pulled up his heavy concho belt and stuck the folded bills into his watch pocket.

"Thanks for the car," I said. The bus was leaving in five minutes for Gallup.

"Sure. Hope you had a good trip."

"It was interesting."

"Run across any snow rattlers?"

"Just two," I said. "Just two."